Also by Tom Turner

Charlie Crawford Mysteries

Palm Beach Nasty

Palm Beach Poison

Palm Beach Deadly

Palm Beach Bones

Palm Beach Pretenders

Palm Beach Predator

Palm Beach Broke

Palm Beach Bedlam

Palm Beach Blues

Palm Beach Taboo

Palm Beach Piranha

Palm Beach Perfidious

Palm Beach Betrayers

Nick Janzek Charleston Mysteries

Killing Time in Charleston

Charleston Buzz Kill

Charleston Noir

Savannah Sleuth Sisters Murder Mysteries

The Savannah Madam

Savannah Road Kill

Dying for a Cocktail

Matt Braddock Delray Beach Series

Delray Deadly

Broken House

Dead in the Water

Killers on the Doorstep

BROKEN HOUSE

TOM TURNER

TRIBECA PRESS

JOIN TOM'S AUTHOR NEWSLETTER

Get the latest news on Tom's upcoming novels when you sign up for his free author newsletter at
tomturnerbooks.com/news

ACKNOWLEDGMENTS

To the gang at Silverhill. Hope you're all doing well.

Chapter 1

Tell you right now, you're not going to like this guy at first.

For starters, he's way too handsome—square jaw, piercing avocado-green eyes, thick dirty-blond hair. Too rich, too. Twenty- nine-year-old managing director of a New York hedge fund, pulling down six mil a year. Then there's his car: a shimmering midnight- blue Bentley. And the clincher, his license plate: *RAINMAKR.*

Case closed? Heard enough?

Hold on...half the people you talk to will say Cameron Crawford is big-hearted, sweet, and utterly charming. The other half? Probably something along the lines of superficial, immature and shallow. Fatuous, even.

Maybe all the above.

But, hey, give him a chance. He might grow on you... *or not.*

The only thing not in dispute is that Cam is an alcoholic and substance abuser of Herculean proportions—a half bottle of Johnny Walker Blue and a side of pharmaceuticals on his nightly menu.

He works with his older brother Evan, and together they manage a billion-dollar fund. Evan is the brains behind the operation. Or at least that's what he hammers into Cam's head all day long. But besides being an MIT summa and brilliant at currency futures and every known derivative, Evan is beyond socially awkward. Schmoozing billionaire clients in the company box at Giants stadium....*so* not Evan's gig.

That's where Cam steps up. Bottom half of his class at the University of Virginia, but valedictorian of the party-hearty crowd, he's the contact guy with clients. Goes to their charity balls, wines and dines 'em, takes 'em out for eighteen at Shinnecock. Not that he particularly likes all that, he's just a total natural. Cam is also one of those guys who is conversant in a vast spectrum of subjects, though not particularly fluent in any. Except maybe where to find bartenders who go heavy on the pour, light on the chitchat.

One time Evan told Cam he was the virtual master of the fluffy conversation, spinning it like it was a compliment. Cam, accustomed to Evan rubbing his nose in it, nodded, smiled and told him to go fuck himself.

One thing you wouldn't expect about Cam is his extraordinary knack for explaining to clients the complex mix of investments his brother puts their money into. And yes, he understands it all. If they listened to Evan, they'd stall out on his first sentence, the one where he monotones on about "systematic/qualitative" versus "quantitative directional" investing or the snore-inducing Dodd-Frank Act. That's where Cam steps in and breaks it all down. Simple. Clear. Concise.

So, the question is with good looks, the aforementioned charm, and enough intelligence to get by, why is Cam pedal to the metal on the self-destruction highway? The answer is not entirely clear at the moment, but at least he's finally realized he'd better do something quick, before he pitches off a barstool while they administer last rites to his liver.

*****

Weaving toward Clairmount Hospital in the pastoral hills of Connecticut, Cam was singing along to a Mumford & Sons CD to stay awake. It was five in the morning, and he was slumped down in the driver's seat of his *look-at-me* wheels, formerly owned by his boss. What happened was, six months before, Trey MacLeod handed Cam the keys to the Bentley when he saw Cam pull into the company garage in a banged-up three-year-old Prius. "That shit-box has gotta go. Not exactly the image we're tryin' to project," MacLeod had said with a monster scowl. When Cam had started in on how good the gas mileage was, MacLeod cut him off. "Who gives a shit? Jesus, Cam, you some kind of tree hugger or something?"

Macleod, whose net worth was half a billion dollars and could give away a $150,000 automobile like it was a ten-dollar tip, didn't want to hear it when Cam said he wasn't much into cars. As for the lame license plate, Cam kept putting off going down to the DMV and waiting in line for hours to change it. So, at least for the time being, he was stuck with it.

Clairmount Hospital, according to its website, specialized in "the treatment of psychiatric and addictive disorders" and was a "unique and extraordinary place that helps people find the path back to mental health and wellness."

At the moment, Cam was just trying to find the path to the admissions office.

Check-in time at Clairmount was nine o'clock Friday morning, so he figured he had one last blowout in him on Thursday night. So, after closing up Eugenia's on Gansevoort Street at four in the morning, Cam stumbled back to his car and aimed it in the general direction of Connecticut. Straying off course more than once, he almost took out a wild turkey on a winding back road in New Canaan. But finally, he GPSed his way into Clairmount, spotted the red *Admissions* sign, and pulled into the parking lot. He still had two and a half hours to kill.

Parking his car in the handicapped spot—because he certainly was—he reached over, pushed a button, and opened the burled walnut glove compartment of the Bentley. He grabbed a small dark-tinted bottle, twisted off the cap, then shook out a crooked line of white powder on his Black Amex card. He snorted half the bulky line, then switched to his other nostril and polished it off. Reaching into the console, he pulled out the bottle of Johnny Blue that had been three-quarters full when he started his little misadventure seven hours before. Taking a long, heroic pull, he winced and shook his head a couple of times.

"Whoa," he said to his steering wheel, shoving the bottle back in the console.

Then, pushing open the weighty Bentley door, he tried to get out to take a leak. But as he slid to his left, he went too far and thumped down onto the asphalt parking lot, his left elbow and butt absorbing the fall.

"Shit," he muttered, searching his addled brain for the best way to achieve verticality. Pushing up from the pocked pavement, he staggered over to a nearby tree, hugged it like he was in the middle of a cat 5 hurricane, and relieved himself.

Next thing he remembered was waking up in his car to a tapping sound. A woodpecker? Rain? He wondered how he could have nodded off with all the coke coursing through his veins. Cam looked up and saw a small older woman in a nurse's uniform knocking on his windshield, a frown etched deeply into her forehead.

She put her hands up to her mouth and bellowed at Cam. "Will you pleeease get out of your automobile, sir?"

His head racked with hellish pain, he hit the button, and his window descended noiselessly. The woman walked around to the driver's side.

He smiled up at her and couldn't resist. "Yes, please. Two Egg McMuffins, hash browns, and a coupla Bud tall boys."

She just sighed and shook her head. "Follow me," she commanded, as if to a misbehaving twelve-year-old.

Cam did as he was told. She reminded him of his grandmother— triple chinned and mad-dog mean. Used to grab him by the ear and haul him off to the woodshed whenever he pulled one of his adolescent shenanigans.

He saw the woman's eyes zoom in on his jacket lapel. He glanced down and saw a slick pool of drool. She just shook her head, realizing she had a major-league fuck-up on her hands.

He followed her into the big open sitting room in Admissions. Martha Stewart's fingerprints were all over the place: lots of chintz, all warm and cheery, with three vases of fresh-cut flowers on tables surrounded with bright-colored club chairs and couches. On one wall hung a large watercolor of a sailboat in the ocean, its blood-red spinnaker ballooning out. The upscale homey look was spoiled, though, by a shiny defibrillator mounted on a rustic hand-hewed beam and a straitjacket hanging next to a raincoat in a half-open closet.

A woman at the desk gave Cam a clipboard with several pages of forms on it and asked him to fill them out.

Cam looked over at a man in his fifties with his head in his hands. He sat in a straight-back chair next to a woman who had the sad gray eyes of a long-suffering wife. When the man moved his hands, Cam caught a glimpse of his face: tortoiseshell glasses and a sickly pallor. He looked massively depressed.

"You going to be okay, honey?" the wife asked as Cam struggled to fill out the form with head-scratchers like 'age' and 'home address.'

"I don't know," the man mumbled without looking up. "Don't know *anything* anymore."

Cam felt sorry...for *her*. The man sounded like he was ready to swan dive off the GW Bridge. Dude needed to suck it up a little.

After a few minutes, the outside door opened and a woman with sunglasses strolled in and sat down next to Cam. She shot him a glance, as if trying to sniff out his affliction. He smiled at her, then went back to the questionnaire, his right leg bouncing up and down as if to some driving hip-hop beat.

Cam looked over again at the man. His head had slumped farther forward. The wife patted him on the knee.

"It's going to be okay, Ted," she whispered.

Cam envied Ted. No way Cam's wife, Charlotte, would ever be so supportive. She had volunteered to come home a day early from her quarterly tune-up at the Canyon Ranch in Arizona and drive him to

Clairmount. But when he said he could manage it alone, she didn't push it. He wondered if maybe she had rendezvoused with her boyfriend out there. The boyfriend he wasn't supposed to know about.

He could tell Ted's wife had insisted on coming, probably arranged the whole thing. Ted didn't look capable of much on his own.

Meanwhile, Ted's head had dropped another six inches, just above waist level now. Like it was a twenty-pound medicine ball. His glasses had slid down to the tip of his nose. Cam started to say something to Ted's wife, but her eyes were locked in a thousand-yard stare, focused on something far, far away. Remembering better days, Cam guessed.

Without warning, Ted pitched off the chair and his head bounced off the beige Berber rug. His glasses snapped and went flying. His wife dropped down on all fours next to him.

"Teddy! Teddy!" she cried out, cradling his head in her lap. "Oh my God, are you all right?"

Cam slid out of his chair and crouched on the other side of the fallen man.

A muffled chuckle from Ted rumbled into a full-scale laugh. "I don't know what happened," he said at last.

His wife patted his head sweetly, smiled, and kissed his forehead. "That's the first time I've heard you laugh in years."

Ted looked over at Cam, embarrassed a little. "How'd you like my little Nagasaki nose dive?"

"A perfect ten." Cam picked up half of Ted's glasses. "Gonna need a little Krazy Glue here. I'm Cam, by the way."

"Ted," Ted said, getting to his feet.

Cam stood too and sat in his chair. After a few seconds, he looked over at the woman in dark glasses next to him.

"You know, you remind me of someone," he said.

"You remind me of someone too," she said, deep into her *Vanity Fair*.

"Oh yeah? Who?"

"A guy who hangs out in gin mills too much."

Cam laughed. "Opium dens too."

She raked him with scorn. "I believe it."

Cam dropped his voice. "Could I tempt you with a cocktail. Out in my car?" he asked, momentarily forgetting he had killed the Johnny Blue.

She turned and glared through the thick dark glasses. She had beautiful skin, jutting cheekbones, and a major-league scowl.

Cam held up his hands. "Hey, we're not officially inmates yet." She shook her head with withering disdain.

Turning to Ted, Cam asked, "How 'bout you?"

"How 'bout me what?" Ted asked.

Cam shielded his mouth and stage-whispered, "A pop...out in my car?"

Ted's eyes brightened. "I wouldn't mind a beer if you got one."

Ted's wife looked up. "Okay, you two, you're all done with that."

"Sorry," Cam said, chastened yet again.

"I usually have a couple beers a day," Ted said.

"A couple?" his wife said. She turned to Cam. "The doctor said alcohol makes his depression much worse."

Ted nodded. "It's true. A black cloud literally comes over me."

A male attendant walked up to Cam. "Mr. Crawford, if you're ready, I need to get you to the lab," he said. "Take a little blood, then up to Main House."

Cam smiled and rose, his balance wobbly.

"Just a couple things first," the attendant said.

"What?" Cam asked.

"I went through your suitcase. That candy, sorry, you can't have that in your room."

"No?"

The attendant shook his head.

"Well, how 'bout if..." Cam went over, opened his suitcase, and pulled out a large bag of M&Ms.

He tore open the bag and offered it to Ted's wife. "Sweet tooth?"

"Thank you," she said and took a handful.

Cam turned to the woman with the sunglasses and held out the bag. She ignored him.

Cam shook the bag.

Seeing he wasn't going away, she asked, "Plain or peanut?"

"Peanut."

She shook her head. "Yuck."

Cam laughed. "But thanks for asking, Cam. That's very kind of you."

Nothing.

Cam turned to Ted. "How 'bout you? Black Cloud?"

"No, thanks," Ted said.

Cam shook out a handful for himself, then handed the bag to the attendant.

"Here you go. All yours, bro."

"Thanks," the attendant said, pointing to Cam's suitcase. "Oh, and that green T-shirt of yours—"

"The Heineken one?"

The attendant nodded.

"Kinda sends the wrong message, huh?" Cam said.

Chapter 2

Avril pulled up in a black stretch to the Admissions building later that day. Her driver, Lenny, scurried around and opened her door. She stepped out, sucked in a deep breath, and started toward the little house with the red *Admissions* sign on the door. She caught her reflection in the passenger-side mirror and didn't like what she saw. She U-turned back to the car and told Lenny to cool his heels while she worked on her face. The face that the boy director had just told her looked "haggard" on the set of the big budget rom-com they were shooting in Westchester County. The same face that had graced the cover of *OK!* magazine only a month ago. That was an all-time low, Avril's picture right below the lead story: "Kim Jong Un's Plan To Snatch Jennifer Anniston!" She thought she looked like a hooker who had just crawled out of a Sunset Strip crack house at five in the morning.

The headline screamed, "Avril's On-Set, Off-Color Antics!" It was a bogus headline, designed to get readers to fork over five bucks to paw through the pathetic rag, expecting sin and salaciousness, only to find vague references to Avril being "tortured and tormented."

Well, Christ, she thought, who the hell wasn't? Avril had been tense and edgy from day one on the rom-com set, having just crash-landed from a manic high. It was brutal playing the perky, high-spirited news anchor as she slogged her way through the thick mud of a full-blown depression. Then there was the whole mess with her co-star, Rankin Hanley.

"Do I look puffy, Larry?" she asked.

She knew she had screwed up his name, but couldn't be bothered.

"You look beautiful, Ms. Ensor," Lenny said as he opened the door again for her.

Bullshit, she thought.

Avril Ensor was about to become Colleen Higgins, her rehab alias so the tabloids wouldn't get wind of her being at Clairmount. Colleen Higgins was actually the name of her seventh-grade drama teacher, the one who had picked her to play Dorothy in *The Wizard of Oz*, her first nibble at applause and adulation.

She wore a black beret pulled low and big wraparounds as she opened the door to the Admissions building and walked up to the desk. Trying to be invisible, she whispered to the woman in charge, "Hi, I'm Colleen—"

"I know," the woman said, then winked at her like they were co- conspirators. "There's quite a bit of paperwork so if you're ready, we can get started."

She handed Avril a clipboard with a form on it. Avril handed it right back to her. "Fill it in and I'll sign it."

"Ah, Colleen, I'm afraid that's not how—"

But Avril was halfway across the room.

She sat and looked over at an older man opposite her. Shaking, the man was bent forward, folds of skin dangling from his chin and neck. His eyes were glassy. He looked like he was on the tail end of something. Beside him sat a stern-looking, older woman staring at a dog-eared *Cosmo*. She looked like she'd rather be at a Megadeth concert. Avril's eyes shifted to another woman in her thirties, dead still, like a mannequin. Her eyes had a glint of terror in them, as if she was reeling back through a scene of some dark, personal hell.

Avril checked out another woman in a turtleneck. Something was a little off. Then it occurred to her. Well, yeah, no shit, everyone at this place was going to be at least a *little* off. Whether it was drugs or alcohol, drugs *and* alcohol, borderline personality disorder, post-traumatic stress, depression, or God-knows-what, people didn't come to Clairmount for the ambiance.

She pulled her beret lower, stood, and walked around.

Antsy as hell.

She saw an ambulance pull up outside. An attendant in a white jumpsuit went around and opened the back door. He stepped up into the back of the ambulance. A minute later, he hopped back down and was followed by a tall, skinny redheaded girl. Late teens, max. Her hair was the color of a Key West sunset and surrounded her pale freckled face like a halo.

Avril saw a six-inch-wide bandage on her left wrist as the girl followed the tech toward Admissions.

Seven sets of eyes zoomed in on her bandage as she walked inside.

"Okay, so what," the girl said loudly, seeing everyone staring. "Tried and failed. What are your lame-ass stories?" Her eyes strafed the room.

A tech put his hand on her shoulder and tried to steer her toward the check-in desk. "Come on, Rachel," the tech said, "let's just get through the process, nice and—"

But there was no stopping her—she was in fifth gear.

"Goddamn roomful of zombies—" she said, zeroing in on a mousey, older man standing nearby.

"I just work here," he said.

"Coulda fooled me," she shot back.

Her eyes flicked to the older woman next to the glassy-eyed man, trembling now like he was on top of an L.A. quake.

"Just a wild guess: pill popper?" Rachel said.

The woman rolled her eyes. "I happen to be a family member."

Rachel nodded.

"You tellin' me you never knocked back a Xanax or two in the last sixty years?"

She didn't wait around for an answer.

The social worker was suddenly in her face.

"Okay, miss, you need to stop talking right now," she said, hand on hips. "You're being very disruptive."

Rachel ignored her and looked across the room, spotting Avril for the first time.

"Hey, I really dig those Jackie Os," she said about Avril's sunglasses, "and that funky *chapeau*."

Avril was in no mood. "Listen, you little—"

"That'll be enough," said the social worker, taking a step toward her.

But Avril wasn't done. "You come in here like some loud-mouthed drama queen... whatever your problem is, how 'bout keeping it to yourself? Everything was nice and peaceful till you showed up."

The social worker and the tech moved between them like hockey refs. Then the social worker took one of Rachel's arms.

"Let's go, Rachel," he said, guiding her across the room toward a door.

Rachel didn't resist and walked zombie-like to the door. But then suddenly she turned, caught Avril's disapproving eyes, raised her right hand, and extended her long, skinny middle finger.

Chapter 3

Cam and Ted were detoxing in Main House, even though Ted wasn't convinced he needed to be. Cam, on the other hand, had no doubt about it. He had the shakes, nausea, killer headaches, and a feeling that his life had, thus far, been a colossal waste of time. He also had a massive craving for anything with alcohol in it, plus a cigarette, a habit he had given up two years before.

He and Ted had been there three days and were with twenty-two other patients in various stages of drying out and trying to get used to life without their lifelong sidekicks, alcohol and drugs. The patients had single rooms on the second and third floors. On the first floor was the dining room, which facilitated Main House and the seven other residence houses. Main House was a majestic 1890s Colonial perched on a hill that looked out over a field, an old clay tennis court, then across a meandering two-lane road that bisected Clairmount's campus.

In spite of how he felt, Cam—people person he was—was already on a first-name basis with most of the nurses and techs at Main House. On his second night there, sitting on his bed jittery and hyper, he'd heard a light knock on his door. He said "come in," and a sparrow-like woman, sixty or so, had walked in so quietly Cam barely heard her footsteps.

"Hi, I'm Alice," she said. "I've been keeping an eye on you. You're not doing so hot, are you?"

He just shook his head, not comfortable talking about himself or his problems.

Nevertheless, they'd talked for an hour and a half. She was very sweet and comforting. After a while, Alice had confided that she had a lot of drinkers in her family and let it go at that. Cam had asked her a few questions about Clairmount, and she knew everything about the place, having worked there for over thirty years.

The next day, when Cam was muscling his way through a hefty tome called *Healing the Addicted Brain*, he heard the light knock on his door again. Alice came in and suggested they take a walk.

"It's unhealthy, being cooped up all day," she said, gesturing toward his door. "You need to smell the flowers, hear the birds chirp."

He followed her out, happy to give the book a breather. Alice pointed to the various buildings as they walked. Below Main House, and to its left through a stand of maple trees, was a red brick Colonial.

"That's Schechter," Alice said. "You'll probably go there after you get stabilized here."

"That's where they stick us alkie's, huh?"

She laughed.

Below it was Admissions, and across from it, on the other side of Main House, were three separate buildings housing acute-care patients, an office and administrative building, the library, and a laboratory.

Across the street, the land flattened out and a twisting fifteen-foot-wide brook ran through the property. There were three residential houses on that side and another one in the later stages of being constructed. In between the residential houses, and over a bridge spanning the brook, was a one-story 1970s plain-Jane, boxy brick building where classrooms and doctors' and social workers' offices were located.

At the end of the walk, Cam said how much he enjoyed it and asked Alice if they could do it again.

The next day came a knock. "Yesterday was geography. Today is history," Alice said with an inscrutable smile. "And a somewhat nefarious history it is."

She proceeded to explain how Clairmount came into existence. How Main House had been lived in for three generations by a family named Craig until Bradley Craig willed it to a Dr. Harold Rasmussen back in 1961. Rasmussen had treated Craig for depression for fifteen years, and over time, a rapport had developed between the two.

One day after a session, Rasmussen had shared a vision with Craig: how he wanted to create a unique rehabilitation facility where he could help alleviate suffering and provide a lasting cure for patients in distress from acute depression. Rasmussen explained to Craig how certain men were put on earth to make mountains of money, others to lead nations, but he would be satisfied helping as many people as he could navigate the treacherous shoals of addictive anguish. It was a good rap.

On September 14, 1961, Craig died heirless at age seventy-three, the result of fifty-some odd years of alcohol, Cuban cigars he inhaled down to his toes, and daily slabs of red meat. In his will, he gifted his thirty-six-acre estate to Rasmussen so the doctor could fulfill his noble vision.

Alice turned to Cam and raised her eyebrows. "And within days Rasmussen had contacted four luxury home builders and a demolition company. A month later, he had architectural plans to build eighteen quite ostentatious Georgian Colonial houses."

Cam hadn't seen that coming. "Wait, what? I think I missed something."

Alice sighed. "I think it's safe to say the good doctor was something of a con man. He was in it for the money," she said. "Turned out there was a fly in the ointment, though. Craig had never mentioned he put a clause in his will that said his house and land when gifted to Rasmussen could only be used as a hospital or medical facility."

"So much for the get-rich-quick scheme, I guess," Cam said, caught up now. "So, what happened?"

"Well, Rasmussen, being a resourceful man, put an ad in several medical journals and within six months found three doctors with sincere aspirations to create a drug, alcohol, and mental health facility. They were financed by a Yale University endowment fund and saw this as the perfect site for their project. Close to New York City, a beautiful pastoral setting, and near a number of rich communities which—I'm sure they figured—tend to spawn disproportionate numbers of alcohol and drug-addicted individuals."

"Yeah, so I've noticed," Cam said. "So, they bought it?"

"Yup."

"And what happened to Rasmussen?"

"The good doctor, it seems, retired to Palm Beach, ditched his wife, took up polo, and apparently never missed hearing about other people's problems."

Chapter 4

Ted and Cam were sitting at a table with two others in the living room of Main House, playing Scrabble in front of an old brick fireplace. A group of three women were at the next table, playing Hearts, and a few feet from them a man was gesturing and conversing with a person invisible to everyone but himself. And outside, a cluster of patients were on a smoke break.

"What the hell's a *magwa*?" a man with a silver-and-black pony tail next to Cam asked. Cam had just spelled the word out on the Scrabble board.

"A kind of goose," Cam said earnestly. "A Canadian goose. Quacks really loud while in the act of fornicating."

"Bullshit," the man said, shaking his head and reaching for the Scrabble dictionary. "You're making up another one."

Ted and a twenty-year-old girl with Mike Tyson-like tattoos on either side of her neck eyed Cam skeptically as they pondered their next word. On one side of the living room was a wall of shelves that contained games, books, and a collection of old movie DVDs. Looking through the DVDs, Cam had spotted *The Big Lebowski* and wondered how it had snuck by the censors. Supposedly, patients could request movies that weren't on the shelves, but Cam hadn't had much luck when he asked for *The Hangover*. Instead what he got was a withering look from a female tech, which seemed to give the impression his suggestion might be a bit sophomoric.

"So, would it be a flock of magwa's or a gaggle?" the girl asked.

"A gaggle," Cam said without hesitation.

The man with the ponytail looked up from the dictionary. "No such word," he said, shaking his head in disdain. "Try another."

"Let me see that," Cam said, reaching for the dictionary.

Cam pretended to look for the word he had just invented. Out of the corner of his eye, he saw Ted put a "U" and an "N" next to a "G" on the board.

"Hey, Black Cloud," Cam said, "it's not your turn. And by the way, your words...they're a little dark, man."

"What do you mean?"

"What do you think I mean? Just look at 'em," Cam said, pointing. "Pills, jump, gun—see any theme there?"

A word in the dictionary suddenly caught Cam's attention.

He looked down at his letters, grinned, and started spelling out, 'M-A-G-P, then the I next to the E already on the board.

"Magpie," he said, raising his arms in triumph. "It's a bird."

"It's a plane," Ted said.

Cam counted his points. "Twenty...twenty-eight...thirty-five...forty points—" He pumped his fist. "Yeesss."

"Yeah," said the girl, "but you cheated again."

"What are you talking about?"

"You saw that word in the dictionary," she said.

"Sore loser... Tyson."

"Don't call me that," the girl said.

Cam patted her shoulder lightly. "Sorry. What's your name again?"

"Emily."

"And what are you in here for?" The girl picked up a Scrabble letter.

"Oxy was my drug of choice. Huffing turpentine and Freon were close seconds," she said. "Toss a little depression into the mix."

Ted perked up. "Hey, me too."

The girl's eyes narrowed. "Freon?"

"Depression," Ted said, his eyes blinking. "Suicidal too, I guess."

The man with the ponytail turned to Ted, mildly interested. "Ever try to off yourself?"

"Jesus, Pony, how 'bout a little sensitivity here," Cam said.

"Just askin'." He turned to Cam. "What's with you and all the nicknames anyway?"

Cam just shrugged.

Pony eyed him. "So, what are you in for, hotshot?"

"A gallon a day Johnny Walker Blue," Cam said.

"That's all?"

"Sometimes two."

"I'm guessing a lawyer," Pony said.

Cam shook his head. "Guess again, my man. I work for something called a hedge fund. Probably don't know what that is."

"I know what a hedge fund is," Pony said. "Where Bernie Madoff worked."

"Bernie Madoff was a fuckin' con man," Cam said, then glanced at the girl. "Sorry, 'bout my language, Tyson."

The girl backhanded him on the arm.

"Owww, shit," Cam said. "I meant Emily."

*****

After flimflamming his way to victory, Cam walked down the corridor with Ted.

"I'm worried about you, man," Cam said when they got to Ted's door.

"What do you mean?"

"Your state of mind."

Ted put his hand on Cam's shoulder and smiled. "Just worry about yourself."

He turned and went into his room.

Cam walked up to the main desk and saw his friend Alice. "Do me a favor," he said. "Keep an eye on Ted, will you?"

She smiled and nodded.

"Thanks," he said. "Might wanna take his belt, too."

Chapter 5

The red-haired Rachel and three other women twice her age were watching a movie in a little room off the "observation deck." The observation deck—the patients' name for it—was where the techs sat and kept an eye on things. It was a big glass-enclosed oval, twenty feet long, with work stations that faced out and was right in the middle of everything. On one side, it faced the locked front entrance to Acute Care. Another looked out at the dining area, which doubled as a game and meeting room. On the third side was a room where medications were dispensed, and the fourth side was a long corridor with patients' rooms off of it.

"OCD John" was making his rounds around the perimeter of the observation deck. That was his route. Dressed in perma-pressed blue jeans, red waffle-soled Nikes, and a Phoenix Suns T-shirt, John would circle the observation deck—like he was on an oval track—from eight in the morning until lights out at eleven. He only stopped for meals and bathroom breaks, hundreds of times every day. Word was that John had been in Acute Care Unit for over two months, and they couldn't figure out where to ship him off to next. Sometimes people would join John on his endless loop just to get a little exercise. John was friendly and a willing conversationalist, only problem was that what came out of his mouth was 98-percent gibberish.

One of his favorite topics was how the US government and members of the reconstituted Baader-Meinhof gang were in league to discredit alternative energy sources such as solar and windmills because they were on the take from a major oil company. When someone asked which oil company, John said he didn't know for sure but heard it was secretly owned by Venezuelan dictator Hugo Chavez and Sean Penn had a piece of it. When someone said Hugo Chavez was dead, he said maybe it was Baby Doc Duvalier. When they said he was dead too, he said, okay, Putin then.

Rachel had picked a movie and put it into the DVD machine ten minutes before. The older women deferred to her because—even though just eighteen—Rachel was decisive, opinionated, and bossy. She had her heels up on the sofa in front of her, where two of the women were sitting. She was leaning back on the rear legs of a burnt- orange plastic chair. They were watching *Nevada Sky*.

Rachel glanced up and saw the shades and hat as Avril swept into the room. Avril heard just one line of dialogue, spun, and walked toward the door.

"It just started," Rachel said.

"I've seen it already," Avril said, picking up speed.

"Oh my God," Rachel said. Her eyes went wide, and she put her hand up to her mouth.

"Oh my God," she said again.

Avril jerked to a stop.

"That's you," Rachel said, her eyes going from the TV screen to Avril's face. "I just noticed...the voice."

The two other women swung around and their mouths dropped simultaneously.

"Oh my God—"

"—you're Avril Ensor," the tall, plump one finished the short, skinny one's sentence. "I heard someone famous was coming here."

Avril slowly turned around and took a few steps toward them. "If you're going to watch something," she said, motioning the screen, "why did you pick *that* dog?"

She looked at herself on the screen and noticed she didn't have crow's feet back then.

"Ho-ly shit," Rachel said, still taking it in.

The tall, fat one looked like she was hyperventilating.

"I just read something," Rachel said, "how you got busted for doing 'ludes, shooting a mov—"

"Get your drugs straight, honey. It was Molly."

"Least you got good taste," Rachel said.

Avril's drug and mood bouts were legendary, but up until the Westchester shoot, she had always delivered the goods. The director, who had a low threshold for diva antics and a strung-out star, had talked the studio into substituting Priscilla Farr for Avril. Priscilla was their second choice for the role and—it just so happened—the director's girlfriend.

Rachel got up from her chair, hit the pause button, and went back and sat down.

"So, what didn't you like about the film?" Rachel asked, pointing at the screen.

"The 'film,'" Avril said. "Jesus, that's so goddamn pretentious."

Rachel's arms flew up. "Well, ex-*cuse* me," she said. "The fucking *movie* then."

Avril had a sudden urge to bolt up to the front desk and tell them she was out of there. They couldn't stop her. She could just pack up and go. Then she imagined what the tabloids would say: *Avril Couldn't Hack Ritzy Rehab* or *Troubled Avril Jumps Ship*. She had no choice except to gut it out.

"What didn't I like about it?" Avril said acidly.

Rachel nodded.

"Well, for starters, the director, my costar Rankin Hanley, not to mention the whole fucking state of Nevada."

"Wait? Rankin Hanley?" Rachel said. "He's such a hottie."

"Get to know him a little, honey."

Rachel's eyes scrunched up. "Really?"

The woman with a yellow smiley face on her sweatshirt turned to Avril. "Well, I for one really liked it."

"Well, no offense, Gertrude," Avril said, "but you have shitty taste."

The woman looked like a bucket of freezing water had been tossed in her face.

"My name is Mary, and I think you gave a fine performance."

"What?" Avril said. "Nuanced? Layered?"

Rachel laughed. The woman looked confused.

"Aren't you at least flattered we're watching it?" Rachel asked.

Avril took a few steps toward Rachel. "No, I'm not. What's wrong with a nice Harry Potter *film*?"

"We probably would, if we had one."

Avril turned to go.

"Come on, princess. Sit down," Rachel said, gesturing to a brown Naugahyde chair. "We'll put something else on. Just let us bask in your aura. Plee-eeese."

Avril turned to her. "Sarcastic little bitch, aren't you?"

"Yeah, but it grows on you."

Avril fought off a smile.

"Where you goin'?" Rachel asked.

"Get my meds. See my doctor."

"Come back after that."

Avril turned and disappeared.

Chapter 6

Dr. Davidenko knocked on the door and pushed it open in one motion, like he hoped to catch Avril undressing. He had showed signs of advanced Dirty Old Man syndrome before. He made his rounds every second day and talked to patients for five minutes max, like he got paid by how many patients he churned. Since getting there four days before, Avril had gotten twenty minutes to a half hour per session. Not that she played prima donna and demanded it, but fact was, she did expect it. And the doctor, no surprise, wanted to spend more time with her than his other patients. She was a movie star, after all. Beautiful, charismatic, vulnerable, and, until he worked his psychiatric magic, shattered. He had already told friends at a cocktail party that he was treating a famous movie actress and let them ask enough questions to figure out who she was.

So much for doctor-patient confidentiality.

"It's been four days. Have you noticed progress?" he asked.

The doctor was standing, arms crossed. She was slouched in a wooden chair opposite a bare-bones desk.

"Not much. Depression's still horrible. Withdrawal's maybe a little better."

The doctor scratched the back of his head. "So...you think you're ready for the next stage?"

"Do *you*?"

"Pretty soon, I'd say."

"Tell me about it, I've never done a program before."

"Sure," he said and sat down at the end of her bed.

That struck her as totally inappropriate, but she didn't say anything. That had always been part of her problem.

"It's a combination of things. A structured program, where you get up at a certain time, have activities in the morning, classes in the afternoon. AA and NA meetings at night."

"So, it's much more intense?"

"Yes, more intense and meant to give you discipline, education, and—as I said—structure. You'll go to Brook House, learn DBT, do homework—you know, how to cope better with your issues. Plus, there are chores: clean the kitchen, make your bed, things like that."

Avril's long eyelashes batted several times. "I like it when people do those things for me."

Davidenko laughed like she was Jimmy Kimmel.

"So, what exactly is DBT again?"

"Dialectical behavior therapy is a fancy name for teaching you how to make problems easier to deal with," he said earnestly. "We teach you several strategies for how to cope with things and people better. Plus, handle stress and anxiety caused by your disease."

She raised her arms. "Well, bring it on, Doc, I'm ready." Davidenko smiled his thick rubbery-lips smile.

"You'll have two classes in the afternoon, then homework about what you learned," he said and patted her on her knee, definitely way over the line. She shot up out of the bed and headed toward the door.

"So, when do I go to Brook House?" she asked, avoiding eye contact.

"In a few days," he said, glancing at her long, tanned legs. "Am I going to have a roommate?"

"I assumed you wouldn't want one, so I put you in a single."

"No, I want one. I haven't had a roommate since my sister."

Davidenko nodded. "Okay, I think that's good. Socialization is definitely a good thing."

Avril nodded back. She had a strong urge to get away from this man.

"I'm going to go watch a movie." She knew, unlike other patients, she could call the shots.

Davidenko stood up and smiled. "Which one?"

"I'm not really sure."

She walked out of the room, feeling safe at last.

Avril walked back into the TV room. It was packed now. The cat was out of the bag she could tell. Word had spread.

Rachel saw her. "An oldie but a goody," she said, motioning to the screen.

Avril glanced up and saw the character played by James Mason. Then she saw the young blond girl next to him, played by Sue Lyon. It felt like a steel fist to her stomach. "I can't watch this," she said.

Rachel held up a hand. "It's just—"

"No, no," Avril said and ran out of the room.

Rachel's first reaction was to run after her. But she let her go. The other women all looked at each other.

"What's the big deal? It's just *Lolita*," one woman said.

Another one looked at Rachel, then shrugged her shoulders, bewildered.

But Rachel had a theory.

Chapter 7

D r. Paul Crockett, wearing a Dartmouth baseball cap, was sitting on the porch of the Acute Care Unit at Clairmount. Being an Ivy League graduate was a big deal to him because in high school he had always been Paul Crockett, the geeky grind, or Paul Crockett, the last guy on earth girls would ever catch a movie with. The hat also helped prevent a sunburn, and since Paul was 80-percent bald and 20-percent nose, he wore it a lot outside.

It was his third session with Arthur Petit, a twenty-five year-old- patient who suffered from schizoaffective disorder, Cotard's delusion, dissociative identity disorder, and possibly a few yet-to-be diagnosed afflictions. Arthur, who had family money, had checked himself in five days before and had glibly told Crockett that he needed a "change of scenery" and how the pictures of Clairmount on the website looked nice.

Arthur reminded Crockett of a photo he had seen of Truman Capote as a kid. Towheaded, androgynous, and—you could just tell—bad news. But if Capote was short, Arthur was shorter, because Arthur was a dwarf. Almost normal from the waist up, he had legs that were the length of a ventriloquist's dummy.

It was such a cruel joke, Paul thought, Arthur's last name being Petit. Arthur was talking about his childhood in London, though he was as American as a '57 Chevy.

"So, me and my brother were out in the garage of the house in Highgate," Arthur said, "Guess I was about nine or ten. Garage was big enough for like twelve cars—"

The doctor was leaning forward in his chair, hands pressed together, his goateed chin resting on his thumbs.

"Your father was working there...in London?"

Arthur blinked, turned his head to one side, and took in the clustered pack of Clairmount patients on their smoke break thirty feet away.

"Working?" Arthur said. "Thought I told you, he was ambassador to England. Court of St. James. Pip, pip, cheerio." Then he added, "Not exactly a job...*job*."

The doctor nodded. Arthur had never mentioned this before. Crockett made a mental note to Google Ambassador Petit. See if there really was such a guy.

"All you told me was that you were in England for a few years."

"And a messed-up few years it was," Arthur said, flicking something invisible off his pants.

Crockett leaned back in his chair. "So, tell me what happened, Arthur?"

"Well, my father was a car collector. Triumphs and Healey's, mainly," Arthur said eyeing the twelve-foot wall surrounding the Acute Care Unit. "He also had this old black coach, s'posedly an eighteen-hundreds London taxi. Looked like an old stage coach—you know, driver up on top, passengers inside."

The doctor nodded.

"So, one day I said to my brother, Robbie, 'Let's play Cowboys and Indians. You be the cowboy inside the coach, shooting out at me. I'll be on my horse, firing arrows—'"

"Wait, a pretend horse, right?" Crockett asked.

Arthur squinted and turned his head. "Well, yeah, of course. A pretend horse, pretend bullets, but *real* arrows."

The doctor frowned slightly, imagining Arthur catching his brother in the eye with an arrow. Then he figured they probably had those rubber tips on them.

"So, I squirted lighter fluid on the tip of an arrow like I saw in a movie, then lit it up—"

The doctor swallowed hard and pushed up his cap.

"First one flamed out. Second one bounced off the stagecoach, but the third one..."

The doctor's hand was back on his chin, squeezing it now.

"It hit the coach and caught fire. The thing was really dry. Went up in flames in a flash. Then the whole garage caught fire. I got out of there just in time."

The doctor was having trouble asking the obvious question. Finally. "And your brother?"

"He didn't make it," Arthur said matter-of-factly.

Arthur's tiny feet jiggled.

The doctor searched Arthur's eyes. They didn't look sad or guilty or remorseful. He didn't even blink. His eyes just looked very dark. The color of ashes.

"Did this really happen, Arthur, or—"

"Did I make it up?" Arthur said, looking amused. "You tell me. You're the shrink."

The doctor sighed and looked over at the smokers going back inside, one attendant leading them, one bringing up the rear. He locked onto Arthur's eerie, disturbing eyes for as long as he could, then had to look away.

Chapter 8

Cam's wife, Charlotte, came up to see him five days after he got to Clairmount. It was five-thirty, and they were in the library of Main House. Cam asked her if she felt like having dinner.

She turned her head and looked at him funny. "Since when do you have dinner at five-thirty?" she asked. "Did you turn into a farmer up here?"

Cam shrugged, remembering how just about any subject could turn into a fight. "What can I tell you? That's just when it is."

"Fine," she said, throwing up her hands.

As they stood in line, Cam introduced her to Pony, Emily, and a guy with Tourette's syndrome. She didn't seem impressed with any of them.

He noticed Arthur Petit looking her over. Cam got an unsettling feeling that he was mentally undressing her. He had seen Arthur look the same way at a girl in AA. Just staring and staring, his tongue gliding around his upper lip like a serpent's, his beady eyes zeroing in on her breasts, then slowly working their way down. The girl had no idea. Neither did Charlotte.

As unimpressed with Cam's new friends as Charlotte was, she was even less impressed with the food. She didn't need to say anything to Cam. The tiny portions she put on her plate said it all. A little clump of brown rice and some army-green asparagus was about it.

"Billy Joel didn't think much of it either," Cam said, pointing to her plate as he sat across from her at the eight-person dining room table. Another couple was at the far end.

Charlotte looked up with a frown after a bite of the asparagus. "Was he here too?"

"Yeah, a res told me he did a stint after that model dumped him," Cam said. "Told me he was always bitching about how much the food sucked."

Charlotte smiled. "*A-men* to that."

One thing for sure, Charlotte had a killer smile—freckles, cheek bones, and big lips all working together nice and harmoniously.

"This place gets its share of celebrities, I heard," she said. She was dressed in a light-green skirt and a white silk top with black polka dots and enough cleavage so you'd notice but not ogle.

"Supposedly some actress just came here on the down low," Cam said, taking a bite of bone-dry chicken.

Charlotte leaned closer. "Where'd you hear that?"

"I'm tight with the staff. Want me to get you a salad? They can't mess that up...too much."

"Romaine lettuce?"

Cam glanced over at the brown-edged lettuce, then saw one of the waiters put something down on the buffet table.

"How 'bout a nice piece of carrot cake?" he asked.

Charlotte shook her head. Violently almost. Like he was suggesting she knock back a gallon of Ben & Jerry's.

"Five hundred calories. Are you kidding? So, who is she?"

Cam's mind was still on the carrot cake.

"Oh, you mean the actress? No clue. Maybe just the rumor mill." Charlotte reached across for Cam's hand. It always surprised him how her hands were a little clammy. Even in winter.

"Charlie came up to see me," Cam said.

Charlotte smiled and put her hand on his arm. "That was nice of him. That's a long way to come."

Cam nodded. His brother Charlie was a homicide detective in Palm Beach, Florida. He used to work in New York City, but had burned out and moved down to the Sunshine State. Cam was the youngest, Evan the oldest, and Charlie in between. Evan was the odd man out. Charlie and Cam had been athletes, Evan was on the debate team. Charlie and Cam had been kids who liked to have a good time, Evan was the serious one. Charlie and Cam were popular with girls, Evan was popular with librarians.

"What did you guys talk about?"

"Oh, you know, random stuff."

"No, Cam, I don't know. What kind of random stuff?"

Cam shrugged. "Well, like I told him I was getting ECT, where they zap you with electric shocks. He got all concerned. I told him not to worry, it wasn't like *One Flew over the Cuckoo's Nest.*"

"Glad to hear it," Charlotte said, flicking a strand of shiny brown hair out of her eye. "So, what are *we* going to do, Cam?"

She hadn't bothered with any of the usual Q&A. Even something really basic like *How are you feeling, Cam?* That would have been nice. Or, *How is it not drinking?* That would have been normal. But he wasn't really surprised.

"What do *you* want to do, Char?" He slid his hand out of hers and leaned back in his chair.

"I don't know," she furrowed her brow and tapped the table, "I love you, but..."

"The old, 'I love you, but.'"

She nervously scratched the back of her head. "It's complicated."

"You mean, because of Antoine?"

Her head snapped back a full six inches.

"Yeah, I know about him."

"I'm sorry, Cam," she said. "He and I—"

Cam held up his hands. "Spare me the details."

"It's Ashton, by the way."

"What?"

"It's Ashton, not Antoine."

"That's such a bogus name." He couldn't hold back. "What did he change it from?"

Charlotte stood up and wiped her mouth with her napkin. Cam noticed how toned her legs were. Canyon Ranch was delivering the goods. He saw Arthur Petit's eyes zoom in on her breasts again from a table away.

Charlotte put her hands on her hips and glared at Cam. "You know, Cam, sometimes you can be such an—"

"Asshole?" Cam said under his breath.

"I was going to say, 'jerk.'"

"Oh, right," Cam said. "*An* jerk, huh?"

Charlotte stormed out of the dining room. Cam watched Arthur Petit's eyes trained on the wiggle-waggle of her perfectly rounded ass.

Chapter 9

Avril picked up a phone, dialed a number, and waited. The two phones in Acute Care were right next to each other, which made it tough to have a private conversation. Her sister, Terry, answered.

"Hey, it's me," Avril said.

"Hey, Av," she said "Things any better?"

"No."

"The depression?"

"Yeah, plus the food, the people, the routine. Never had it like this," Avril said, watching Rachel go to the dispensary, get her pills, toss them in her mouth, then take a swig of water like she was knocking back a shot of tequila.

"Did that bastard Hanley ever call?" Terry asked.

"Emailed me," Avril said sadly. "Sixteen words to be exact."

"What a dick."

Avril wrote his initials on the whiteboard like she was carving them into a tree.

"Hey, it wasn't like I never heard the rumors. He was just so incredibly sweet to me at first. Treated me like nobody had in a long time. Those perfect manners, no raging alpha-male ego, and he is so damn handsome."

"Damn it, Avril, it was all an act," Terry said, her voice amped up. "The guy used you to get the part, then his publicist got you two in all the cheesy supermarket rags and gossip shows. Guy had three duds in a row—he needed a makeover."

"You are so damn loyal. It ever occur to you that maybe I thought I was some goddess with the power to turn gay men straight?"

Rankin Hanley had been in Santa Barbara to play in a celebrity golf tournament along with a handful of entertainers and jocks. He and Avril had met at a dinner party, and two weekends later they had gone down to a spa in Palm Springs together. Within a month, their affair was leaked to *Access Hollywood*. Terry's theory was that Rankin Hanley, or maybe his agent, had planned it from the beginning—the "chance" meeting at the dinner party, how he had come onto her with his mesmerizing eyes, bouquets of roses every day, and yes, even the pathetic poetry...which, Terry figured, his agent probably wrote.

It had been a three-month torrid affair until the night she, Rankin, and the makeup guy went out for dinner during the shoot. Avril told Terry how it might just as well have been the two men at the table with their secret shared laughs, their eye contact that lasted a beat too long, even her suspicion at one point that they might actually be holding hands under the table. It was either thoughtlessly cruel or intentionally sadistic.

The next day Avril called Rankin and said they had to talk. He stole her thunder by telling her he really liked her but was "sporadically un-heterosexual." Then in case she didn't get it, he said he liked girls and boys. She felt exactly like she did after the failure of her marriage— pummeled, bruised and crushed—and the dark, heavy blanket of depression came on its coattails and deadened and debilitated her. Amazingly, she had never had a relationship with an actor before. One of the grips on the set had a stash of pot that numbed the pain. But she needed a lot more than just to be numbed.

"Guy's a complete shithead. Movie'll bomb without you in it," Terry said. "They should rename it *The Fag and the Stand-In*."

Avril laughed. "Oh, nice, Terry. And you, always the politically correct one."

"Is there anybody there you can talk to?"

"No, I wake up and just feel horrible. I'm so damn negative."

"Like how?"

"Like I can't get out of bed—all these scary thoughts racing around in my head."

"About what?"

"Like I can't act, I look like shit, my face is nothing but crow's feet and wrinkles—"

"You're only thirty years old, for Chrissakes!"

"Yeah, well, I don't feel it. I got myself convinced no one likes me, I'm worthless, everything sucks. Plus, I totally lost it the other night, completely freaked out. This movie reminded me..."

"Of what, honey?"

Avril sighed. "You know...of what happened."

"Oh God, sweetie, I'm coming out there to see you."

"You're in California."

"So?"

"'Cause you're always coming to see me. Stay there and take care of your perfect husband, perfect children, and perfect goddamn mutt," Avril said. "Christ, I'm sorry. Self-pity much?"

"Your doctor there any good?"

"He looks at me like he wants to get in my pants."

"So? You're used to that."

"Yeah, but he's, like, seventy."

Avril heard her sister say something to someone. Avril's five-year-old niece, she guessed.

"You know," Avril said, "I look at my pathetic life—I mean, no husband, no boyfriend, no kids, no cute little fur ball of a dog, and realize I'm this goddamn cliché in a mental institution."

"What do you mean?"

"You know, beautiful, rich, talented, but oh-so-tragically fucked up."

"You've got a very serious illness, honey."

"Yeah, but so? Suck it up, Avril. I'm *so* sick of letting it rule my life."

Terry thought for a second. "You know, I've said this before, but you're really way too tough on yourself."

"Yeah, maybe," Avril said, seeing one of the techs tap his watch, signaling it was almost eleven o'clock and time to hang up and go to her room. "Hey, I just got the word from the moron in charge—time for Avril to go nighty-night."

Terry laughed. "I'll call you tomorrow. Hang in there, kid, and by the way, I don't know anyone who's got the perfect husband, perfect kids, and perfect mutt."

Avril laughed. "I'll take just one."

She hung up and walked away from the phones, eyes cast down. Rachel walked past her. Not a word between the two.

*****

Rachel had been given a little pink message slip that said *Call Regis Furth, urgent re. mother's estate. Call anytime.*

She dialed the number and finally connected with Furth, who explained he was an attorney for her stepfather, Phil Eppersley. She thought about hanging up right away, but was scared. She didn't know what he could do to her—he was a lawyer, after all.

She told him she only had a few minutes until they shut the phones off.

"This won't take long," Furth said. "Your stepfather has engaged me to make sure there is an equitable distribution of the estate of your late mother, Evelyn Eppersley—"

He paused, and Rachel just waited as she watched OCD John circle the observation deck, then stop and walk toward his room after the tech said something to him. She flashed to her stepfather, a nasty bully who used to bend her over his knee and spank her for really trivial stuff. Like leaving the milk out overnight. What was really creepy was how he used to pull down her underpants when she was younger, turn his signet ring around on his finger so the initials were face down, then spank her. Afterward, she'd look back and see the initials PE on her bottom in blocky letters. Like she was a steer he had just branded.

Ten out of ten creep factor.

Not that her real father was any bargain. He had stiffed her mother on child support, until the day the tables suddenly turned. Most painful to Rachel was him refusing to take her sobbing phone calls. That had crushed her fragile teenage heart.

"Phil just wants his due, Rachel."

Regis Furth's nasal rasp snapped her back.

Rachel always lost her bravado talking to male authority figures.

"I don't know about any of this,"

"You do know that your mother left you everything?"

"Yeah, I guess."

"What do you mean, you 'guess'?"

Rachel picked up the black dry erase marker and started nervously doodling on the whiteboard.

"Well, it's not that big a deal to me," she said, regretting the words immediately.

Why was she even talking to this guy?

"Well, if that's the case, then we don't have an issue?" .

"What do you mean?"

"If you don't care about the money," Furth said. "In any case, my client—your stepfather—is entitled to a substantial share of your mother's estate. Half, to be exact."

"Why is that?" Rachel asked, nodding at the tech who had just signaled that she needed to hang up.

"Because he was her husband at her time of death last month."

"But my mother didn't want to give him anything—"

"Doesn't matter. The law is very clear on this—marital assets are evenly divided at time of death."

"Am I going to need a lawyer?"

"Sure, be my guest, but he's going to tell you exactly what I just told you," Furth said. "I'll caution you, though, if there is any litigation between me and an attorney you might engage, and it is resolved in our favor, which it will be," Furst droned on, "I will recommend to my client that as part of any judgment, our attorney's fees will be borne by the losing attorney. And they will be...considerable."

Rachel took the black marker, pressed hard onto the whiteboard, and slowly started writing. She watched Mary, the girl whose room was next to hers, pad leadenly down the corridor from the medical dispensary after getting her evening Remeron fix.

"How much money is it again?" Rachel asked.

There was a pause on the other end.

"Eighteen million dollars, give or take."

Rachel said she had to go and quickly hung up before he could protest, then looked down at what she had written.

Get me out of this life in bold, stark letters. In quick, violent swipes she crossed it all out.

It wasn't right to give other people ideas.

Chapter 10

Paul Crockett had his yellow lined pad out. He had asked Arthur to go back to the beginning.

"Okay, for starters, Doc," Arthur said, "I grew up in Normal, Illinois. *Not!*"

Arthur said it so loud a woman across the room turned and looked.

Arthur blew her a kiss. "So, when I was a kid, I dreamed of becoming either the president of a college or someone who came up with the cure for a disease. Not a major one, just something that would get me a few pages in one of the medical journals. Yeah, I know, not the dreams of a normal kid."

Crockett looked up. "Tell me about your family, Arthur."

Arthur's eyes darted around like he didn't know where to start. "Okay. My father owned a chain of drugstores that got bought out by Walgreen's. I was the youngest of eleven kids—all of them nauseatingly *normal*. Right after the old man sold his business, when I was ten, we moved east." Arthur sighed and tapped the side of his chair. "Nobody ever bothered to tell me why. But what did I care. Not like I had a bunch of buddies I was leaving behind."

"What was your relationship with your brothers and sister like?" Crockett asked.

Arthur thought for a second. "Strained to nonexistent."

"Can you tell me what you mean by that?"

"I'd rather not," Arthur said. "But I'll give you a taste. Three of my brothers were jocks in high school, and my father went to all their games. So not exactly being basketball material, I became the star of the debate team. Think my father showed up for any of my debates? I got the sense he wished he'd had his tubes tied after ten kids."

"What about your mother?"

"I'm not going to talk about her at all."

Crockett decided to let it go for now. "But your father neglected you?"

"Fuck, yeah," Arthur said. "Only thing I ever got out of him was learning how to shoot. Me and the oafs—"

"You mean, your brothers?"

"Yeah. We'd go out behind the house and shoot at these Schlitz beer cans with .22s. That's what my mother drank. By the case, I might add. I got so good I could dot the 'i' in Schlitz with a bullet. Every time."

"You mentioned that you started seeing a psychiatrist at a pretty young age."

"Yeah, around twelve," Arthur said. "No one told me why I had to see the creepy old guy. Wore aviators inside. First time I told him about wanting to be a college president or a guy who invented a cure for something, he looked at me like I was a total freak show. I could just tell what was going through his head: 'Why don't you want to be fireman or a baseball player like every other kid?'"

It was time for Crockett to chime in with an insightful observation. "Well, you couldn't, because of your size."

"No shit, Doc," Arthur said. "So, I kept talking to this guy, like it was important for him to understand me. Told him if I was a college president, they'd maybe name a prize after me, or a dorm. Or hang my picture in some room with all the other presidents. Or if I found the cure for a disease, people would have to say my name every once in a while. The shrink just looked at me like I had a tree growing out of my nose"—Arthur shook his head slowly— "I mean, like he should talk, sitting there looking like some perv in those aviators."

Chapter 11

Ted had been stuck on the third page of his book for the last twenty minutes. Concentrating for more than five seconds was impossible.

Every morning his first image was of the stretch when he hit rock bottom—a little over two years before—and he'd replay it constantly throughout the day. He hadn't been able to make peace with it or leave it behind, even though his shrink had given him a dozen visual images how to jettison the whole bad patch.

The shrink suggested that he visualize putting all his baggage on a cloud, then watch the cloud slowly drift away. Or stick it in a small box, put it in a stream and watch it float away. That might work for some, but not for him. His mind would simply race ahead and project into the future. And the places it went were unbearably dark.

*****

Cam walked into the game room and tapped Ted on the shoulder. "Time for AA, Black Cloud."

Cam wasn't doing much better than Ted. The craving was still there, especially around six at night, when—back in the good old days —he'd load up on his first five fingers of Johnny Walker Blue. Charlotte had called once since the night she came for dinner. She'd asked him how he was, but before he could answer, she launched into a story about how a forty-year-old friend of theirs had had a heart attack and dropped dead on the squash court.

"Come on," Cam said to Ted. "Time to hear all the alkie's and addicts spill their guts."

Ted put the book down and managed a meager smile.

"It's like you're talking about a bunch of foreigners."

Cam pointed a finger at Ted and shot him a wink. "You got me there. Pot calling the kettle black, huh?"

"Yeah, well, all your war stories: cocaine and Jack Daniels, grass and Jack Daniels—"

"Johnny Walker," Cam said. "And I got an update for you: They call it weed these days. Pot in some circles, but never grass."

A nearby tech had her antennae up.

"Gentleman," she admonished. "Change the channel, please."

Cam had been reprimanded by her before. "Okay," he said for her benefit, "guess we gotta get back to talking about bondage and discipline."

She rolled her eyes and slowly shook her head. "Don't you have AA now?" She checked her watch.

"On our way," Cam said.

*****

The van pulled away from the Acute Care Center, carrying a cargo that included Rachel, her posse of older women friends, a woman in holey blue jeans, and Avril. They were being taken to the AA meeting held in the auditorium at the south end of campus.

Rachel was mulling over her theory that something bad had happened to Avril when she was a kid.

Avril was sitting up front with the driver, who kept giving her furtive glances. She had been completely outed. Everyone knew. All the Clairmount employees now referred to her as, "the starlet."

"You been to one of these before?" Rachel asked Avril.

Avril didn't answer.

"Bet you're a veteran," Rachel said.

"Are you talking to me?" Avril asked.

"Yes, *dah-ling*."

"Been going to these since before you were born."

"Cut the shit. You're only ten years older than me."

"Yeah, but light years in maturity," Avril said.

Rachel laughed. "Oooooh," she said, raising her hands and shaking them side to side, "good one, girl."

Avril just shook her head. Girl could push her buttons.

"Bet they got meetings on every street corner in Hollywood." Rachel said.

"I wouldn't know. I live in Santa Barbara."

"Oooh, pardonnez-moi...San-ta Bar-bar-a."

Avril turned, shook her head, and threw Rachel a look of heavy disdain. "Such a child."

"Bite me."

"Moron," Avril said, turning back.

Rachel laughed. "You know, people from the outside come to these meetings."

No one said anything.

"Probably some star gazers will show up. Word's out about you, you know," Rachel said.

Christ, she had a point, Avril realized.

This was her first open meeting. Up until now, there had been alternating nights of AA and NA meetings just for Clairmount patients. Once a week there was an open meeting for both Clairmount patients and people from the surrounding area.

"It'll be cool seeing guys who aren't Acute Care losers for a change," Rachel said.

Holey Jeans turned to Rachel. "You got a problem with the manic Hispanic? Or the dude with his pants halfway down his ass?"

Rachel laughed and shot a look at Avril. "You mean, the guy with the jones for the princess?"

"Fuck off," Avril said as she noticed the driver stifle a laugh.

The driver pulled up to the auditorium. The five women got out, walked up the steps, and went through the front door of the auditorium. Avril lagged back a step or two. It was a big cavernous room with a wood floor and about fifty gray metal folding chairs arranged in a circle. Avril got behind Rachel, who was the tallest, and tried to slump down and be invisible.

It didn't work. A woman sitting down in front spotted her, pointed a finger, and whispered to a friend.

Rachel turned back to Avril. "You didn't really think you were just going to be one of the girls, did you?"

Avril felt like turning and running, which wasn't her usual reaction. She actually liked making entrances, liked it when people pointed at her and recognized her, though she played it like it was all such a tremendous hassle. But this time was different.

The four women had unknowingly formed a lopsided blocking formation, and Avril followed them, head down, as they crossed to the far side of the room. She sat down and didn't look up.

A few minutes later a man welcomed everyone, and the meeting began. Then he asked, "Are there any people here at the open meeting for the first time?"

A woman raised her hand. "Hi, Cindy. Alcoholic, ten days clean."

Applause and a chorus of, "Hi, Cindy."

The chair recognized another man with his hand up.

"Hi, name's Dennis," he said. "Fourteen days."

More applause and a chorus of, "Hi, Dennis."

On the other side of the room, a man raised his hand, and the meeting facilitator acknowledged him. "Hi, I'm Cam—"

A chorus of, "Hi, Cam."

"Six days." Cam went on. "I know...big deal, right? Hey, longest I've gone since tenth grade."

A few scattered laughs, followed by applause.

Avril raised her head for the first time and looked at the man who had just spoken.

Pretty boy, somewhere around her age, she figured. Kind of a dirty-blond version of Jack Nicholson in his early days. Circa *Easy Rider* maybe. Clearly had issues—she could tell—hyper, had the whole toe-tapping thing going. Stubbly cheeks and chin. His hair could use a comb, but he could probably clean up nice. She pictured his girl-friend's—tall, good looking, legs to the sky, a tad on the vacuous side.

Then she noticed about thirty sets of eyes drilling into her and looked back down at the floor again.

A moment later she glanced up at the man running the group. He was staring at her. Like he knew it was her first open meeting and wanted her to say something. So he could tell his wife. She stared back defiantly but did not raise her hand.

Finally, he looked away and turned to the man next to him, who was the night's speaker.

He introduced the man as Bill and assured everyone that Bill had a "whale of a story to tell." A man with darting eyes, a fleshy Irish-looking face, and sandals with black socks, Bill didn't take long to get into his two relapses, which he covered in anguishing detail.

"Then after the second one, I knew I had to do something dif-ferent, so I did. It wasn't enough to just cut out the Wall Street martini lunches and all the boozing after work. No, I had to do something drastic—"

He paused for drama.

"So, I shit canned three guys in my shop who I drank with. I know, pretty harsh," he said, putting up his hands, "but I had to get rid of every vestige of my drinking life. I stopped seeing all the friends I used to drink with. I had to. I wasn't strong enough to do it any other way. Ended up with a lot fewer friends, but the ones I had were *real* friends."

Cam poked Ted with his elbow, leaned close, and whispered. "This is what we have to look forward to."

Bill paused and scanned the room.

"It gets worse. My wife was my number one drinking buddy. No, I didn't fire her, but I got rid of every bottle in the house. Every ounce of booze, into the garbage. Beer, wine, the hard stuff, you name it—"

"What a waste," Cam whispered to Ted.

"The last thing I did," Bill said. "No, not demand that she quit, but if she was going to drink, she had to go out to the guest house—"

"What a dick," Cam said.

"No drinking at dinner, no drinking in the same house with me. I didn't even want to smell it on her. I know—sounds pretty hardcore, but that was the only way I was going to make it stick. *The only way.* Not only that, I never go to parties or restaurants or anywhere where people are drinking. That's the discipline I have to enforce. My wife can go alone, that's fine, but I don't go. I can't. I just can't."

Bill's eyes swept the room. He looked extremely pleased with himself. He waited for comments or questions.

No one raised a hand at first. Like they were afraid of him. Finally, Cam's hand shot up.

"Yes?" Bill said.

"Don't take this the wrong way, Bill, but my question is, is there any fun left in your life?"

There were several snorts of suppressed laughter. The majority, though, seemed to regard the question as highly inappropriate, not in keeping with AA protocol.

Avril looked up at him, a faint trace of a smile on her face.

Bill's eyes narrowed. He sat up straight in his chair and folded his arms.

"Guess you think you're pretty funny, Six Days. Well, there's nothing funny about this. To kick it, you gotta do things that are hard. Probably not gonna make you too popular, but you gotta do what you gotta do."

"Thanks a lot, Bill," said the facilitator, looking everywhere but at Cam. "Great story. Thanks for sharing."

A few minutes later the meeting was over, and they all gathered in a circle, held hands, and said the Serenity Prayer.

On their way out, all eyes fell on Avril. People were showing just enough respect for her privacy so no one got too close, but there was plenty of scrambling to get near enough for a good look. Avril's blocking wedge of Rachel and the other three women had broken down.

A large woman with stringy gray hair and denim overalls veered into Avril's path with a magazine in one hand. "Avril, can you sign this for me, please?"

Avril saw that the magazine was opened to an article in *Hello!* She hadn't seen it before but saw her picture, which had been taken by a particularly odious paparazzi as she stumbled out of a LA celebistro.

Avril took the magazine and, not breaking stride, signed it and handed it back to the woman, who said thanks and how she was a "huge fan."

"Thank you," Avril said.

"No, thank you. Hope it goes well at Clairmount."

Avril nodded as she went out the door of the auditorium.

"Over there," Avril heard one of the women say, pointing to the van, like she was Secret Service.

The white van was parked twenty feet away.

"What a party, huh?" said a man's voice behind Avril.

She turned, recognizing the voice.

It was Cam.

One of the girls opened the van door for her.

"Yeah," she said, "a subject you probably know a lot about."

She climbed into the van and stared straight ahead.

Chapter 12

C am looked down at the large whiteboard above the public phone at the end of the Main House corridor. People had written phone numbers, messages, doodles, and graffiti on it.

Time for a lobotomy, Margo, read one chicken-scratch message.

Another said, in bold red slashes in the middle of the board, *Dr. McQuack is whacked.*

"It sucks, Evan," Cam said into the worn, pea soup-colored public phone. "Shakes, nausea, sweating... shit, and the craving I got is off the charts. They got me on benzos, but they ain't cuttin' it."

Evan had asked how he was doing, but clearly, he would have preferred a succinct answer like, "fine." Or even, "shitty" would work.

"We gotta get Humphries to make up for losing Kreutzel," Evan said, his brother's health already in the rearview mirror.

"Christ. You gonna rub my face in it again?"

"It doesn't go away just 'cause you want it to," Evan said.

Greg Kreutzel had had a $200 million account with Cam and Evan's fund.

Operative word...*had.*

Kreutzel's wife was why they'd lost it, and she had a lot to do with Cam checking in to Clairmount. Kreutzel had been a client of Cam and Evan's for five years and had suggested they have dinner with him to review the account and discuss his investment mix—a standard thing they did with clients, sometimes in their office, sometimes at breakfast, sometimes lunch. Kreutzel was more than satisfied with what

Trajectory Partners had done for him—his returns beat all but 5-percent of other funds.

Cam and Evan had arrived at La Parnesse at 7:30, and Cam ordered ginger ale, his standard client drink. Evan ordered a weak scotch and soda.

Kreutzel, a perpetually tanned guy with really convincing hair plugs, walked in ten minutes later. Behind him was a blond woman twenty years younger, a million dollars' worth of bling hanging off her.

"Oh, Christ," Evan whispered, looking up, "he brought the trophy wife."

Cam stood as the couple approached.

"Gentleman," Kreutzel said, "nice to see you again. Cam, I don't think you've met my wife, Genevieve."

She looked like a Genevieve. Exotic, self-assured, sexy as hell. "Nice to meet you," Cam said.

"I've heard all about you," she said, her eyes lingering on Cam's longer than he was comfortable with. "You're married to one of the Englehardt twins, right?"

Cam nodded. "Charlotte."

She turned to Evan. "So nice to see you again, Evan."

"Thank you, Genevieve. The pleasure's indeed mine," Evan said, like he took notes watching the soaps.

Cam held Genevieve's chair, and they all sat down.

Greg Kreutzel took a sip of water. "Rather than bore the hell out of Genevieve with a bunch of shop talk about currency swaps," he said, "let's just have a nice business-free dinner. Couple of bottles of the best champagne, toast you guys for doing a hell of a job."

Kreutzel flagged down the waiter and ordered a bottle of Cristal, and Cam broke his vow to never have more than one drink with clients. Why not? Kreutzel had declared it a celebration, not a business dinner. But despite what Kreutzel had said, he and Evan got right into the shop talk. That left Cam with Genevieve. Genevieve chattered about a couple they both knew. The husband was having an affair with the nanny, and the wife was having one with her female yoga teacher. Genevieve—because she was French, maybe— put away champagne without getting sloppy and flirted without her husband catching on. At one point, her face leaned so close that her lips grazed Cam's chin.

La Parnesse had a small wood-floored dance area, and after dinner the restaurant played music. Cam had gone from champagne to cappuccino when Genevieve suggested they dance.

It wasn't like he could say he had a broken leg.

It was a slow dance, and he put his hand in her hand and his other one on her back. Lightly.

"You're a good dancer," she said at the end of the song. "But it's like you're dancing with your sister."

Precisely.

"One more," she said. It was almost a command.

This time she pressed close to him. Cam tried to pull back, but she pushed tighter. He looked over at the table. Kreutzel had his hand up for the waiter, then he looked around. Cam quickly steered Genevieve behind another couple between them and the table.

He felt her breath on his chin, smelled her expensive perfume, and concentrated hard on how he was going to put backspin on his nine-iron shot the next day.

"You seem scared of me, Cam," Genevieve said, blue eyes blinking, breasts pressing.

"French women intimidate me."

"We don't bite," she said, "too hard."

Cam was praying Kreutzel would cut in.

Finally, the song ended. She stayed pressed up against him for too long.

"Thanks," Cam said, pushing away from her. "I don't want to monopolize you."

He took long, quick steps back to the table.

Then, the worst part. She called him two days later. At ten in the morning.

"Cam, it's Genevieve Kreutzel," she said in her breathy voice. "This is a business call...how's our account doing?"

Well, actually you have several, he thought, detecting a slur in her voice. Like she was washing down her morning croissant with a Bloody Mary.

"Ah, I'm not too sure, Genevieve," Cam said. "How 'bout I have Evan give you a call?"

She laughed. "Don't bother. Business call's over. I want to buy you lunch at a nice, quiet, out-of-the-way place tomorrow."

"I don't think that's a good idea."

"I do, and I was under the impression you work for me."

Cam wanted to slam the phone down on the receiver. "Well, yes, but—"

"No buts. Lunch, a drink or two, then we go somewhere and make mad, passionate love."

"Genevieve, I'm a happily married man," he lied.

Then he hung up.

Four days later, Evan and Trey MacLeod walked into Cam's office and told Cam they had just lost the Kreutzel account. Trey looked pale and out-of-breath. Evan looked like a priest who had just heard a particularly disturbing confessional.

"Greg found out about you and Genevieve," Trey said. "Said if he couldn't trust you with his wife, how could he trust you with his money? Went on about you dancing with her all-night long."

Cam looked across his desk at Trey in disbelief.

"Are you fucking kidding me?" he said. "That's complete bullshit. She asked me to dance. What was I supposed to say? I didn't know how? It was two whole dances, ten minutes max. When she called, I said, thanks, but no thanks. End of story."

Trey booted up his avuncular smile.

"You know how much I value you, Cam," he said, stroking his nicotine-colored mustache, "but your drinking...well, it's a problem. I mean, tell me to mind my own business, but I think Charlotte might just agree."

Evan went into auto-nod. Cam wanted to lean across his desk and cold cock the brown-nosing bastard. Jerk probably couldn't wait to tell Trey all was not matrimonial bliss in the Crawford household.

"Trey, I'll deal with my wife," Cam said, grabbing a pen and tapping it on his desk. "No way my drinking had anything to do with what happened with Genevieve Kreutzel. I had two glasses of champagne. Probably less than you."

Evan was waiting for that. "Yeah, but *we* know how to handle it." Cam's face went brilliant red.

"Always got my back, don't you, Evan." Then to Trey. "Drinking was a fucking non-issue...except for her."

Trey looked at Evan and raised his eyebrows.

"Don't deflect, Cam," Trey said. "We're not talking about anyone's drinking here but yours."

"And don't kid yourself," Evan said, piling on. "It's a problem."

Cam wanted to jab the pen into his brother's sycophantic eyeballs. "I drink too much. Okay, you happy?" Cam said. "But it doesn't affect my work."

"Dragging your ass in late doesn't affect your work?" Evan said.

Cam was seething now. "You know, Evan, you're such an asshole. I came in late once or twice, but I never missed anything important."

"What about the time—"

Cam shot out of his chair. "I don't want to fucking hear it—"

Trey held up his hands. "Cam, take it easy," he said. "You're in denial. You need to go somewhere and get clean. For your sake, the sake of your marriage, and yes, for the sake of Trajectory Partners."

Trey had walked out of Cam's office with Evan in his wake, the subject clearly not up for further discussion.

*****

Now Cam found himself gripping the public phone handset like it was his brother's neck. "So, Evan, are we done here?"

"Yeah, just wanted to check up on you," Evan said. "See how it's going. We miss you."

That was Evan's bullshit conciliatory tone. Drop his bombs, then get all solicitous.

Cam knew Evan *really* did miss him. Because Cam was the point man for client relations, and no matter how much Evan played that down, he knew how critical it was.

"I gotta go," Cam said.

"Is there anything you need? Anything I can send you?" Evan said, because he definitely wasn't going to come there and drop it off.

"No, I gotta go," Cam said again. "As usual, it's been a barrel of laughs."

"Hey, Cam, you don't have to—"

Cam slammed the phone down so hard that a piece of the mouthpiece broke off and flew across the room.

He stormed down the corridor and out the front door of Main House. One of the techs followed him out.

"Where you going, Cam?" the tech asked.

Cam knew where he *wanted* to go.

Marquis Liquors. 323 Main Street.

He had looked them up on the internet his first day at Clairmount. He had called and asked what time they closed. Just in case.

Chapter 13

Arthur saw her over in the corner of the dining room. The vibe she was putting out couldn't have been more clear: don't come within fifty miles of me. She wasn't wearing the beret, but her big black sunglasses seemed to cover half her face. You could still see the frown, though. It stuck out like a stop sign.

It was working, too, because the other people in the room were clumped together at tables a long way away from her.

Arthur walked right up to her table and put his green tray down opposite her. He knew she wasn't about to look up.

"Hi," he said. "My name's Arthur. Figured you could use some intelligent conversation, instead of what dribbles outta the pie holes of these mooks here."

No reaction from her.

"*Sure, have a seat, Arthur,*" he said. "*Love to have you join me.*" He sat down, stuck his spoon into his Grape Nuts and took a bite. "Ever wonder why they call 'em Grape Nuts?" he said, "I mean, what the hell do these little brown BBs have to do with grapes?"

"I never wondered," came the flat response.

"I like the taste, but the grape thing, I just don't get what that's all about."

Avril looked up, wondering who the odd ramble was coming from. She took him in.

"Yeah," he said. "A dwarf, a midget, a runt, or as one guy called me yesterday, a 'wiseass, uppity little cretin.'"

Avril laughed. "Fuck 'em," she said.

Arthur raised his orange juice glass in toast. "Exactly. Fuck 'em all."

"My name's Avril."

"No shit, really?"

Avril laughed again.

"You're way better looking close up, and I'm not just suckin' up to you."

"Thank you. That's very kind of you."

"When I heard you were here, I figured we were two people with something in common."

"Really, and what would that be?"

Arthur poured some more milk onto his Grape Nuts. "Ever notice how Grape Nuts dry up so much? How you constantly gotta water them with more milk?"

Avril nodded. "I like Cheerios," she said. "They float."

Arthur shrugged. "So, what we have in common is we both stand out," he said. "The two of us, kind of freaks of nature. You, in a good way. Me, in a, well, vertically challenged, big-headed, ugly kind of way."

Avril laughed and took off her glasses. "You're funny."

"Thank you," he said. "I've been saving it up. Didn't want to waste it on these clowns."

Avril chewed on the end of her sunglasses. "Thought they were mooks," she said. "By the way, what exactly is a *mook* anyway?"

Arthur looked around the breakfast room, and his eyes lighted on a bald man in a frayed bathrobe with thickets of hair sprouting out of both ears.

"See that guy over there?" he said, pointing.

Avril turned and looked. "Yeah?"

"One hundred percent, pure-bred, All-American mook."

Chapter 14

Dr. Paul Crockett and Arthur Petit were out on the flag stone deck of the Acute Care Building on the chilly May afternoon.

"So how was lunch?" Crockett asked, giving his Dartmouth cap a little tug.

"Lunch is lunch," Arthur said, following it with a gaping yawn.

Crockett leaned closer. "What you told me a while back...about your brother and that fire in the coach in London. Turns out he's alive and well, living on Long Island with a wife, two kids, and a dog."

Arthur tapped his foot a few times, then gave Crockett a big grin. "Didn't know about the dog," he said. "So what are you, Crock, a shrink or a private eye?"

"I asked you to not call me that," Crockett said.

"Sorry...Doc."

Crockett looked appeased. "Arthur, I've said it before and I'll say it again, it's completely pointless if you're just going to lie to me all the time."

Arthur slumped down in the metal chair and didn't look the least bit chastened.

"I deny the accusation. I don't lie to you all the time. Just some of the time. Like when it's more interesting than the stultifyingly boring truth."

"I'm not sure that's a word."

"Boring?"

"No, stultifyingly."

"Look it up, dude."

Crockett turned his baseball cap so the bill was facing backward. "Don't do that, man," Arthur said shaking his head. "A backward hat looks ridiculous on you. You trying to bridge the thirty-year age gap or something?"

Crockett decided to leave the cap facing backward. He didn't want Arthur thinking he could run the show.

"So, what would you say?" Crockett said. "Fifty percent of the time? Sixty?"

Arthur looked blank at first, then smiled. "Me lying? Nah, I'd say only about twenty-five, thirty percent. I mean, I do get it that you can't help me slay my demons if I lie all the time."

"How 'bout telling me the truth *all the time*, Arthur? Would that be so hard?"

"Are we negotiating?" Arthur asked, his head tilted to one side.

Crockett gave him his theatrical sigh and, when Arthur wasn't looking, turned his cap back around.

"I got me a new girlfriend," Arthur said.

Crockett smiled. "Oh yeah? Who's that?"

"The movie star, Avril," Arthur said, holding up his hands. "I know what you're thinking—here he goes again."

Crockett fought hard to maintain a straight face. "No, keep going. You have my undivided attention."

"I don't know. We're just kind of like on the same wavelength," Arthur said, tilting back in his chair. He couldn't go back very far because his legs were so short.

"Well, tell me about her," Crockett said. "I haven't met her yet."

"Well, she's really hot, for one thing."

Crockett started to sigh, but knew that was the reaction Arthur wanted.

"She gets my sardonic humor, laughs at my jokes. We had this awesome conversation about nightmares. Turns out hers are, like, way darker than mine."

"About what, for instance?"

"Snakes, for one thing, and, like...gothic churches?"

"Gothic churches?"

"Well, 'haunted gothic churches' was how she described 'em," Arthur said. "With real creepy priests dressed in prison garb."

Crockett had interpreted a few dreams in his day, but decided to steer clear of this one.

Arthur put his hands on his knees, then leaned back in his chair again. "You know what I was thinking?"

Crockett cocked his head to one side and stroked his beard, which was the color of dirty snow.

"No, what were you thinking, Arthur?"

"I was thinking about that smokin'hot Australian actress. Kate something. Married to this bald, dumpy guy with a pudgy face. Looks like Mr. Potato Head."

Crockett slowly shook his head. "I don't get where you're going."

"Meaning, you don't necessarily have to look like George Clooney to get the girl."

Crockett regarded all this Hollywood drivel as being beneath him and just nodded.

Arthur looked as though he had a few more thoughts on the subject. "I also was thinking—" Arthur rocked back and forth in his chair and put his arms in a flattened cross over his chest— "take a look at Tom Cruise."

"What about Tom Cruise?" Crockett asked.

"Well, he's a short little fucker too."

Chapter 15

"Is this seat taken?" Cam asked.

Avril looked up. Cam kind of reminded her of the architect she had gone out with.

It was fifteen minutes until the start of AA. There were only a couple of other people in the auditorium.

"All yours," she said, motioning to the chair. "Did you get here early to make sure you get your ten-day clean-and-sober chip?"

"Nah. One day short, only got nine."

Somewhere in his good looks and easy manner, she thought she spotted a wounded bird. Took one to know one.

"So, the guest speaker is gonna call you 'Nine Days' this time?"

He laughed. A good, natural laugh, she thought, nothing held back.

"It's a closed group tonight. No townies, just us inmates. You know, I was thinking, until I got here, I've had a drink *every single* day of my life for the last eleven and a half years."

"*A* drink?"

Cam laughed. "Okay, *lotsa* drinks. Every single day, no matter how hungover, or sick, or lousy I felt."

Avril nodded. "I think you got a lot of company," she said, blowing a strand of hair away from her eye.

"By the way, I don't think you get a chip until you have at least thirty days," Cam said, looking around and seeing Ted straggle in.

"Think you're gonna make it?" Avril asked.

"Thirty days? Yeah, piece a cake."

His eyes slowly wandered around her face. They lit on something. "What are you staring at?" she asked.

"What do you mean?"

"You were..." She hated her unreliable instincts. "Nothing."

"Sor-*ry*. I was just trying to make eye contact," he said with a shrug. "I do that when I'm having a conversation with somebody. Weird, I know."

Avril laughed. "Sorry. Just another paranoid schizophrenic," she said. "So, what exactly is your story? Cam, right?"

She knew perfectly well what his name was.

He nodded, put his hand on the back of her chair, and leaned back.

"How much time you got?"

She thought she saw a glint of pain. "Well, the meeting starts in ten minutes."

"I can do it in twenty-five words or less," he said. "Booze and drug abuse stemming from self-esteem issues and/or not being fulfilled in job, wife, and life. Deep-seated issue...father always loved big brothers more than me, thereby creating feelings of inadequacy and insecurity."

She smiled.

"Wow, that was impressive. But I think it was a little more than twenty-five words. Wish I had as good a handle on all my stuff."

"It's easy when you're as self-absorbed as me," Cam said

"Oh, trust me—I've got you beat on that," she said. "So, you're married?"

"Just barely," he said. "It was a mistake."

"I'm sorry."

"Thanks. I was no great shakes in the husband department. She deserved a more stable guy."

Avril heard a noise and looked up. She knew who it was. Arthur Petit dragged his right leg. It was longer than his left one, he had told her.

"Hi, Arthur," she said.

"Hey," he said, smiling at Avril. Then he eyed Cam like he was a trespasser.

Cam nodded.

Arthur scowled.

"Can I join you?" Arthur asked Avril and sat down before he got an answer. "Talking about your wife, huh?"

"We had moved on," Cam said.

"I saw her the other day," Arthur said. "Very hot. But I could tell, no soul."

Cam's eyes bored into Arthur's. "You're talking about my wife, who you've never met before."

"How do you know?" Arthur tossed a smile at Avril.

She didn't return it.

"I was kidding," Arthur said. "But it's true, right?"

"Look, Arthur," Cam said, like he was struggling to hold his temper. "Talking about my wife is totally off limits. Got it?"

"Hey, man, don't get all bent out of shape," Arthur said, raising his arms in protest. "Gonna beat me up 'cause I said she was hot?"

*****

The AA meeting came to order, and Ted had the floor. Unlike other people, Ted always stood when he spoke.

"It was nine years ago—2008—and I just finished this real estate development."

"Poor bastard," someone in the back said. "Shitty timing."

"Yeah, I had a hundred-sixteen houses. Every cent I had was tied up in them. First ten sold pretty quick. Then the shit hit the fan. Bear Stearns. Lehmann Brothers, that old, bald bastard, Henry Paulsen—"

"You tell 'em, Ted." Same guy in the back.

"It was like somebody said real estate was toxic. I mean, one Sunday I had two people show up to go through my model home. Three months before that, my broker toured forty people through it—"

"Where you going with this, Ted?" Arthur cut in from off to the side. "We all got hard-luck stories."

Cam leaned forward and shot Arthur a look. "Let him talk."

Avril snuck a look at Cam. By his own admission, he was damaged, tormented, and troubled. But he seemed like a guy you could definitely count on. Not only that, self-effacing and spoke his mind. Kind of funny, too.

And so damn good looking.

"Long story short," Ted went on, "I got my ass handed to me."

"Aww," Arthur said. "Poor baby."

Avril saw Cam's body tense. "Okay, Arthur, cut the shit." Then turning to Ted, "Keep going, man."

"I was done," Ted said, eyeing Arthur warily.

"No, you weren't," Cam said. "We wanted to hear about what happened."

Ted's eyes darted around the room. "Okay, I'll tell you," he said. "The real estate market totally dried up, house prices dropped by a third to a half. The depression that they insist on calling the *Great Recession* is what happened. Sure as hell wasn't anything *great* about it—" he shot Arthur a look— "know what I mean, Arthur?"

Cam patted him on the shoulder.

Chapter 16

Rachel and an overweight woman named Esther were sitting at the gold Formica breakfast table in Acute Care. Esther had her usual plateful of bacon that was all stuck together and undercooked. The fat bubbles looked like toes that had been in the ocean too long. Esther was someone who glommed onto people until they either told her to leave them alone—usually in much stronger language—or they succumbed to her relentless barrage of questions.

Rachel had come to breakfast a half hour earlier than usual to avoid Esther, but Esther walked in three minutes later, almost as if she had Rachel vectored in on some secret radar screen.

"So, how long did you go out for?" Esther asked out of the blue, shoveling four pieces of intertwined bacon into her mouth. She liked to root around in people's love lives, and Rachel had made the mistake of once mentioning her old boyfriend, Harlan.

"A year and change," Rachel said. "Up until, like, eight months ago."

"Was he cute?"

"Very cute, for a psycho."

Esther rubbed her hands together in glee, like this was going to be good.

"So what happened?"

"What didn't is the question."

And damned if Rachel didn't tell Esther the whole story. It was just easier than getting badgered to death with a million questions.

Harlan DeKalb—tall, rangy, off kilter—had an IQ of 161. He was two classes ahead of Rachel in high school and had graduated and gone to Harvard on a full scholarship. But right after he got there, he inexplicably started to veer off track. In mid-November, he was put on probation by Harvard's notoriously lax disciplinary committee for having a stripper move into his dorm room at Eliot House. Harlan's strait-laced roommate from Ohio had pleaded with him to ask her to leave, but Harlan was smitten and refused. Finally, claiming that his grades were suffering from the distraction, Harlan's roommate complained to the disciplinary committee. The girl was evicted and Harlan put on probation.

Two months later, Harlan was summarily bounced. His offense was original and unique. Drunk, he had broken into the hockey stadium with another boy and found the Zamboni ice-surfacing machine parked near the rink. Handy with engines and machines, he hot-wired the Zamboni and proceeded to drive it—miraculously, undetected—from the Harvard hockey rink out onto the frozen Charles River. Underestimating the weight of the Zamboni, it crashed through the ice twenty yards from the shore and quickly sank. He and the other boy almost drowned in the icy waters, but somehow made it to shore, where an off-duty fireman threw them a rope and hauled them both to dry land.

"What an inspired fuck-up," said Esther admiringly.

Rachel looked down at her bloated Corn Flakes. She had stopped eating them because she was going to gag watching Esther's two-handed attack on the greasy bacon pile.

"Yeah, so he came back home last year. We started going out again while, according to him, he 'contemplated the next chapter' of his life."

"I like this guy," Esther said.

"You wouldn't in real life. He treated me like shit. Finally, one day, he just split. Disappeared. Which was okay with me."

"Okay then what happened?"

"Nothing. Two months went by, and I didn't hear a word, and I'm going, 'Phew.' Then he calls up really late one night and asks me to fucking marry him."

"Oh my God," Esther said, clapping her hands, "the guy's a total freak show."

"I said, never, ever call me again or I'll call the cops, and he goes, 'What are they gonna do, arrest me? For asking you to marry me? Last time I checked, they didn't put you in the slammer for that.' Turns out he was out west somewhere."

"Doing what?"

"I have no idea. Been there, like, five months. I haven't talked to him since that night. I just know I haven't heard the last of him."

Esther patted her on the shoulder.

"Well, the good news is you're safe here."

"Huh?" Rachel laughed. "Never really thought of being here as 'good news.'"

Chapter 17

7 a.m. Main House. Ted woke up to a flashback of the Heron's Landing fiasco like it was an endlessly looping newsreel. It was always right there waiting for him the second he woke up. And usually it was what he drifted off to at night, after his bludgeoning dose of sleeping pills. He'd escape it for seven hours, then wake up to it all over again. A faceless, foreboding presence, he imagined sitting at the end of his bed.

Ted was awake when he heard the knock. It was five past seven. "Your wife's on the phone," the voice said.

A jolt of fear shot through him. It was only 4 a.m. in California. Something bad had happened. Christie, maybe?

He bolted out of bed in his pajama bottoms, not bothering to put on his pajama top. He opened his door. The tech saw him. "You need slippers and something on top, Ted."

Ted ignored him and barreled past him to the phone. "Hi, honey, what's wrong?"

"Ted, it's bad. They're really going through with it—"

"The foreclosure?"

"They served me papers ten minutes ago. Said a notice was going in the papers, then a sale on the courthouse steps."

He wanted to track down the process server and ream him out. Sadistic bastard, calling her up in the middle of the night.

"I'm sorry. I'm so, so sorry," he said.

She was silent. She'd heard it before.

He had a sudden urge to run and dive through the window at the end of the hallway and crash head first to the asphalt below. End the fucking nightmare. Then he wondered whether the drugs he had stockpiled were enough to do the job. He had heard a train's whistle the night before and imagined stepping out in front of it.

What a pathetic coward. Sure, killing himself would end his problems. But leave Katie and Christie holding the bag.

"I don't know what to do," she said helplessly.

He was totally powerless. He didn't have an answer. He would have had one a few years back.

"Why don't I come home and help," he said finally.

"No, I need you to get better. Then you can help. You can't do anything the way you are."

He could never kill himself. Because of what it would do to Katie and Christie. Especially Christie. She'd think she'd been stuck with the suicide gene. Plus, people feeling sorry for them. *Poor Katie*, he could hear them say, *the bum left her to clean up his mess.*

"Ted?"

"Yes."

"Oh, I thought we got disconnected," she said. "The good news is I might be getting an offer on the house on Bahia Mar."

"That's great. What are they asking?"

"A million eight."

"How much is the offer gonna be, you think?"

"A million four."

He tried to be upbeat. "You can do it, girl."

She sighed. "I can tell you don't really think so."

"Kate, 'you can do it' is what I said."

"I can hear it in your voice—you don't really think so."

"I do. I do. I know you can. Have you heard anything from Christie?"

Katie didn't say anything at first.

"She didn't call you?" she asked after a few moments.

"No."

"I asked her to."

He was crushed. "Well, thanks, honey. Let's talk soon. Keep me up to speed."

Ted hung up. First, he thought about Heron's Landing. Then about his daughter, Christie.

He had put the shovel in the ground for Heron's Landing in the Spring of 2009. He had staved off going belly up in a couple of housing busts and socked away some decent money in the boom times. From his first project on, he always built houses for his friends—not literally—but with guys like Peter Moseley in mind. Moseley was someone who would piss and moan if the grout was cracked in his bathroom floor or if the mortis rusted out on his front door lockset. Ted built houses to the highest level of quality so he didn't have to hear it on the golf course from the Peter Moseley's of the world. Also, because he liked to create the best. No shortcuts. Being that way didn't generate the biggest profit margins, but it gave him huge peace of mind.

By the fall, they had sixteen contracts out of a hundred-and-twenty houses at Heron's Landing. Then one of the buyers dropped his deposit, then a second, then the wind changed direction. Subtle, and Ted was not the only one to feel it. The word for it was a "pause," as in the markets were pausing to take a breath. Out of those sixteen contracts, only seven closed. Then the market went stone-cold dead. It was eerie. Still, developers thought it was only temporary.

To carry the construction financing and pay his expenses, Ted sold off part of his stock portfolio. It wasn't the first time he had done it, and it didn't scare him. Until that one Sunday when only two people showed up to go through the model home.

By summer, Ted knew the downturn was bad. His monthly carry was huge and escalating. He sold the rest of his stock portfolio and took out a second mortgage on his house. He lost his best saleswoman because she wasn't anywhere close to making her numbers.

Then Katie volunteered to fill in. She was good, and she was game, but what could you do if no buyers showed up? Ted slashed prices to paper-thin margins, but still there were few takers.

Ted sold their place in Maine and got harangued by his nervous bankers twice a day. Same guys who were throwing money at him and asking him to play golf all the time three years before. They wanted more collateral now. Ted ended up cashing in his life insurance policy. Gave up his country club membership. Even sold the one painting he loved.

About the only good thing that came out of it was realizing that at least he had gotten one thing right. His daughter. He and Katie had been partly subsidizing Christie, who had just started her first job in publishing in New York. Sensing what was happening—her parents' dire financial situation—she called Katie one Sunday and told her she had just gotten a part-time weekend job. They didn't need to send her any more monthly checks. Not only that, she sold the car they had bought her two years before and was Fedexing them an $11,000 check. Ted put it in a checking account for her, knowing Christie had not only gotten her mother's looks but her character as well.

Finally, Ted lost Heron's Landing to the bank. The bank didn't want it, and neither did anyone else.

As for Christie, she talked to her mother on a regular basis, but five months ago she'd stopped returning Ted's phone calls.

Chapter 18

Cam was having dinner with Ted, Pony, and Emily—the Scrabble crew—at Main House.

"Why do you keep looking around?" Pony asked Cam.

"Yeah, you been doing it since we first got here," Emily said.

"Expecting a pizza delivery or something?" Pony asked.

"Why would I ever want a pizza delivery when I got all this five- star gourmet chow in front of me?" Cam said.

"Five-star ptomaine," Ted mumbled.

Cam had a piece of carrot cake for dessert and was about to give up when Avril walked in.

He tried not to let it show.

"Is that who you've been waiting for, lover boy?" Emily asked, flicking her head.

"Who?" Cam said, looking over. "Nah, not my type."

"*Really?*" Ted said.

Avril glanced over at their table and locked eyes with Cam.

"She wants you." Emily leaned forward and whispered. "Desperately."

"Nah, she wants Pony," Cam said.

Everyone but Pony laughed.

"Go on over," Emily said. "Now's your chance. None of the paparazzi's around her."

Cam shook his head. "You know, you people think you're so damn funny."

He stood up and fake glowered at them.

Pony snickered. "You're good, Cam. As an actor, I mean." Then he flicked his head in Avril's direction. "Probably give her a run for her money."

"You jerks are driving me out of here," Cam said shaking his head and walking over to Avril's table.

"Hi," he said, "mind if I join you?"

"Yeah, sure," she said with a smile.

"So, everybody too star-struck to sit down with you?"

She smiled again.

"Lonely at the top, huh?" he said.

"Terribly."

"You're a woman of few words."

"Well, that's 'cause I usually have people write them for me," Avril said, straight-faced. "Coming up with my own original thoughts...it's not as easy as you'd think."

He studied her for a few moments. "I think you're putting me on, but I'm not really sure."

"Why would I do that?"

He studied her for a few more moments.

"You are, right?"

She gave him a faint smile.

"On another subject, what's your take on the food?" he asked.

"I like the peas," she said.

He laughed. "Yeah, I agree. Damn good peas."

Cam saw Arthur walk in, go over to the buffet, and load up. "I see your friend Arthur likes the peas too," Cam said.

Arthur, looking around for a place to sit, spotted them. A malevolent frown appeared on his face.

"I don't think he likes seeing me with you."

"Oh, come on," Avril said. "How do you get that?"

"I'm sure of it. Take a look at his face."

Avril glanced over at Arthur.

Arthur quickly glanced away.

"Did you see?" Cam asked.

"I just saw a short man with a tray."

"Yeah, well, you gotta just trust me on this. He's not a happy camper."

Avril pushed some rice around on her plate, then looked up. "Not a lot of people here are."

"You got a point there."

"So, tell me about your day, Cam."

"Oh man, was it ever exciting," he said. "I had this amazing breakfast. French toast and oatmeal. Then I went to pet therapy and patted this Airedale for half an hour. Then met with my shrink, who told me there was absolutely no hope."

Avril laughed.

"After that, a less-than-average lunch of meat loaf and hash browns, then group and the usual psychobabble, followed by a *Judge Judy* rerun on the tube." He smiled up at Avril. "How about you? How was yours?"

"Glad you asked," Avril said. "I kicked it off with some of that *dee-licious* oatmeal you just mentioned. Then I tried to sneak back to bed, but the res caught me, so I went and watched Dr. Phil. As if there aren't enough doctors in *this* place. Then I skipped lunch, went to the library, and got online to see what was happening in the real world. And trust me—you really don't want to know. After that I got into a heated game of Monopoly. I ended up with hotels on Boardwalk, Park Place, and the green ones—"

"Oh man, you can't lose with that lineup."

"Yeah, you'd think," Avril said. "Only problem was one of the people I was playing with got pissed, God knows why. He grabbed the board and threw it across the room. My little red hotels went flying."

Cam threw up his arms. "Just another day in paradise."

Chapter 19

Cam was on the phone again with Evan, twirling the cord nervously and reading stuff on the whiteboard. A list going down the right side of the board caught his attention: *vodka, scotch, bourbon, gin, vermouth, tonic, soda water, V-8 juice, lemons, limes.* He glanced to the top of the list, which said, *I miss my friends:*

So did he. Except for gin.

"Trey and I owe you an apology," Evan said. "Seems like you weren't the first guy Genevieve Kreutzel ever stalked."

"Well, no shit, Evan," Cam said. "Maybe you assholes should listen to me once in a while."

"Okay, calm down. Let's get past that," Evan said. "Trey spoke to David Humphries, and we've got a pitch scheduled for next Tuesday. Account's worth over two hundred mil."

"You and Trey gonna do it?"

"Yeah, he wanted to wait til you got back, but Hustead already did his pitch."

"When?"

"A few days ago," Evan said. "Word is he heard you're on 'sabbatical.'"

Clark Hustead was a competitor with an irritatingly grating ego but whose big returns helped clients overlook it.

"Where'd you get that?" Cam asked.

"I hear stuff," Evan said, meaning he had his investigator nosing around.

"So, you think Hustead would drop that on David Humphries? About me being up here?"

"Oh, you bet he would," Evan said. "Even though I'd tell Humphries I call the shots."

Cam thought for a second. "How 'bout I get out of here for half a day, go to the meeting. We do a breakfast. I get back before noon."

"You crazy? They'd never let you out."

"Who's asking? They'd never miss me. Nothing much goes on in the mornings anyway."

Cam spotted Arthur Petit at the end of the corridor, picking his nose and thinking no one was looking.

"You seriously think you could pull it off?" Evan asked.

"Piece of cake."

"I'll check with Trey," Evan said.

"So, you really think that asshole Hustead would go to Humphries and tell him I'm up here?" Cam asked again.

"No, he's way too subtle for that," Evan said. "He'd just make sure they found out somehow. You know, anonymous letter by carrier pigeon?"

Cam once told Evan he should avoid all attempts at humor.

"But our numbers beat his, right?" Cam asked. "I mean, five and seven percent better than the S&P in the last two years."

"His were six and eight percent."

Cam watched Arthur leer at a girl who walked past him.

"So, Humphries would go with that arrogant prick for one lousy percentage point?" Cam asked.

"He might when he figures it works out to a million bucks or so," Evan said.

He had something there.

"How's it going with Charlotte?" Evan asked.

"Oh, swell. She's got a thing going with an artist. Wants half my money."

"What are you gonna do?"

"Give it to her. I have no interest in going to war with the woman."

"You know, Cam, you're a real chump. Been married to her for three whole years and you're going to give her half of everything. The fuck you thinking? Call that lawyer I told you about. She'll end up *paying you*."

Cam was pacing back and forth now. A couple more conversations like this, he figured he'd have the hardwood down to the sub flooring.

"Listen, man. I don't want to end up with us hating each other," Cam said. "Spare me a goddamn scorched-earth divorce. Plus, I feel like shit 'cause the whole thing blew up."

He knew both barrels would be coming at him now.

"So, let me get this straight. The fact that she's fucking some other guy—"

"Shut the hell up!" Cam said, so loud a res twenty-feet away swung around.

"I mean, seriously, what the hell are you thinking?"

Cam did a modified count to ten. "Look. I may not like what she did, but I get it. I mean, I proposed to her when I was drunk. I married her when I was high, had sex with her when I was drunk *and* high. I mean, for Chrissakes, put yourself in her shoes. It's no day at the beach being Mrs. Cameron Crawford."

Evan, for once, had no response.

Cam had had enough of the conversation with Evan. "Hey, connect me with Darcy, will you," he said. Darcy was an assistant in their office.

"Sure," Evan said. "We'll be talking."

"Uh-huh."

Cam waited a few seconds.

"Hey, Cam," a perky voice said, "how you doin'? I miss you." Then lowering her voice, "it's no fun around here without you."

"I'll be back before you know it, kid," Cam said. "I got a big job for you. I'm gonna double your salary for the day tomorrow and give you a town car and a driver."

He outlined her mission.

Darcy showed up at Clairmount the next morning with a gold shopping bag. He thanked her and took it back to his room. Then he wrote Avril a note.

Chapter 20

Marvin Garfield was a thirty-three-year old Wharton graduate who had a shaved head, ears that stuck out two inches, and a combative nature. He was Avril's agent at William Morris Endeavor. They had last talked when she was on her way to Clairmount.

"Figured you wrote me off," she'd said, looking out the window at a dead spruce tree that had fallen onto two pines. "You do realize I'm massively insecure and require at least three calls a day to tell me how great I am and how much you and my millions of fans love me."

"I still love you. Course I'd love you more if you'd finish a goddamn picture," Marv said.

Despite his relative youth, Marv was a throwback. Talked like an agent from the thirties, calling movies "pictures" and women, "dolls" or "babes." In a nod to the present, however, he referred to men as "dudes," or more often, "assholes."

"So, what's the feedback? What do you hear?" Avril asked.

"About *Slumming?*" *Slumming with the Martins* was the name of the movie that Avril got fired from. "I hear that boy wonder's not so thrilled with his new co-star."

"But she's his girlfriend?"

"Ahhhh...maybe not anymore."

"That is fabulous news," Avril said, then laughed. "Who me... catty?"

Marv's deep laugh rumbled. "How you feeling now, seriously?"

"At first it was really bad. Now it's just bad."

"I'm sorry," Marv said.

"What pisses me off is not being able to deal with it. But you know me—never one to let the opportunity to pity myself slip by. But enough about me. Got any scripts...for me?"

Marv laughed again, nervously this time. He'd known the question was coming.

"We got this pilot. You play a fashion editor, a widow with two kids."

"Jesus, a widow?" Avril said in a panic. "How old am I supposed to be?"

"Around your age, thirty-two, thirty-three—"

"For Chrissakes, I'm only *thirty.*"

"Sorry. They must've figured you had these kids when you were like fourteen," he said, trying to pump enthusiasm into a project he was not even lukewarm about.

Avril couldn't picture the role. "What about movies? I mean, that *is* what I do, Marv."

Marv heard the rebuke but ignored it.

"Nothing much you'd go for. It's summer, you know."

"Yeah. Were you surprised I didn't react more when you said TV?"

Marv laughed. "I didn't say 'TV.' I said 'pilot.' Scared you'd bite my head off if I said 'TV.'"

"A year ago, I would have, but I'm a realist. The shitty economy, studio's just shooting sequels and comic books. I mean, I do know what's goin' on. How some people in the business look at me as a liability. I just don't want to go the way of Kate Hudson. Or Hayden Panettierre. You know, can't get arrested."

"Ain't gonna happen, babe," Marv said. "Besides, don't look down your nose at TV. You know how good it's gotten. Attracting the big names now."

Then Avril heard a voice in the background on Marv's end.

"Oh, hey, this is a call I been waitin' days for," he said. "Can I get right back to you, Av?"

Two days later, in her Clairmount room, she was still waiting. And still trying not to think about the pilot where she'd play a widow with two children. Hell, there was no assurance she'd even get *offered* the part.

There was a knock on the door. It was a tech. Dale.

"Avril?"

"Yes?"

"Something for you. Not s'posed to let you have it, but, hey, why not?"

Cam had sized up Dale correctly: a tech who'd bend the rules for a hundred-dollar bill.

Avril got up and opened the door.

Dale held out a bag for her.

"Thank you. I appreciate it," she said, taking it and closing the door.

There was a card on top. She opened it, saw it was signed "Cam," and started reading.

> *Avril,*
> *Smuggled these in through my underground network. Hope you're feeling better and that I see your frowning face at NA tonight. In the meantime, enjoy them.*
> *Best,*
> *Cam*

She put the card down on her desk and pulled out the gold box with a brown bow on it. Last thing she'd ever tell him was that she was allergic to chocolate.

Chapter 21

At least Ted wasn't feeling as suicidal. Negative, hopeless and depressed. Yes, yes and, yes. Yet some of the fog had lifted. Still, he had a long way to go. He was on the phone with Katie. It was Saturday.

She had pulled off the real estate deal he thought would never happen.

He had to figure out a way to get rid of his pessimism and negativity next. It seemed stacked high like heavy, wet blankets.

"Not that it's a huge commission," Katie said, "but I figure if we offer it to the bank, it might keep the wolf away from the door."

"You're the best," he said. "Hey, Kate?"

"Yes?"

"I still haven't heard from Christie."

Katie sighed. "I'm sorry, honey, but I don't know what to tell you."

She was right. It was between him and Christie.

A few moments later, he hung up. The phone immediately rang. He answered it. It was for Cam, who was chatting up a res across the room.

Ted held up the phone.

"Yo, Crawford."

Cam walked over. A wide grin. "Yo?"

Ted shrugged.

"Hello?" Cam said.

It was Evan.

"Hey, so me and Trey had a long conversation—"

Cam bet it was pretty one-sided.

"Trey thought you doing the dog-and-pony show with David Humphries was a good idea. But, as I said to him, only if you weren't gonna get in trouble up there at Fairmount—"

"It's Clairmount, and as I told you, they'll never miss me."

"Okay, let's do it then," Evan said. "I'll set it up for the end of the week. I'll call you back with the details. You can be back there by eleven. Oh, hey, by the way, Humphries's wife is coming, so you gotta promise me—no dancing."

Evan's laugh was more like a bray.

Cam shook his head. "I gotta tell you, Evan, that's what I've missed the most."

"What's that?"

"You and that incredible sense of humor of yours."

Chapter 22

Later that night, Cam spotted Rachel in the library and pulled up a chair next to her. "Hey, Big Red."

She looked at him and rolled her eyes.

"Is that the best you got, Crawford? *Big Red?* Your nicknames are so frickin' lame."

Cam shrugged.

"Like that guy with the ponytail. You nicknamed him *Ponytail?* I mean, *really?*"

"Just *Pony.*" He shrugged again. "What can I tell you—I like literal nicknames."

"Clearly."

"See, when I come up with a nickname, everybody knows who I'm talking about. But if I called somebody, I don't know, let's say Sparky, you'd have no idea who I was talking about."

"Who the hell is Sparky?"

"See what I mean."

Rachel just stared at him. "Anybody ever tell you, Cam, you're fucked up in the head?"

"All the time... Hey, where's your BFF, Avril?"

She nudged his shoulder with her fist. "You two got a little thing going?"

"Very little," Cam said, hoping there was room for growth.

"She's been kinda rocky lately. Course, she covers it up pretty well with that protective layer of entitled bitchiness. But then...she is a movie star, so—"

"—what would you expect, right?"

*****

After the library, Rachel went back to Main House. She got a call just as she walked in.

"Hello?"

"Hey, sweetness, how's it going up there?"

Her stepfather, Phil Eppersley, had a really annoying personality.

Rachel had no idea what her mother ever saw in him, except he was game-show-host handsome. Like he could have been prom king at a medium-size high school. Or a guy who could have ended up being a so-so insurance man having affairs with lonely hearts down at the bowling alley.

But the man had a swaggering self-confidence, which was difficult to fathom since he had struck out with four women and hadn't had a job in years. Phil told people that he had owned fourteen Harley Fat Boys, but failed to mention that number thirteen had killed wife number four—Rachel's mother, Evelyn.

What happened was a stoned-out kid who had just gotten his license decided to crack open his car's front door to air out the pot smell, and Phil and Evelyn—going sixty—plowed right into it. Barely a scratch on Phil after they crashed on the potholed asphalt, but Evelyn had sustained massive head and brain injuries.

*****

Evelyn Diamond Kornbluth Eppersley had won the New York lottery four years before. It was a bittersweet year for her. Two months before she hit the $26 million jackpot—$18 million after taxes—her husband, Judd Kornbluth, had left her. Bad timing for Judd, some had thought. The money was a nice consolation, but she felt that she had struck out as a wife and had come up short as a mother. She and Rachel had had a stormy relationship—Rachel did what she pleased —but they had loved each other unconditionally.

A month after her mother's tragic death, Rachel checked into Clairmount.

"So, how're you doin'?" Phil asked.

Rachel jerked the phone away from her ear. The voice had nothing but bad associations. Her instinct was just to hang up on him, but she didn't dare. Like somehow he had the power to reach through the phone and grab her by the throat.

"I'm all right," she answered, pumped full of dread.

"Place is costing me a grand a day," Eppersley said. "You better be getting something out of it."

She wasn't going to bother pointing out it was her mother's money.

"I'm going to need you to sign some paperwork, Rach."

She hated him calling her that. It suggested they were close. He knew she hated it too. Almost as much as "sweetness."

"What paperwork?"

"Paperwork that turns over half your mother's estate to me. Trusts and estate law."

She knew Phil got that from Regis Furth. Phil didn't know the difference between trusts and estates and a carburetor.

"I said to that lawyer that if Mom wanted you to have half, why wasn't it in her will?"

"That's not the question. The question is what the law stipulates. Like I said, trust and estates."

The fact of the matter was, Rachel didn't care whether she inherited $18 million or 18 cents. Money didn't mean anything to her. If it did when she got older, she figured she could always find a way to get by. The last thing she wanted, though, was for Phil to get a dime. Not after all the physical and psychic pain he had inflicted on her mother and her.

"I think I should hire a lawyer, let him and Furst work it out," She said, surprising herself.

"Are you out of your goddamn mind? Didn't Furst tell you if there's a lawsuit, you'll end up paying his legal fees?"

"Lawsuit? Why does there have to be a lawsuit? I can't handle something like that. Please, Phil—"

"Just sign the papers, Rach. Simple as that."

"I just, you know. I can't, you know—" She always got a bad case of the "you knows" when he bullied her and beat her down.

"For Chrissakes, Rachel, just do it and be done with it. You don't want me coming up there, bending you over my knee, spanking your little bottom do you—"

Rachel's whole body seized up. The memories came surging back.

"I'm just kiddin.' You lost your sense of humor, Rach?"

"I'm going to hang up now," she said, like she was asking permission.

"Don't you dare hang up on me. We're going to get this settled right now."

"I'm going to," she said again, and this time she did. Her body was quivering. She felt as though she was going to collapse and fall on the hardwood floor. She needed something.

She needed to see the boy whose brother smuggled in the Oxy. But really, she needed something much stronger.

Chapter 23

Avril was buzzed out of the front entrance of the Acute Care Unit. She was psyched about her move, about leaving ACU behind. She was also nervous, and didn't quite know why. Fear of the unknown, maybe.

She walked outside and saw the idling van. A man got out, nodded at her, took her suitcase, and put it in the back seat of the van. It was 6:35 at night.

She looked at the driver.

"You know where I'm going, right?"

The driver didn't look directly at her, like someone had told him not to gawk.

"Yes, ma'am, across the street, over to Brook House."

"Please, God," she pleaded. "Do I really look like a ma'am?"

"No, ma'am. I mean—"

She just laughed.

He drove down to the main road, took a right, went several hundred yards then turned into the driveway of a three-story Tudor house with a slate roof. A woman waited for them up at the front door of the house.

She was in her thirties, had bottle-blond hair, and looked like she was trying hard to make it seem like she was welcoming just another patient.

Avril stepped out of the van, and the driver handed her one suitcase, then the other.

"Hi, I'm Tanya," said the woman on the porch, "one of the residents in charge. Can I give you a hand with your bags?"

Avril walked up the steps. "Thanks. I got 'em."

She reached the top of the steps and shook Tanya's hand.

"Looks a lot nicer than ACU," Avril said, looking around.

"I think you'll like it here," Tanya said. She was having trouble making eye contact.

"I'll just follow you," Avril said.

"Okay, you're all the way up, third floor." Tanya went inside and started up a flight of stairs.

"Penthouse suite, huh?"

"Exactly," Tanya said with a nervous laugh.

The room was bigger than Avril expected, with windows on three sides and light streaming in through them. There were two single beds on opposite sides of the room, two homely brown wooden desks from the eighties, and two dressers that looked like they were from a garage sale. Avril went over and pushed down on the bed with both hands. There was a crackling noise.

"Jesus, what's that?" she asked, turning to Tanya.

"Oh, it's a plastic liner, just in case—"

"Just in case I lose control of my bladder?"

Tanya laughed self-consciously.

"Okay, here's what I need you to do, Tanya," Avril said, waving a hand imperially in the air. "Call up a bed place and order their top-of-the-line king-size bed. Immediate delivery. I can't possibly sleep on this."

Panic swept Tanya's face, like she needed her supervisor. "But, I—"

"Tanya, please."

Tanya squinted and turned her head. "I'll...I'll have to do it after tonight's meeting," she said, her eyes going side to side like windshield wipers.

"What meeting?"

"We have meetings every night at 7:00," Tanya said. "Then there's NA after that."

"Your little meeting...sorry, I'm gonna be late."

Tanya turned to go.

"Oh, hey," Avril said. "Extra firm, please."

Tanya's mouth opened. She just turned and walked out.

Avril took her time unpacking, putting her clothes in the wooden bureau and hanging blouses in her closet, then walked down the two flights. The meeting had been going for ten minutes. Her eyes swept the large living room and the eleven women sitting in easy chairs and sofas arranged in a circle. When she stepped into the room, the conversation stopped immediately as they took her in.

She was used to making entrances and was good at it, but like at the AA meeting, she felt palpably uneasy, and suddenly realized what it was. People were studying her, knowing she was damaged, scrutinizing her for tics and telltale signs of what was wrong. She felt wobbly. Afraid she might trip. Out of control. Spinning. She sat down as quickly as she could on the nearest sofa.

Tanya sat facing the group in front of a flat-screen TV.

"Welcome," Tanya said, nodding, her eyes steadier now, like she got braver with people around her.

Avril nodded back.

"Ladies, this is, ah, Avril," Tanya said. "Now, go around the room, please, and introduce yourselves."

They did. To Avril, it was a blur of voices and names. They wore everything from blue jeans to short skirts, from young women to several in their forties and fifties.

"What we do here," Tanya explained to Avril, "is repeat our goal of the day we made at the morning meeting. Say whether we achieved it or not, then tell the group what our moment of the day was."

Avril looked skeptical. "Moment of the day?"

The woman next to her, ponytail and high forehead, giggled.

"Bryn, why don't you lead us off?" Tanya said.

Bryn, who Avril guessed was about forty, had flawless skin, prominent cheekbones, and no makeup. She kept her eyes on the floor as she monotoned, "My goal was not to have any panic attacks, which didn't quite work out, and my moment of the day was feeding the ducks."

"Thank you, Bryn. Very good," Tanya said.

She pointed to the woman next to Bryn.

"Lindsay?"

Lindsay was in her early thirties, a large-breasted woman just shy of six feet tall with a rigid, contorted face.

"My goal was to talk to my doctor about changing my meds, which I did, but...he didn't. The fucking Nazi."

"Lindsay," Tanya said. "We avoid personal judgments here."

"Since when?" Lindsay said under her breath.

"Next," Tanya said. "Oh, wait a minute. What was your moment of the day, Lindsay?"

"Talking to my boyfriend on the phone. I just hope that jerk's being faithful to me while I'm up here at Shangri-fuckin'-La."

"Okay, that's enough," Tanya said.

Avril remained stone-faced as the women spoke.

They went around the circle, then Avril was next.

"Avril, I don't mean to put you on the spot since you just got here," Tanya said, "but you mind telling us what your moment of the day was?"

Avril scratched her head.

"Ah, okay, my moment of the day was getting the hell out of ACU, away from all the drama queens."

"We got plenty of 'em right here," said a munchkin-like woman whose feet didn't reach the floor.

"Now, Abby," Tanya said. "That's a judgment, too."

"And hers wasn't?" Abby glanced at Avril.

Tanya let it go. Avril could see that, at best, Tanya was a soft disciplinarian. She'd scold a person, then a minute later another one would do the exact same thing.

"Okay, ladies"—Tanya clapped her hands— "that's the end of the meeting. Bryn, come on up and meet your new roommate."

Bryn, who was trembling so badly she looked like she was about to quake apart, tiptoed over.

"Bryn, this is Avril," Tanya said.

"Hi," Bryn said, her eyes flitting side to side.

"Hi," Avril said. "I get panic attacks too."

"You do? Really?" Bryn's eyes lit up, like she had just been supremely validated.

"Oh yeah, really bad," Avril said. "Hot flashes, the room starts spinning, I can't breathe. I tremble, shake, sweat, hyperventilate, sometimes roll up into a ball and feel like I'm going crazy."

Bryn's mouth had dropped a full inch.

Avril smiled at her. "I'm guessing you don't get 'em quite that bad?"

Chapter 24

NA meetings, which stood for Narcotics Anonymous, weren't required, just *strongly* recommended. Everybody from Brook House went.

NA was the same format as AA meetings, with a few wrinkles. For one thing, there was a lot more hugging, which Avril told her sister she couldn't stand. Because, the fact was, people wanted to hug her. Especially creepy old men and hormone-frenzied twentysomethings. She had gotten to the meeting before Cam and Ted. They walked in, saw her, and sat down beside her.

She gave Cam a big smile.

"I loved my Godiva chocolates," she said. "Thank you so much. That was so thoughtful."

"Yeah, well, my spies told me you were going through kind of a rough patch."

"I'm better, first day at Brook House. Doing a thirty-day thing there."

"Oh yeah? How's it goin'?"

"Too early to tell."

Then Rachel walked in. Avril noticed something was off right away. Rachel was shambling across the room, not her usual purposeful stride, and scratching her face so hard it looked she was going to scrape off a layer of skin. She looked flushed, her smile too big, her eyes dilated.

She spotted them and gave a little wiggle of the fingers, something that was so *not* Rachel. She crossed the room and sat down next to Avril.

"Hiya, princess," she said, the volume too loud.

"Shhhh. Jesus," Avril said, checking Rachel's eyes.

She was on something, Avril's sensitively tuned antennae told her. Rachel's smile barely fit onto her face. "Cool," she said.

"What?" Avril said.

"Nothing."

Rachel pushed her chair back. The front two legs of the metal folding chair lifted off the ground and teetered precariously.

"What's going on with you?" Avril whispered.

"Bring on the entertainment," Rachel said, loud enough so the man who ran the meetings heard her and frowned.

Rachel's head bounced up and down as if she were rocking to some jungle beat.

"What are you on?" Avril whispered.

"Just high on life," Rachel gave her the thumbs up.

"Yeah, right. How did—"

But Avril didn't need to know the particulars. She just needed to get Rachel the hell out of there.

Rachel's eyes dropped to the floor.

"Rachel, listen to me," Avril whispered. "Walk out of here towards the bathroom to the left. I'll meet you out there in a few minutes."

"Why?"

"Goddamn it, just do it."

Rachel shrugged. "Whatev."

Avril put a hand on the side of Rachel's chair and pushed it down so all four legs were on the floor. She was afraid Rachel would topple over and crack her head open.

"For Chrissakes, go," Avril said. *"Now."*

Rachel stood up, hesitated, then headed for the door.

Avril turned to Cam. "She's on something."

Cam nodded. "I thought so. What can I do?"

"Nothing. I got it."

A minute later, Avril walked out.

She caught up with Rachel just outside the front door. Rachel was humming something that sounded like a slow version of *In-A-Godda-Da-Vida.*

Avril got in her face.

"What'd you take?"

Rachel smiled dreamily. "Smack."

Avril's mouth popped open.

"How the hell'd you get—"

"Todd's a dealer. Dealers have their ways."

Avril had no idea who Todd was.

"We're going to my room at Brook."

Rachel started frantically gesturing with her hands, but no words came out.

Then finally, she said, "I can't. It's...it's against the rules."

Avril laughed, grabbed Rachel's hand, and started walking fast. "And smack isn't? You gotta be fucking kidding."

She shook her head. "Look, I'm no angel, but are you out of your mind? High at an NA meeting?"

Brook House had three doors. The front door, the door to the living room, and the back door. Avril went around and tried the back door first, but it was locked. Then she came around to the living room door.

"I'm going in first, to make sure the res is in her office."

"What are we doing?" Rachel asked.

"Just wait here, and don't talk to anyone," Avril said, opening the door and going in.

Avril walked up the stairs to the resident's cluttered office. Tanya, doing paperwork, looked up.

"Hi," Avril said. "I was feeling really nauseous, I had to leave NA."

Tanya started to rise.

"Stay there," Avril held up a hand. "I feel better just walking around. I'm gonna get something in the kitchen, then up to my room. A shower might do the trick."

Tanya furrowed her brow and cocked her head slightly. "Let me know how you feel after that."

Avril nodded.

"Will do."

Avril walked down the stairs, went outside, and motioned to Rachel. They went through the living room and crept up the back stairway, two flights up. Avril opened her door and led Rachel in. Avril realized she was doing something that could get her kicked out. She went into her bathroom and turned the shower on cold. Rachel followed her.

"Get in," Avril said, motioning.

"What? Why?"

"Just do it. I'm going down to make some coffee. Take your clothes off and get in there."

Rachel pulled down her blue jeans, hopping on one foot and almost falling over.

Avril went to the kitchen. She knew coffee sobered drunks, but had no idea whether it helped someone on heroin. She made a pot and filled a mug, dumping two spoons of sugar into it. She opened the refrigerator to get milk and saw the printed piece of paper scotch taped to the refrigerator door. It said *Brook House Chores,* then specific jobs and the names assigned to do them. Someone had slashed out the second O in Brook and added the letters *EN* after the *K,* in blood-red letters.

Avril felt a sharp stab in her stomach as the words hit home. She walked up the back stairway with the coffee.

Rachel was in the shower, singing some rap song.

"Jesus, Rachel, stop."

"Sorry."

A few minutes later, Rachel turned off the shower, stepped out and dried off.

Avril went into the small bathroom.

"You have a roommate, right?" Rachel asked.

"Yeah, she was sitting beside me at NA."

"Hmm," Rachel said. "Don't remember."

"Course not. You were out of it." Avril said. "Okay, here's the plan. They find out you're using, you're out of here."

"I know. I know, but you don't know the stress I—"

"I don't want to hear it." Avril placed her hands on Rachel's shoulders. "However you're feeling right now, you gotta fake it and act straight. You're a better actress than me anyway. I'm gonna put you in that van. You go back to your room and get in bed. Then we'll worry about the weekly drug test. It's tomorrow. Great timing, girl. You gotta get somebody clean to pee in a cup for you, then swap 'em somehow, or else you're fucked."

Rachel's troubled eyes showed that what Avril said had just sunk in.

"I can't get kicked out of here," Rachel said, panic in her voice. "I can't go home. Christ, I don't even have a home."

"Shoulda thought of that before you shot up," Avril said, leading Rachel out to her room and handing her the coffee.

Rachel took a long sip. "Avril?"

"What?"

"I didn't shoot up. I just snorted."

Avril laughed. "Oh, well, in that case, don't worry about. No big deal."

*****

Avril waited for Cam after Rachel got in the van after the NA meeting.

"How's your patient?" he asked under his breath, walking up to her.

"You believe that," she said, then lowered her voice to a whisper, "she was on heroin."

"Where the hell'd she get it?"

"Some guy named Todd."

Cam thought for a second.

"I'll find out who he is, have me a little man-to-man with him."

Chapter 25

"I'm regressing, Doc," Cam said, sitting with his arms so tightly clenched a crowbar couldn't pry them apart.

Dr. Boylen and Cam were sitting outside of Main House on the patio at three in the afternoon.

"What do you mean you're 'regressing?'" the doctor asked.

"Well, like, the idea is to come here and get rid of bad habits, right?"

Boylen nodded. "That's part of it."

"Like in my case, booze and drugs, right?"

The doctor nodded again.

"So instead, I'm going back to shit I used to do," Cam said. "Like smoking. Quit two years ago, and now I'm back on the butts. With a vengeance."

Boylen took notes on a yellow pad. "What happened?"

"Well, I was checking out the smokers on their break, right over there"—he pointed—"and it's like they're at a big cocktail party. Meantime, I'm stuck inside with the nonsmokers. And it's like a god-damn morgue. So, I think, hey, what's a few Marlboros?"

Boylen was scribbling. "So, what did you do?"

"Next smoke break, I was out there smokin' up a storm," Cam said. "Gotta tell you, it felt pretty damn good to have a vice again."

Boylen chuckled.

Cam unclasped his hands and put them behind his head. "Took me about three seconds to get re-hooked on nicotine. Addictive personality, much?"

Boylen set his pen down on the table. "I think you're just about ready for a thirty-day program."

"When?"

"In a couple days. I'm thinking either Schechter or Brook House. Kind of leaning toward Schechter."

That was the all-male house for drug and alcohol patients. Brook was where Avril was.

"Do I have a say in the matter?"

"Of course."

"Schechter would be fine," Cam said, "but I think Brook might be a better fit."

Boylen cocked his head. "Why's that?"

"'Cause it's not just about drugs and alcohol for me," Cam said, "but all the other issues I got too. You know, the whole self-image thing. My other shit too. Like Schechter seems good for drunks and druggies. Brook House for drunks, druggies, *and* head cases."

Boylen laughed. "So, you're all three?"

"Oh, yeah, bro, in fucking spades!"

"Maybe you're right," Boylen said. "It's therapeutic to be with patients who run the gamut of issues too—bipolar, depression, border line personality disorder, whatever it may be. You learn a lot about yourself by hearing about what they're going through."

Cam leaned in close to Boylen. "Exactly what I was thinking."

"Plus, Brook House is heavy on DBT, which might be a really good thing for you."

Cam scrunched up his eyes. "That's that thing with meditation, deep breathing and all that shit, right?"

"Among other things."

Cam looked up at Boylen and nodded. "So, Brook House it is?"

"Brook House it is."

Chapter 26

Avril had just returned from breakfast. Unlike ACU, which had its own dining area, Brook House sent patients across the street and up the hill for meals at Main. Brook had its own kitchen where patients could keep food, but didn't serve meals.

She had a ten o'clock meeting with a new doctor but first wanted to make sure Rachel was okay. She walked through the Brook House kitchen to where the public phones were and dialed the number of the phone she had used so many times back when she was at Acute Care. She watched the cleaning lady mop the floor in the kitchen, admiring her. She was swabbing away in short, determined strokes, like she was going to make it cleaner than it had ever been before.

Someone answered.

"Hi, Rachel, please."

"That you, Avril?"

Avril didn't recognize the voice. "Yes."

"It's me, Esther. Fat, self-deprecating sense of humor, 'member?"

"Oh, hi, Esther. How's it going?"

"Sucks. We miss our celebrity," she said. "I'll get Rachel." Avril was relieved to hear Rachel was still there.

"Hi, princess," Rachel said, her voice flat. "Thanks for taking care of me."

"How you doing?"

"Okay, I guess," Rachel said. "Bad move last night, I know."

"Ya think? I mean, Jesus Christ."

"Don't make me feel any worse. I got a killer headache too."

"How'd you do on the pee test?"

"No prob," Rachel said. "Like you suggested, I got Esther to fill up a cup and hide it on the other side of the toilet where the res couldn't see it. Then I switched 'em. The res wasn't watching too closely. I mean, think about it—your job's watching someone take a whiz."

"Good girl. So, you dodged a bullet," Avril said. "Unless, of course, Esther's been snorting smack too."

Rachel laughed. "I don't think so. Girl *may* have had one beer in her whole entire life. Hey, can I come see you? I'm still really shaky."

Avril thought for a second. "I've got to see a shrink in a little while," she said. "Meet me in the library. We'll find a quiet spot."

"Okay, thanks," Rachel said. "What time?"

"Let's say 11:30," Avril said. "We can go to lunch from there."

*****

When she moved from Acute Care to Brook House, a new doctor came with the move. He seemed less star-struck than Davidenko. Made her feel like just another patient. Well, almost. There was always some deference. It just came in varying degrees. With Davidenko, she always felt she could overrule him on decisions about her treatment and he would go along with it. With Dr. Holmgren, she got the sense he would dig in his heels, insist that it be done the way he thought best. He also seemed to have a better handle on bipolar 1 and its subtleties as she described her symptoms —the one-two punch of raging, out-of-control manic behavior, then falling into a pitch-black hole of crippling depression. Holmgren was better at asking questions and actually listening to her answers, too.

They were sitting in the doctor's small office. He was in his mid-thirties, tall, rail thin and either shaved every other day or had an extremely fast-growing beard. He had eyes that didn't miss a thing and an owlish, half smile that almost seemed glued on. He was dressed un-fashionably in a pea-green, long sleeved shirt, grey flannels with barely a crease and black slip-on shoes with oddly upturned toes.

She had just told him how her mother had the disease. Used to cut herself a lot but had never attempted suicide until the day in Febru-ary when she drove all the way from Los Angeles to Mount Shasta, walked to within a thousand feet of the peak in jeans and a T- shirt, lay down on the ground and froze to death. Avril explained how under-standing and considerate her father had always been to both her and her mother and how deeply it hurt him when he'd see the cuts on them. How he'd agonize helplessly over their pain and despair. The worst was when she and her mother went through heavy bouts of de-pression at the same time. He didn't seem to know what to do except hug them all the time. That and tell them how much he loved them.

After his wife's suicide, John Ensor went downhill fast. Now, at age sixty-six, he had full-blown dementia and Avril had been paying for twenty-four-hour care for him in his home in Santa Monica for the last four years.

"So, first time you felt bipolar symptoms was right after you were sexually molested?" Holmgren asked.

Avril nodded, gripping her water bottle tighter.

"And how many manic episodes would you say you've had? Roughly?" he asked, tapping a pencil with a sharp point lightly on his desk.

"Um, maybe twenty, twenty-five. Around there," Avril said, then took a sip from her water bottle.

"So, on average more than one a year?"

"Yes, but sometimes none in a year, sometimes like two or three."

"And definitely bipolar 1?"

Avril gave an exaggerated nod. "Oh, yeah. Bipolar 1, rapid cy-cling, mixed bipolar, none of that wimpy bipolar 2 or cyclothymia for this girl."

Bipolar 2 and cyclothymia were much less intense than bipolar 1. And rapid cycling and mixed bipolar were a more frequent alternating of mania and depression.

"My levels of norepinephrine go up and down like the proverbial roller coaster. I guess same with dopamine and serotonin too."

The doctor nodded.

"They tell me I also may have abnormal thyroid function, circadian rhythm disturbances and probably high levels of cortisol in the mix."

"You really know your stuff," the doctor said with his wry little smile.

"Comes with the territory, when it's all about me."

"So, when you're manic, what are your symptoms?" the doctor asked, putting the pencil down, folding his arms.

Avril smiled. She could talk endlessly about this stuff.

"I guess all the usual suspects: shop till I drop, max out my credit cards, talk a mile a minute, think I'm the queen of the universe, act impulsively, exhibit shaky judgment which I'm convinced is brilliant, and I tend to get a little... promiscuous."

Holmgren reddened slightly. "All pretty much textbook. What about the depression?"

"Probably about the same as everybody," Avril said, brushing a wisp of blond hair aside. "I mean, I'm sad, I feel worthless, I cry, I get pissed off, I'm anxious, don't want to get out of bed, don't want to eat, can't read, can't concentrate, don't want to do anything or see anybody, I think about death a lot. That about covers it."

"I'm sorry," the doctor said, and she could tell he meant it.

It was an unusual but genuine reaction, she thought. Most doctors didn't want to show any soft edges.

"Have you ever tried to kill yourself?"

That, too, was different. Most other doctors preferred the more euphemistic, 'have you ever tried to hurt yourself?'

"No, I'm not suicidal. But ask me again after a few more bad movies."

The doctor searched her eyes.

"That was a joke."

The doctor smiled. "Where did you grow up, Avril?"

"Oklahoma. Moved away, after what happened."

"Do you think 'what happened' might have triggered that first bipolar incident?"

Avril scratched her head and looked down at the floor.

"That's a good question," she said finally, her voice low. "I don't honestly know. I mean, it was already in my genes. But it made me feel pretty lousy about myself. Like I had done something to cause it."

"Why did you feel that way?"

Avril looked him in the eyes, then looked out the window.

"I guess 'cause"—a tear slid down her cheek—"there's some part of guilt that's as comfortable as an old cashmere sweater."

Chapter 27

Avril and Rachel spent two and a half hours talking in a quiet corner of the library. Right through lunch hour.

Rachel was talking about losing her virginity when she was eighteen.

"So, he plied you with margaritas—"

"Yeah, and my inhibitions, poof, gone in a heartbeat," Rachel said.

"Funny how that works. Then you slept with him?"

"Yeah, well, if you could call it that. We were so drunk, it was pathetic. You know, he kind of reminded me of Rankin Hanley. Well, maybe a shorter, pastier version of him. What's he like anyway?"

"It's a sore subject."

Rachel was silent for a few moments.

"You know, you actually seem pretty down to earth," Rachel said. Avril laughed. "Well, thank you, but truth is, I'm utterly self- absorbed."

"Really?"

"Really. Self-absorbed, self-pitying, self—" Avril had to stop herself. *Stop blathering to this teenager.* It was so unlike her.

Usually she was so guarded. She had visions of hearing her words played back on *Entertainment Tonight* or splashed all over *Page Six.*

Avril glanced up at a shelf of CDs.

All of a sudden her mind was flooded with the torrent of torturous flashbacks that had battered her so many times in the past two years. The only good thing was the whole sad parade of images blew by in five seconds. Renny on stage at the Staples Center with a mike in his hand, his mouth moving but no sound. Then meeting him in the dressing room afterward, having too much to drink, and eight months later, him waiting for her as she walked down the aisle in the wedding dress that cost a fortune but didn't really fit. Then their amazing three-week honeymoon in Asia and Australia.

Six months later, she walked into their pool house and found him with a raven-haired groupie with burgundy lipstick. He gave her a convincingly sincere apology about how he had fucked up and it would never happen again. Then two months later, it happened again. Different woman, different place. Almost like he wanted her to catch him. She cut him off quick when he launched into another heartfelt apology. She was *so* out of there that time.

She glanced back at Rachel, who seemed to be miles away too, then reeled back over the recent years...The aftermath of her divorce. How devastated and badly damaged she was. Thinking it was something she did wrong. What she could have done that she hadn't? What she did that she shouldn't have? Then seven men in four years. None of them had really clicked for long. Drew, the party-hearty guy who inherited the football team but had never accomplished anything on his own. Then Michael, the real estate guy with the king- size ego and all the horses. Flying down to the Kentucky Derby on his G-4 so he could show off all his toys. Then it had dawned on her—she was one of them. After him came Landon, the sweet architect. He had actually lasted the longest, and she didn't really know why it had unwound— just that it was slow and painful. The others were just blurs.

Then suddenly, without feeling it coming on, Avril started to sob. She tried to hide it.

"Are you all right?" Rachel said, reaching over and putting a hand on Avril's shoulders.

"No, I'm *not* fucking all right," Avril said, fighting tears.

"It's okay, it's okay. I'll help."

Avril put her hand on Rachel's hand and smiled. "Funny," she said, "I was supposed to be taking care of *you*. Not the other way around."

"Don't worry," Rachel said. "We'll take care of each other."

Avril nodded. Then she started talking. Opening up like she never had before. Not to a shrink. Not to her sister. Not to a lover. Not to anyone.

At the end of it, she felt ten pounds lighter.

She told Rachel about her whole bipolar history. About her manic highs where sex, drugs, and rock 'n' roll were so rapturously, self-destructively out of control and about the depression that then swept down upon her without warning and chased all the hedonistic indulgences away.

She told her about the unrelenting pressure to please that she had always felt.

About how she had to claw to get to where she was and how she felt that where she was...wasn't really anywhere.

She said if she had it to do all over again, she'd be a nurse or a vet and really meant it.

She told her how she always felt fat when she was naked and how she hated sex scenes but how they were always right there in flashing lights in every script she was ever sent.

And finally, she told her about Alan Streeter. The single biggest reason why she had ended up in a bare-bones room at Clairmount.

"How old were you again?" Rachel asked.

"Fourteen."

"What a fuckin' pig!"

"Thing is, I have to take some of the blame," Avril said, looking at a stack of books about addiction.

"Come on, Avril. The guy was twenty-four and you were fourteen."

"Yeah, well, he didn't tie me down and make me smoke that joint."

Rachel shifted in the black leather chair. "Wait a minute. He was your teacher who called you into his office, supposedly to talk about some term paper."

"Yeah, but if I'm being completely honest, I knew something was up. I knew it was more than just a quote-unquote student-teacher conference. Something else was going on."

Rachel shook her head. Violently almost. "I'll say it again," she said. "You were fourteen, and he was your fucking teacher. You told your parents, and the guy got what he deserved. No two ways about it."

Avril looked into Rachel's unblinking eyes. She had been down this terrible road a million times before, and the pain of remembering never got easier.

"For Chrissakes, Avril," Rachel said, "this was a guy in a position of trust. S'posed to be teaching you, not seducing you. It's totally unbelievable to me you could think you're guilty in any way. I mean, hello? That's fucking crazy!"

"Hey, look," Avril said. "I get it. I was a teenager, he was my teacher, but there's just no way I was a hundred percent innocent."

"Really?" Rachel said, slapping her lightly on her shoulder. "Really? Well, how about ninety-nine point nine?"

Avril smiled at her but then her eyes filled with tears again.

"What?" Rachel asked, leaning forward and putting her hands on Avril's shoulders.

"I was just thinking what he took from me," Avril said softly. "How I've never, never completely trusted a man again. Not even my own father"—a few tears fell on her hand—"I remember after what happened, being alone with him, my father...and how in the back of my head I was thinking...maybe—"

"But he never...your father never—"

"Oh, God no. The man was a saint. Point is, the distrust, the fear, the suspicions were in here"—Avril pointed to her head— "about every man, and no matter how hard I tried, I could never completely get rid of it."

"So, with, like, boyfriends and your husband?"

Avril nodded. The tears had stopped, but she looked unspeakably sad. "Yeah"—she tried to laugh—"and you can just imagine how shitty the sex was."

Rachel put her hand on the back of Avril's neck. The weight of Avril's pain seemed to slump her shoulders forward.

"It's a joke. I mean, here I am this sex symbol completely petrified of sex. Unless I have like five bottles of champagne and a few joints." Avril laughed. "Hey, you can't go spreading this around."

"Don't worry, your secrets are safe with me."

"Sorry you had to be the one to get cried on. I warned you I was incredibly self-absorbed." Avril grabbed the corner of her white blouse and wiped her eyes with it.

"So, whatever happened to that sleazeball, Alan Streeter?"

Avril sighed. "Well, I heard some things, but I don't really know. We don't exactly have reunions."

Rachel hugged her, tears all over her blue jean shirt. "I'll tell you what they should have done," she said. "Shoulda castrated the bastard."

Chapter 28

Cam was excited about his move to Brook in a few days. But for now, he had some things to take care of. First on his list was Todd. Then at the end of the week, to try to get the Humphries account.

He had followed Todd to the gym. He had seen him there a couple of times before.

For a hospital that charged a thousand dollars a day, the gym was pathetic. Stairmasters from the eighties, a few broken-down upper-body machines, and lots of corroded free weights.

Todd had just benched two hundred fifty pounds. Fifteen reps. Cam guessed he'd be lucky to do half that. Once.

Wearing a University of Virginia T-shirt and a scowl he hoped would be intimidating, Cam sucked it up and walked over to Todd. Todd, early twenties and buffed out, was on a whining treadmill now, sprinting like Hussein Bolt. He was wearing a tight-fitting Under Armor T-shirt and loose gym shorts. He had slab-like biceps and triceps, a hydrocephalic head, and at least fifty pounds on Cam.

Cam had hoped for someone smaller. He took a few steps and pulled the plug on Todd's treadmill. Todd almost slammed into the front of the machine, then looked around, pissed.

He saw Cam and raised his arms. "What the fuck, bro?"

Cam took one more step forward, while Todd stayed on the frayed black mat of the treadmill.

"You ain't my bro, fuckhead," Cam said. "I got a friend. A tall redhead named Rachel."

Todd toweled his brow.

"And the reason you're tellin' me this shit is—"

"'Cause you sold her something that coulda gotten her kicked out of this place."

"You got the wrong guy, bro," Todd said, with a sneer. "Now turn the fuckin' machine back on."

Cam looked past Todd and saw the attendant in the gym reading something—he was a kid who looked to be no more than sixteen. He was at the far end of the gym, past the basketball court, the Ping-Pong table, and the pool table.

"I don't think I communicated my message to you," Cam said.

Todd hopped off the machine and got in Cam's face. "Yo, bitch, communicate your message up my ass."

Cam fanned his hand up and down. "You got really skanky breath."

Todd shoved Cam so hard he almost toppled over backward. But Cam came storming back and stopped within a foot of Todd's face.

"Message is," Cam said, "you ever sell heroin, or anything else, to Rachel—"

Todd reared back with his left fist and threw a hard, fast punch. Cam turned, and it glanced off the side of his head. Cam came up underneath with a right that slammed into Todd's chin.

Todd looked more surprised than hurt.

"You're dead, asshole."

Todd threw a quick left at Cam. Then a right. The right crashed into Cam's cheekbone and left eye, knocking him to the lumpy gray mat.

"Listen, you piece of shit," Todd said, looking down at Cam. "I'll sell *whatever* the fuck I want to *whoever* the fuck I want *whenever* the fuck I want."

Cam, dazed, saw the kid attendant coming toward them, cell phone up to his ear—clearly, not in a big hurry to get involved.

Cam stood, unsteady, and Todd threw a haymaker at him. Cam tried to duck it, but it hit him in the exact same spot the one before had. He staggered backward. Miraculously, he didn't go down.

Hunched over, hands on his knees, he saw his only shot.

He let loose with everything he had and kicked Todd square in the nuts. Todd flopped over, howling.

Cam felt numb, about to puke.

The kid attendant was ten feet away.

"I called the cops," he said. Cam's knees were wobbly, and his head and left cheek were killing him. Todd was slowly getting back up, holding his balls. Cam thought about running, then had a better idea.

"When the cops show up," he said, "maybe they'd wanna hear all about your little drug operation. Huh, bro?"

Todd stopped, the gears turning slowly.

Finally, he pointed to the door. "Just get the fuck out of here." Cam decided that was probably a good idea.

His last fight had been in college ten years before.

He'd lost that one too.

Chapter 29

Cam was in a far corner of the dining room, where nobody ever sat. Pony had stopped by with his tray of mystery mounds and rice earlier.

"What's with the shiner, dude?" Pony asked, pointing.

Cam hadn't rehearsed a cover story. "Oh, ah, I was sleepwalking. Ran into a goddamn wall."

Pony didn't look like he bought it. "If you say so. But I think you mean *sleep running?*"

Ted came over a few minutes later and sat down next to Cam. "Jesus, what the hell happened to you?"

Cam smiled up at him, painfully. "Sleepwalking."

Ted didn't buy it any more than Pony did. "No, seriously, what happened?"

"Okay, how 'bout I beat the shit out of a guy," Cam said, then added. "But he got in a couple of lucky punches."

Ted looked skeptical. "Sounds like it's half-true," he said and took a bite of a mystery mound. Pork chop was Cam's guess, but then again it could have been Salisbury steak.

Cam saw Avril walk in with an odd-looking woman who was wearing sweatpants and a Kurt Cobain T-shirt.

"Oh shit," he said and put his head down.

"What's wrong?" Ted asked, swinging around and seeing Avril. "Oh."

Avril and her friend beelined over a few seconds later. "Hi, boys," Avril said. "This is my roommate, Bryn."

Cam looked up.

"Jesus, what happened to you?" Avril asked.

"A little accident," Cam said, trying to smile.

He'd seen himself in the mirror. A burgundy-yellow bruise, the color of a Montana sunset, surrounded the lower half of his right eye.

Avril knelt down and studied his face.

"You poor thing...what—"

"Nice to meet you, Bryn," Cam said, trying to change the subject.

"Nice to meet you too," Bryn said.

Avril eyed Cam's battered face. "Okay, so I'm guessing the other guy has a broken nose and a busted jaw?"

Cam lowered his voice. "The other guy's name is Todd."

Avril looked blank. Then her hand went up to her mouth. "Oh...my...God."

Cam nodded. "Not a scratch on the little bastard," he said under his breath. "Well, actually, he's not so little."

Avril put her arm on his shoulder. "Did you see a doctor?"

Cam chuckled. "All we got here are shrinks. Who probably don't know squat about cuts and bruises."

She smiled and touched the back of his head softly. "Can I get you some ice or something for that lump?"

"Thanks, I'm fine," Cam said. "I'm moving down to Brook in a day or two."

"That's great," she said. "When you do, me and the girls will nurse you back to health."

Chapter 30

"We need to talk about the direction of your life, Arthur...after Clairmount," Crockett said.

Arthur groaned. "Oh, fuck."

"Don't react like that. This is critical. You have an IQ that's off the charts—"

Arthur rolled his eyes.

Crockett kept going. "Arthur, listen to me, for God's sakes. You're twenty-six years old. You've got an amazing intellect, the ability to do anything—the sky's the limit. It's time to get engaged in life. It's time to make your mark in the world."

Arthur clapped his hands and whistled.

"Bravissimo, Doc. The old 'sky's the limit' speech. My old man's version was a lot longer. And my last shrink's pitch was that I could actually become a congressman or a senator with all my incredible oratorical abilities." Arthur shook his head and sneered. "You believe that shit? Here's the reality. I'm a fucking midget. When was the last time you saw a midget senator? When was the last time you saw a midget success story in any field? Excluding the circus, of course."

The only person Crockett could come up with was Ricardo Montalban's sidekick in *Fantasy Island*. But he was maybe just a really short guy. Then he came up with someone else.

"Okay, what about the painter, Toulouse-Lautrec?"

Arthur laughed.

"Are you kidding me? His problem was his two grandmothers were sisters. Poor bastard was a victim of inbreeding, which caused a condition called pycnodysostosis, a.k.a. osteogenesis imperfecta. His upper body was normal but his legs were like a ten-year-old's."

Arthur's eyes bored into Crockett's. "No offense, Crock, but I just wonder who's the captain of the ship here, me or you?"

Chapter 31

It was seven o'clock in the morning. Cam walked out of Main House wearing Wayfarers and a Yankee baseball cap. He had borrowed a little makeup from a girl next door to hide the shiner he got from Todd a few days before, and his face looked almost as good as new. Evan had arranged to have a car meet Cam at the back of the Admissions building, where nobody was likely to be at that hour.

Cam walked up to the idling black Lincoln town car and opened the back door.

"Morning," he said, sliding in fast.

"Oh, hi, Mr. Crawford. Didn't see you coming," said the driver. "My name's Hank."

"Hey, Hank, how's traffic into the city?"

"Probably be about an hour-fifteen," Hank said, pulling out of the parking lot and looking back at Cam in the rearview mirror.

Something didn't feel right to Cam as they drove down the windy road. The last time he was on the road, he was colossally drunk and coked up, going the other way, dodging wild turkeys. He expected to feel exhilaration—re-entering the real world for a few hours, getting away from the dysfunctional addicts and head cases. But instead he felt dread. Like this was maybe a really bad idea and he should have just done his stint at Clairmount, let the treatment take its course.

He saw the garment bag hanging from the hook on the far side of the car and knew it was a suit that Evan had gotten from Cam's house and arranged for the driver to pick up. On the seat next to him, he saw his leather attaché case. Evan may suck as a people person, but nobody was better organized. Cam knew without opening it that the case contained the in-depth report about the soup heir David Humphries and his wife, Jessica. Cam had skimmed the report a week ago and remembered a lot of dry stuff about all the investments the Humphries had and how they had performed over the years. There also was ten pages that detailed what the Humphries' favorite charities were, all about their four children and what the Humphries liked to do in their spare time.

Cam never asked Evan how he got his hands on the stock portfolio, which was highly confidential and managed by one of their biggest rivals. Fact was, he didn't want to know. No, fact was, he *did* know, but wished he didn't. He had read something in the *Wall Street Journal* about how one hedge fund company in Greenwich had accused another of hacking into the cell phone of one of their traders. Cam knew Evan had a private detective on the payroll. Evan had hired him to look into the private lives of rivals and potential clients. How else would he know that David Humphries had a six-foot Brazilian model girlfriend he saw twice a week at a Gramercy Park apartment he paid for?

Cam opened the case and saw the twenty-page report. This was Evan's way of telling him to go over it again and memorize every name and number and, while he was at it, brush up on what clubs the Humphries belonged to so he could drop a few names if need be. He saw something new. A two-page account detailing their rival Clark Hustead's DUI, which took place two summers ago in Bridgehampton, and the fact that he had made a substantial contribution to the 2012 Barack Obama campaign. That information alone might get a diehard Republican like Humphries a little disenchanted with Hustead. Cam had never used any of the information that Evan's guy had dug up before. He had a problem with spies. That was a bone of contention between him and Evan because Evan felt they had lost an account when

Cam failed to reveal something that would have put a stake through the heart of a competitive firm's philandering managing partner.

Cam reviewed the paperwork for the next forty-five minutes and when he looked up, saw the Manhattan skyline against a backdrop of vivid blue. It reminded him of the morning of 9/11. His stomach tightened.

He reached for the suit bag.

He unbuckled his belt and slipped it through the belt loops. Then he took off his khaki pants and put on the grey pinstriped ones.

"Don't mind me back here. Just changing into my battle fatigues."

The pants were a little big on him. Cam chalked it up to the Clairmount food. He knew without looking that Evan would have chosen a Paul Stuart tie, probably a blue one. Evan had a theory that Paul Stuart ties worked better on old-money clients, Hermes ties on new money.

It was a *red* Paul Stuart tie. Close enough. Cam knotted it and looked down.

"This on straight, Hank?"

Hank looked back through the rearview mirror. "Perfect, sir."

The brand-new white Brooks Brothers shirt in cellophane sticking out of the oversized pocket of the garment bag was a button-down, which he never wore. This was another theory of Evan's: old money more often than not wore button downs, new money no buttons. Cam amused himself at the thought of how three generations of a family that started a soup company in some Pennsylvania backwater was old money. Same as the forty-year-old woman he'd had as a dinner partner once who was the biggest snob he'd ever met. Her great-grandfather had been the farmer in Moline, Illinois, who had invented a yellow-and-green farm machine with one wheel in front and two in back.

Hank pulled up to the green awning with the number 106 on it— the Leicester Club.

Cam thanked Hank, handed him a fifty-dollar tip, and climbed out of the car. He went inside and up to the reception desk.

"Morning, Mr. Crawford," said the man at the desk. "Breakfast with Mr. MacLeod and your brother?"

"Hey, William. Yup. They here yet?" Cam asked, looking at his watch.

"No, sir, you're the first."

"Also, a Mr. and Mrs. Humphries."

"Yes, your brother left their names."

"Will you tell them I'm up on the second floor?" "Certainly, sir."

*****

Evan was going on about how Trajectory never invested in mortgage-backed securities. Then he segued into his old favorites, swaps and derivatives. Mrs. Humphries was clearly lost, confused, or couldn't care less. David Humphries looked as though he was getting it, but Cam suspected he might be faking it for his wife's benefit— like, *Don't worry, honey, I can keep up with these New York hotshots every day of the week.*

A few minutes later, Evan went totally tech-speak. Trey gave Cam a light kick under the table. Cam knew exactly what it meant: *quick, translate before they slump over on the table, dying of boredom.* Cam swung into action and broke down all the algorithms and metrics-laced lingo his brother was spewing, and before long, the Humphries looked like they had caught up. Within five minutes, Cam had them nodding and smiling.

"You know," Cam said, "there's something else. It sounds like a cliché when guys like us drone on about relationships and how we listen attentively to our client's every need. Well, fact is, *we don't.* Couldn't care less. All we care about is making money. And the only way we make money is to make damn sure you make it. And the more, the merrier—"

David Humphries smiled a smile like he had just gotten off with his Brazilian model.

"Relationships?" Cam said. "Sure, they're important. But a distant second to making you returns that are the envy of our competitors. You know, those guys who get you great tickets to Broadway shows but only so-so returns on your money."

Jessica Humphries smiled at him and—he thought—winked.

Cam had basically cribbed the spiel from Gordon Gekko in the movie *Wall Street* and used a variation on it for all their dog-and-pony shows.

He watched the waiter clear the plates that had scraps of eggs Benedict, toast, and sausage on them and waited for Evan's standard wrap-up.

"Obviously, we can't make any promises—" Evan started.

"—but if history repeats itself," Cam said, as if grabbing the baton in a 440-relay race, "we'll do pretty damn well for you."

David Humphries looked at his wife, then Cam.

"We had pretty much made up our minds after our first meeting," Humphries said.

At that meeting, Evan had hammered away at their double-digit returns on foreign currencies, knowing the competition had only produced seven percent. Ferreting out the fact that Jessica was an avid reader, Cam had had a nice conversation with her about *The Great Gatsby* while Trey had played éminence grise to the hilt, oozing gravitas and polish, though not saying much of real substance.

"So, does that mean—" Cam knew exactly what it meant.

"Yes, we're on board," Humphries said as his wife beamed.

"You know, at first," Jessica Humphries said to Cam, "I'll be honest—I thought you were too young."

Trey leaned forward and put his hand on Jessica Humphries' wrist.

"Cam's just aged well, Jessica," he said. "He's actually forty-five." Trey guffawed, always the biggest fan of his gimpy jokes.

"Just don't let the competition steal you away," Humphries said to Cam, then turned to Evan. "Or you."

"We're not going anywhere," Evan said.

Cam knew Evan was thinking his bonus better be north of $5 million, or he might be tempted.

Jessica put her hand out to Cam. "Cam, you'll just have to come see our paintings sometime."

"I would love to, especially that marvelous Seurat you told me about."

He had never said the word *marvelous* before in his life. It was almost as bad as *iconic* or *robust*.

*****

It was a one-hour $200 million breakfast. Cam felt like he had just shot three under, won the Nobel Prize, and had taken a massive hit of amyl nitrate.

"Good job, guys," Trey said, shaking hands with Evan after the Humphries got into their car and left. "Really good job."

He put his hand out to Cam. "*Nice work*," he said again.

But Cam didn't shake his hand.

"Trey, I just want to say one thing," Cam said. "I don't need a father. I got one"—he paused— "and even though he kind of sucks at the job, I don't need another one."

Evan stepped forward. "Come on, Cam. Don't—"

"Shut the fuck up, Evan," Cam said, looking back at Trey. "I'm giving you fair warning, Trey. You get into my personal life again, I'm history. I bet Clark Hustead might be able to scare up an office for me." Cam put out his hand. "Do we understand each other?"

Trey just smiled, nodded and shook his hand.

He turned and walked toward his Mercedes limo. He slid in, and the long, shiny black car pulled away.

Cam turned to Evan. "I meant every word, Evan."

"I know you did," Evan said.

Cam turned and walked over to where Hank was double parked.

Hank got out and held open the back door. "Hello, sir."

"Hey, Hank," Cam said, getting in. "Back to my little paradise on the hill."

Chapter 32

Dr. Paul Crockett wasn't wearing anything green or with the Dartmouth name or logo, which was about as rare as Arthur without a cynical taunt. Crockett was clad all in black except for a white T-shirt under a Faded Glory black-collared shirt. Arthur had never been impressed with the sartorial splendor of any of his five shrinks. He and Crockett were outdoors sitting in Adirondack chairs, and the wind was having its way with Crockett's comb-over.

Arthur had just announced to Crockett his new policy: total candor at all times. One hundred percent of what he told the doctor henceforward was going to be the truth.

"Here's the only problem," Arthur said. "I'm not sure I can always tell the difference."

"Between what you think happened and what really happened?" Crockett gave his mustache a tug.

"Yeah, exactly, between fantasy and fiction."

Crockett nodded. "Like, can you give me an example?"

"Okay," he said, closing his eyes and smiling. "Like having this serious grope session with Avril Ensor."

Crockett's laugh was automatic.

Arthur whipped his head around to Crockett.

"Sorry, Arthur, but I'm pretty sure that was a fantasy."

"Don't be so fucking sure, Doc. She likes me."

"I'm sure she does, but—"

"Okay, let's change the subject," Arthur said, eyes like a rattle-snake's.

"I am ecstatic to hear that it's going to be all the truth *all the time*, Arthur. That demonstrates a whole new commitment level."

Arthur yawned, still stung. "Then again, I think that bitch likes the pretty boy, Crawford."

"You mean Avril?" Crockett gave his ear a tug.

"Yeah, who the hell you think I'm talking about? Ya know, Doc, you got a lotta tics goin' on. Yanking your mustache, tugging your ear, brushing invisible shit off your pants."

"Something apparently has you very agitated, Arthur?"

"What the hell does she see in that fucking lightweight?"

Crockett started to spin his cap around, but knew Arthur would call him on it.

Crockett cleared his throat. "I feel strongly that romance at institutions like Clairmount is not a good idea."

"Tell that to the all-American couple."

Crockett raised a finger. "Except, obviously, they're not."

Arthur looked quizzical for a second. "Or else what would they be doing in this joint, you mean?"

"Precisely," Crockett said.

Chapter 33

Going up Third Avenue, Cam saw a lot of his old haunts. A few of the bars and restaurants had good associations. Many of them he remembered walking into but not out of. Others were just a blur.

He closed his eyes and rested his head back on the seat.

It was only ten o'clock. It wasn't as though they did head count every five minutes at Clairmount, he thought.

He didn't really feel any better. Not drinking, that was.

He opened his eyes and saw the East Eighty Second street sign. He leaned forward in his seat.

"Hank, pull over in front of that place," Cam said, pointing to a bar called Malachy's. "Just a quick celebratory pop."

Hank pulled over. Cam got out of the car and motioned to Hank to join him. Hank's eyes widened with skepticism.

"Come on," Cam said, motioning, and Hank followed him in. "One ain't gonna kill you."

Cam looked down the long wooden bar with the smoky mirror behind it.

"This is about the only joint on the Upper East Side I don't remember getting shitfaced in," Cam said.

"Nice place," Hank said, looking around.

The bar had dark wood paneling and soft lighting, but its main feature was hundreds of hats that hung from the ceiling. Bowler hats, pork pie hats, baseball caps, fedoras, homburgs, you name it. Cam wasn't curious enough to ask the bartender why this particular theme had been chosen.

"Bloody Bull, please," he said, "and for my friend here, a..."

Hank looked uncomfortable, like he didn't make a habit of drinking with passengers.

"Come on. You're not gonna plow into a tree after just *one*."

"Okay, sure. Maybe a beer."

"What kind you want, Hank? How 'bout a Heineken or something?"

"Bud draft's good," Hank said.

The bartender nodded.

"So, how long you been drivin'?" Cam asked.

"'Bout four years."

"Really? What before that?"

"A stockbroker. Bear Stearns," Hank said, like it was a bad dream.

"You're shitting me. Good shop, bad ending."

The bartender arrived with their drinks.

Cam's Bloody Bull had barely touched the bar top when he picked it up and took a long pull. His big green eyes seemed to light up.

"Oh, man, nectar of the gods," Cam said. "So, you didn't want to stay in the brokerage business?"

"Well, see, thing was, Mr. Crawford—"

Cam wiped his mouth. "Hey, Hank, lose the Mr. Crawford. I'm half your age."

"Okay...Cam. Thing was, I couldn't hack cold-calling people to get their accounts. I mean, at age fifty?"

"I hear ya," Cam said, taking another long sip and finishing off his Bloody Bull. "I never had to do that shit, or I probably would have quit too."

Cam flagged the bartender.

"'Nother one, please. This time hold the tomato juice, bullion, Tabasco, and Worcestershire. Just vodka. You married, Hank?"

"Yep, that's one I got right. Thirty years and it's still good."

Cam was envious. "Hat's off," he said. "I got the dough. You got the happiness. Wanna switch?"

"Nah," Hank said. "I'm good."

"I got a wife," Cam said wistfully. "Not for long, though—"

He caught himself, knowing he was at risk of doing the maudlin-guy-at-a-bar-who-bemoans-his-whole-sorry-ass-life routine. The bartender put the straight vodka in front of Cam.

"So, what's the secret?" Cam asked.

"To...?"

"You know, being happily married."

"Don't bitch about how much she spends on shoes and separate sinks."

Cam raised his glass in a toast, then put it up to his lips and drained it.

The bartender gave Cam a wary look. Like he was thinking maybe Cam should consider pacing himself.

"Ser'ously, Hank, tell me how you got thirty years."

His internal drunkometer chirped an early warning. *Beware: short, choppy, slurred phrases.*

Hank took a sip of his beer. "You know, I think I just got lucky: finding someone I was compatible with. I mean, someone who'd put up with my bullshit."

"Lucky man," Cam said.

"So, you run a hedge fund?"

Cam looked at his empty glass and tried to get the bartender's attention.

"Put it this way, I'm like the junior partner. Work with my brother. He's the brains. I'm the face and the mouth."

Cam started waving his hand at the bartender.

"Don't get me wrong—I work my ass off and get paid a lot, but basically it's just memorizing a bunch of shit and being good with people." Cam finally caught the bartender's attention. Dropping his voice, he said, "Any idiot could do it."

"Somehow, I doubt that," Hank said.

"Trust me."

"Yes, sir," the bartender said. "Another?"

"I'm switching to Johnny Walker Blue and a splash."

The bartender eyed Cam like he was sizing him up: Was he going to be a loud, obnoxious drunk or a quiet, happy one?

Cam turned back to Hank, blinked and gave him a *where was I* look.

"As my dear old Dad used to say—a hundred times a day—'somebody's gotta get A's and someone's gotta get C's."

Hank raised his mug. "To us C guys."

Cam raised his glass. "Hey, while we're at it, here's to Jessica and David."

"Jessica and David?"

"People whose account we just landed," Cam said. "Whole reason for this little celebration."

"To Jessica and David," Hank said. They clinked glasses.

Chapter 34

Hank kept it to just one beer, but lost count how many drinks Cam had. Hank remembered him switching over to Johnny Walker and knowing that was a bad idea. After that, Cam got back onto the subject of his brother again. His brother being the smart one, Cam the fuck up. Went on about Evan winning half the prizes at MIT, an IQ just shy of Einstein. He talked about his other brother, too, and how well they got along. Charlie the homicide cop. Used to be in New York, now down in Florida.

Cam was passed out in the back of the town car as Hank pulled into Clairmount.

"Mr. Crawford," Hank said. "Cam, hey, Cam, rise and shine."

"Huh?" Cam said, a flicker of eye movement.

"We're back at Clairmount."

Cam bolted upright. "Holy shit. What time is it?"

"Just past two."

Cam tried to get his bearings. "I'm still shitfaced," he slurred.

He started taking off his suit fast. Looked like he was wrestling an alligator.

"Do you want me to drop you off where I picked you up?"

"Hang on. Let me think," Cam said, pulling on his khakis, then realizing they were backward.

"No, drive up that road," Cam said, pointing, as he put on his baseball cap then, pulled it down low. He tried to stick his belt through a loop, but missed.

"Okay, now pull up a little. Yeah, okay, stop."

Cam squinted, pretty sure, but not positive, Main was the building two hundred yards ahead of them.

"All right," he said, like confiding to a co-conspirator, "I'm gonna run into the woods, then slip around back of the house."

Hank nodded, glad he wasn't in Cam's shoes.

"Got any gum or mitts...I mean, mints, Hank?" Cam asked, shaking his head. "Jesus, I'm a fuckin' mess."

Hank had neither. Cam handed Hank a fifty-dollar bill.

Hank thanked him and said, "Be careful."

Cam put on his sunglasses, grabbed the door, opened it and took off. Within ten steps he had slipped and gone down.

Hank watched the highly compensated hedge fund manager get up and slalom into the woods.

Cam was behind a tree looking out at the back porch of Main House. There were two people he knew by sight in chairs, talking. He formulated a plan: he would casually walk up to the porch like he had had just gone for an afternoon stroll in the woods. Then go in the back door of Main and try to somehow get to his room without being spotted. That was the tough part, because the only way to his room was past the desk where the techs monitored patients' comings and goings. There was no other way. Once he got to his room, he figured he could sleep it off.

Thoughts started rocketing around in his head. Shit, why hadn't he just stayed in the car until he sobered up? Or gone to a Starbucks and downed a few grandes—after a while he would have been okay. Couldas and shouldas...too bad, because Hank and the car were long gone.

Getting to the porch was the easy part. Cam thought about sitting down in one of the chairs, killing some time, but his head was throbbing and he was dying to get into his bed. Through a window he saw two techs sitting at the desk, one doing paperwork, the other talking on the phone, looking down at a newspaper. He crossed quickly to the far side of the room with just one slight misstep. His balance was definitely shaky. He was now on the side of the room where the long built-in techs' desk was. He inched along the wall toward it. He looked out and saw a patient watching him curiously. He put a finger up to his lips, and the patient nodded but kept staring. He shuffled a little farther and was now ten feet from the long desk. He stopped and thought for a second, a few beads of sweat sliding down his forehead.

The old movie he had watched two nights before, *Platoon*—no, that wasn't it—popped into his head. It had a part where two GIs crawled through the mud, flat on the ground, to avoid a machine-gun nest. He looked around: the coast was clear. He sank down on his knees, then leaned forward, and his chest and stomach hit the floor a little harder than he meant. He looked over and saw the guy still eyeing him, like he couldn't believe he was watching another patient belly his way across the floor.

Cam was parallel to the desk now. He could hear the tech, Sarah, talking on the phone. He kept inching along, sweating profusely now. He was near the far end of the desk. Almost there, the door to his room in sight. He was going to make it. Shitfaced and all.

Then he heard a footstep. He slowly turned his head and saw a size thirteen black wing tip a few inches from his head.

"Uh, Cam?" came the voice of Dr. Boylen six feet above him. "What in God's name do you think you're doing?"

Chapter 35

Rachel was in her room now, talking, for the second time since she'd arrived at Clairmount, to Lenore Peck, a senior social worker who would evaluate Rachel's suitability for moving from Acute Care to a thirty-day program.

Lenore had intense, deep sunken eyes that never seemed to blink and sat at Rachel's desk, taking notes. Rachel rested on her bed, legs straight out, back against a wall.

"Since you've been here, have you felt suicidal?" Lenore asked.

"A day doesn't go by when I don't."

"But do you ever think about how you'd do it? You know, make a plan?" Lenore turned the page on her black- and-white notebook.

"No."

"Well, that's good," Lenore said with a rare smile. "How about, have you had any drug cravings?"

If she only knew...

"Yes, sometimes when we talk about them in NA."

Lenore probably wouldn't buy it if she just gave her a flat no.

"On a scale of one to ten, how intense are your cravings?"

"Um, I'd say about a six or a seven."

"So not too intense?"

"No."

"What do you think about the most here?"

Lenore struck her as a repressed detective.

"My mother, her death. How it left me all alone. How much I miss her, even though we fought like cats and dogs."

Rachel squeezed her hands together tightly.

Lenore put her elbow on her knee and cupped her chin. "I understand, Rachel. I really do."

"Do you?"

"Yes, there's something called 'radical acceptance,' one of the core concepts of DBT—"

"I hear that DBT stuff really helps."

Lenore nodded. "It's something that might be very positive for you. Radical acceptance is what it sounds like: coming to grips with something major that altered or disrupted your life. Accepting what happened and trying to move on. That's a tall order, no question about it. Idea is not to minimize it but to face it. Deal with it, and if possible, build from it."

A very tall order, Rachel thought.

Lenore sat up and put her notebook down on the desk.

"Here's what I recommend: You take the thirty-day program, which consists of two hours of DBT every day. You'll get a lot out of it, I think. You'll move down to Brook House, where there are usually around ten to twelve other patients living in an environment which is structured but also gives you a certain independence."

"So, techs don't hang around my room on suicide watch all night?"

Lenore shook her head.

"They check on you at first, but you'll get a lot more freedom—"

"Unlike this dump."

Lenore smiled and nodded.

"Okay, so when?"

"Tomorrow."

Rachel nodded, mostly okay with it.

"How's it going with your stepfather? You mentioned last time you've had a few conversations."

Rachel put her hand on her forehead and closed her eyes.

"Let's just say they weren't very productive. Leave it at that."

"You two don't get along?"

"'Don't get along?' Guy's a complete and total asshole."

Lenore's head snapped back, and her mouth formed a perfect O.

Rachel smiled. "Aren't you glad you asked?"

*****

Rachel had her father's phone number. A lot of good it had done her. During the first year after he split with her mother, Rachel had probably left close to twenty messages on his machine and none of them had ever been returned. Finally, she'd stopped calling him.

She decided to phone him and let him know she was at Clairmount. Partly as a sympathy play and partly to make him feel guilty. Based on history, she expected chances of him feeling either were slim. But she also needed advice, and Judd Kornbluth was a lawyer.

The phone rang, and of course, he didn't pick up.

"It's your daughter, the only one you got... I think. Course who knows. Maybe by now you got a whole new family," she said into the machine. "I need the advice of a lawyer, and since you fit the bill... Anyway, I'll pay your fee. It's about my mother's estate."

Twenty four hours later, she was still waiting.

But just when she was about to try to find another lawyer, her father called back.

OCD John answered the phone and told her it was, "some guy." She was just hoping it wasn't Harlan. He had called her a few days before, and she'd never called him back.

"Rachel?"

"Yes?"

"It's your dad."

She was angry and joyful at the same time

"I recognized the number. Voice sounds kinda familiar."

He cleared his throat. "Hey, listen, I realize I've been—"

"Don't bother. I just need some legal advice, which, like I said, I'll pay for."

"You don't need to pay me for anything. I'll help, if I can. If I can't, maybe I can steer you in the right direction."

She was suspicious. "I insist on paying you."

"Okay, make the check out to your favorite charity, if that's how you feel."

She vaguely remembered a glib charm.

"Is there something in trusts and estates common law that says the husband automatically gets fifty percent of an estate?" Rachel did her damnedest to sound like a client.

Judd Kornbluth laughed. "No. Why? Is that what Eppersley's telling you?"

"Yes."

"Listen, Rachel. I guarantee you your mother made him sign a prenup. She had that money she inherited from your grandfather," Kornbluth said. "She made me sign one, and that was back before she hit the jackpot."

"That son of a bitch. Will you call him and his lawyer, tell 'em to get off my case?"

"Sure, just give me their numbers. I'll call them right away."

*****

He got back to her the next day and said technically Phil Eppersley wasn't entitled to a dime, but that to make him go away, Judd's advice was to give him $50,000 which ought to shut him up. He added that Phil would need to pay his lawyer out of that. He told her he needed to review the prenup, which Phil finally confessed existed, but was 90-percent sure the money in the bank was all hers.

He also explained that he needed to read over the will, and that it had to be filed in probate court and accepted by a judge before any distributions were made.

Rachel said she was in no hurry.

"Sounds like all this might take a lot of time?" she said.

"Listen. I've got about five years of guilt to make up for. So, don't worry about it."

A million questions flooded Rachel's head. At first, she didn't want to give him the satisfaction of knowing that she cared. But she had to ask.

"Why didn't you ever call me back?"

"I wish I had a good excuse," Kornbluth sighed. "Let's just say I was going through some pretty heavy issues at the time."

"Like what?"

He didn't answer.

"Tell me."

"Oh, Christ, Rachel—"

"You can't just let me guess, for God's sake." She amped up the volume.

"Okay, like just this really self-destructive behavior. My life was an out-of-control disaster."

A few seconds of silence passed like a glacier. Then Rachel laughed.

"It's funny?" he said.

"No, but at least I know where I got it from."

Chapter 36

Ted had told a white lie, but had done it convincingly. He had told the tech at the desk that he had gotten a call from the woman in charge of billing and she needed him to bring over his Blue Cross/Blue Shield card in order to submit insurance papers. The tech looked at him funny.

"Who was it who called, Ted?"

"Ah, I forget the name."

"'Cause usually one of us would just take it over for you," the tech said.

Ted shrugged. "I don't know what to tell you, but she asked me to do it as soon as possible."

Now he was outright lying.

"Okay," said the tech, buzzing the front door open, "but don't stop off at any bars, like your buddy."

Ted forced a laugh.

He knew there was just the one administration building and figured that was where the head of the hospital had his office.

He was right.

He saw the man's name on the directory. Room 202. He rode the elevator up to the second floor with the manila envelope under his arm.

He walked into room 202 and saw a woman at a desk in a small reception area.

"Yes, sir, may I help you?" she asked.

"I'm here to see Dr. Wittman," Ted said. "I don't have an appointment. I'm actually a patient."

The woman looked wary. "Yes, and—"

"I need to talk to him about something very important," Ted said, walking past her toward the door.

She moved in front of him and cut him off like an offensive lineman protecting his quarterback.

"Dr. Wittman is busy. If you would just tell me the nature—" Ted saw a tall, bald, frowning man come out of his office.

"What can I do for you, sir?" the man asked.

"My name is Ted Purvis and I just need ten minutes of your time, Dr. Wittman."

The man's frown faded. "Sure," he said, "come on in."

Ted followed Wittman into his office. Wittman pointed to a wooden chair opposite his desk. Ted sat down and put the manila envelope on top of Wittman's desk.

"Dr. Wittman, I came here on behalf of Cam Crawford. I know you know the whole story—"

Wittman nodded.

"Cam had a bad slip up," Ted said, "which probably a few other patients at Clairmount have had at one time or other. He is a good man, with a positive attitude and is greatly respected by his fellow patients. He goes out of his way to help the rest of us and keep our spirits up. I've brought with me thirty-four letters"—Ted pointed to the manila envelope—"from patients at Main House and a bunch of others from people who have come in contact with Cam at either AA or NA meetings. They all vouch for Cam's, ah, exemplary character and generosity of spirit—" Ted felt as if he was filibustering. "Not only that, but I think if you spoke to most members of the staff they would—"

"Excuse me, Ted, but I've already made my decision about Mr. Crawford."

Ted blinked nervously. "You have?"

"Yes, I have," Wittman smiled broadly. "One of my oldest and most trusted employees who's a member of our advisory board spoke very highly of him. Frankly, that was enough for me. As you said, we all have had our slip ups. Just make sure you tell your friend that one he had yesterday has to be his last one here. Or anywhere, for that matter."

Ted got up from his chair and pumped Wittman's hand. "Oh, that is great news. You won't regret it, Dr. Wittman. Thank you so much."

"You're welcome," Wittman said, walking Ted to the door. "I just wish I could dig up thirty-four people who'd write letters for me."

Chapter 37

Cam went up to the desk, and Alice, the nurse who had taken him under her wing the first few days, looked up from her paperwork.

"Hi, Cam, you been behaving yourself?" she said, a twinkle in her tranquil blue eyes.

Cam hadn't seen her since "the incident" but had found out she was the main reason he hadn't gotten tossed from Clairmount. He'd heard about what Ted did too. When he thanked Ted, all he got was a quick shrug and a *hey, it was nothing* look.

Cam had always just thought Alice was a sweet, old nurse who had been a good listener when he spilled his guts right after he first arrived. But it turned out she was on the advisory board of the hospital, not to mention the sister of Dr. Wittman.

At the meeting to decide Cam's fate, most of the board thought it was time for him to pack his bags. Not Alice and Dr. Boylen.

"Could I talk to you, Alice?" Cam asked.

"Sure, give me two seconds. I just need to finish this up."

"Want to just come to my room?"

She nodded.

Cam paced around his room, trying to figure out what to say, when she walked in.

He gestured toward the chair, and she smiled at him and sat down.

Cam sat down on his bed. "I just wanted to tell you how much I appreciate you going to bat for me. I think I really need this place and if I had been kicked out, well, I don't know what would have happened. But it wouldn't have been good."

Alice pushed her glasses up. "You remember, Cam, when you first got here I told you I had a lot of drinkers in my family?"

"I remember."

"Well, what I didn't tell you was that I was the worst offender." She hesitated, like she was trying to decide whether to go on or not.

Then, she exhaled deeply. "What the heck. I'm going to tell you the story. When I was twenty-eight years old, I was a bad alcoholic. I was also a mother. And not a very good mother. One time when I was very drunk, I left my three-year-old daughter in the bathtub and went downstairs to get another glass of—I remember what it was to this day—Boone's Farm Apple wine. When I came back up, my daughter was on her side, her head underwater."

Cam put his hand up to his mouth. "Oh my God."

Alice held up her hand. "Fortunately, she hadn't drowned, but pretty close to it." Alice brushed a tear from her eye. "She was never going to be normal, the lack of oxygen to her brain."

Cam reached over and patted her on the shoulder.

She looked up and stared him in the eyes. "I really don't know why I'm telling you this. Except I know you're someone with a really good heart. Your concern for Ted that night, that he might do something to himself. Your...your basic kindness."

"Thank you, but—"

"You know my daughter."

"I do?"

"Daphne. She works in the dining hall serving food behind the counter."

It took a few moments to register.

"Daph, the tall one—"

"That's right. With the stutter. She's the one I was telling you about. She told me how nice you always are to her. Always ask her what dessert she recommends. Compliment her on how good the shrimp pasta was." Alice winked. "We both know that food's marginally better than prison food."

Cam laughed.

"Anyway, I put in a good word for you not because you were nice to my daughter, but because some people—not all of them—need, and deserve, one more chance. No matter how many they've already had. I never got one—my husband left me over what happened—and I understand that. I ruined the life of his only child. Of course, we're talking about two very different things. You just snuck out of Clairmount and had a few drinks—"

Cam laughed. "I gotta come clean with you, Alice. It was more than a few."

Alice smiled. "Whatever. You're a good person and I think this place can turn you around. Not only that—men like you can be positive forces here. Help other people make their experience better. So, think of it as partly a selfish thing. You can make this place that I love an even better place."

"Thank you, Alice. Thank you very much. Sappy as it sounds, I think this just might be a turning point in my life."

Chapter 38

Cam dialed his brother, Charlie, in Florida. "Hey, Chas, it's your fuck-up brother."

"You mean my *former* fuck-up brother," Charlie Crawford said.

There was a long pause. "Nah, 'fraid not," Cam said, grimly. "I had what you'd call a little relapse."

"Oh, shit, what happened?" Charlie asked. "Hang on. I'm pulling over to the side of the road."

Cam gave him the details.

"Well, at least you dodged a bullet," Charlie said. "You know what it is?"

"What *what* is?"

"You got the Crawford pleasing gene," Charlie said. "You wanted to please Trey by doing your bit to win that account."

Cam thought for a second. "Swell. So not only did I get the Crawford depression gene, but I'm trying to please everyone too?"

Charlie laughed. "Well, maybe not everyone," he said. "Dude, just take care of yourself, okay? What happened may have been a good wake-up call."

"Yeah, thanks," Cam said as he saw Ted give him a wave from across the room. "Gotta go, man. Time for the next activity here at the fun house."

*****

Ted and Cam and twelve other patients waited in the living room of Main House for pet therapy. A few patients looked like dog lovers, but most of them just looked bored. Dog therapy was a specific event on the Clairmount activities calendar, every Tuesday at ten o'clock. A consultant had recently suggested that the living room, also known as the "brown room" because it was a mix of heavy brown wooden furniture and brown upholstered furniture, be redecorated, as the colors probably did little to lift patients' spirits.

"You believe they make this shit mandatory, Black Cloud?" Cam whispered, patting a well-coiffed Airedale.

"What did you say?" the dog lady asked.

She was about sixty, had a short pageboy, and dressed in corduroy pants and a blue LaCoste shirt. Her collar was popped, which Cam always felt was a somewhat lame fashion statement, particularly on an older woman.

"Nothing," Cam said, patting the Airedale again. "Nice doggy."

Ted made an attempt to laugh, but being so out of practice, had trouble coordinating the required mouth muscles.

"A friend of mine suggested entering Falstaff in the Westminster Dog Show," the dog lady proclaimed proudly to no one in particular.

Cam looked at Ted, then back to the dog lady.

"I'd say this old dude would be a shoo-in for top dog."

The dog lady frowned, like 'dude' was a moniker well beneath the regal Falstaff.

They were in the same room where Cam, Ted, and the others played games. Scrabble was still their favorite, but they played Boggle and Scattergories too. Their first day there, Cam had told Ted it would have been nice to play Beirut too, but Ted had just looked at him blankly.

Seven hands were patting Falstaff, and though he was a fairly big dog, there wasn't any room left on him. Pony thumped Falstaff's head, like he was dribbling a basketball.

"What exactly is this s'posed to do?" Pony asked the dog lady.

Her eyes crinkled. "I'm not sure I know what you're asking, sir."

"You coming around with Falshaft," Pony said, "s'posed to boost our morale or something?"

The dog lady looked uncomfortable with the question.

Cam smiled at her. "If I may," he said, "I think the idea is for us to get off focusing on ourselves, dwelling on our own sh...stuff. Right?"

The dog lady pondered. "Could be. I've just been doing it for as long as I can remember. Before Falstaff, I came here with my setter, Iago."

"Got kind of a Shakespeare thing going, huh?" Cam said.

"Yes. My husband's the same way with his boats. Calls his Whaler *Othello*."

"Is that right?"

The dog lady nodded and crinkled her eyes again.

"They pay you?" Pony asked loudly.

"That's a tacky question, Pony," Cam said. Then to the dog lady: "Don't mind him. He's, you know, socially maladjusted."

"I do it"—the dog lady frowned—"to bring pleasure to my fellow—"

"When was the last time you washed Falshaft?" Pony smelled his hand.

The woman's eyes narrowed. "It's Falstaff," she said. "Three times a week, and he's as clean as a whistle."

Pony looked up at her skeptically. "I seen some pretty nasty-looking whistles in my day."

Cam took Pony's hand and peeled it off the dog's head. "Give it a rest, man."

The dog lady looked at her watch. "Well, it's about time I—"

"I notice that Falshaft farts," Pony said.

Cam grabbed Pony's arm. "Okay, Pony, come on. It's time to—"

He suddenly noticed Arthur Petit's head at elbow level. He had just walked in.

"Marvelous-looking creature," Arthur said. "We had one just like him."

The dog lady nodded, eager to leave, but clearly feeling it politically incorrect to not acknowledge the comments of a small, disadvantaged person.

"Ours used to love shagging tennis balls," Arthur went on. "This guy like to do that?"

The dog lady nodded enthusiastically.

"This one time"—a few patients shuffled toward the door, veterans of Arthur's dubious tales—"me and my brother had just smoked a little ganj—"

The dog lady cringed.

"And we took a tennis ball, cut out a hole about the size of a penny—"

The dog lady took a step toward the door.

"Then we shoved this cherry bomb in it—pretty tight squeeze—"

The dog lady's mouth tightened.

"Hey, Arthur," Cam said, "let this poor lady go home. She's been here—"

Arthur raised a hand. "Almost done. So, my brother lit it. Then I chucked it as far as I could, and Frodie—that was his name—went running after it—"

The dog lady snapped the leash, and her bandy legs started to churn.

"And guess what happened?" Arthur asked, raising his voice so she could hear.

"What?" Pony was dying to know.

Arthur shot Cam a sly smile.

"Blew ol' Frodie's head into the next county."

Chapter 39

"So, let me get this straight. You were crawling on the floor, drunk, trying to get to your room?" Evan said.

Cam had twisted the black phone cord around his wrist several times as he stared at something in loopy handwriting on the whiteboard.

"Who told you?" Cam asked his brother.

"Your fucking doctor."

"Since when did you become my guardian, Evan?"

Evan was silent.

Cam knew Evan was doing his version of counting to ten. Evan had a hot temper and sometimes had to fight his instinct to yell and break things. He also had a knack for making Cam feel like an undisciplined child.

"Cam," he said finally, his voice thick with condescension, "are you trying to commit financial suicide? What if your little shenanigan gets out to the competition?"

"For Chrissakes, don't give me that shit. I fucked up and take full responsibility for it," Cam said, pacing. "It was a really bad idea leaving this place and doing that dog-and-pony. I was just doing it for the team."

Evan went off. "You gotta be fucking kidding. So, it's our fault you left Clairmount and pounded cocktails all morning? Is that what you're telling me?"

"What I'm saying is I shoulda let my treatment run its course," Cam said, straining mightily to rein himself in. "You didn't twist my arm to go to the meeting and, obviously, you have nothing to do with my drinking."

"Well, thank you for that," Evan said, still boiling. "You do realize that any one of our investors can pull their accounts any time they want. I mean, what if Humphries hears you been crawling around the floor, drunk at rehab—"

"Okay, Evan, I know you get pleasure rubbing my face in it, but let's just end it right now. Leave me the fuck alone to do what I gotta do here. Okay? If I leave and I still have a problem, then I guess you and Trey have a decision to make—"

"Whoa, whoa, I didn't say anything like that. I just don't want—"

"Goodbye, Evan, it's been swell talking to you."

Click.

Cam looked around the room for something to throw. That was about the only thing he had in common with Evan. Instead he just fell limply into a black leather chair.

"Fuck!" he yelled.

No one was around to hear.

*****

Cam was meeting a res named Tanya down at Brook House in an hour. He was ready for a change of scenery but had a few things to take care of before he left.

He dialed Charlotte's cell phone.

"Hi," he said, "now an okay time to talk?"

He asked because 90-percent of the time when his wife answered, she'd say, "I gotta call you right back."

Then maybe five hours later she would. Cam didn't get how an unemployed woman with no kids was always so damn busy.

"Sure, now's fine," Charlotte said, surprising him.

Cam exhaled. "Listen, Char. I just don't want to go to war with you and make the lawyers rich. I also don't want us to end up hating each other. I mean, what's the point?"

"So, what *do* you want, Cam?" Charlotte asked.

"To split everything right down the middle. Fifty-fifty."

Charlotte paused. "Okay, but what do we do with something like a car?"

"Simple. Figure out how much it's worth, then if you keep it, you give me half of what it's worth. I keep it, I give you half."

"Yes, but say it's your car and you think it's worth more than what the dealer says it's worth. How do we decide—"

"Jesus, Char, trust me that won't happen," he was pacing. "I just want to resolve this thing and be done with it so we can go our separate ways. Nice and amicably."

"What about stuff you gave me? You know, jewelry and stuff like that?"

"Of course, that's a hundred percent yours."

"What about the house? I paid for half with my own money."

"Yes, you did. Tell you what, you can have it—the house is all yours. One hundred percent."

Charlotte didn't say anything. Like she was waiting for a catch. "That's very generous of you, Cam," she said finally.

"I'm a very generous guy."

She laughed. "You know, you really are. So... is that it?"

"Yeah, I think so. Why don't you have your lawyer write it up. Should take him about three hours max."

"Okay."

"Char?"

"Yes?"

"Your lawyer's going to be a very unhappy man. He was counting on World War III."

Cam hung up and slowly unwrapped the telephone cord from around his wrist.

He heard footsteps coming through the kitchen and looked up. It was Pony.

"Yo, Pony, what's up?"

Pony smiled and stuck out his hand. "I just wanted to wish you well, man."

Cam reached out and shook hands. "Well, thanks. I appreciate it."

Pony crossed his arms. "You know, when I first met you, I thought you were just this spoiled rich asshole who didn't give a shit about anything. Turns out you're all right."

Cam slapped him on the shoulder.

"Well, thanks, dude. But knock it off, or we'll have to start hugging."

Pony laughed and held up his hands. "Do I *really* look like a hugger?"

Cam ran his hand through his hair. "So, what's your plan? Where do you go next?"

"Home," Pony said.

"Yeah? You ready for that?"

"No."

"Why are you then?"

"Insurance wouldn't cover me going to Schechter for the 30-Day thing."

"Shit, that's a bummer."

"Yeah, well, what can you do?"

"Go to a lot of meetings, for one thing." Cam said.

"Yep. And stay away from the dudes I used to run with, right?"

"Easier said than done, huh?"

Pony nodded.

"Think you can do it?"

Pony shrugged. "We'll see."

Cam reached into his back pocket and pulled out his wallet. He took out a card and handed it to Pony. "I fucked up the other day, didn't set the best example—"

Pony laughed.

"—but, swear to God, I'm gonna quit. I got a big scare that day."

"What do you mean?"

"I was like a man on a mission," Cam said, his fists tightening. "To fucking drink till I dropped. Two days later and I'm still hung over."

"Been there, bro."

"Yeah," Cam said. "I don't know about you, but I start to hate myself. I mean, the guy I turn into when I drink."

Pony nodded slowly. "Been there too."

"So anyway," Cam said. "I'm done with that shit. This time I mean it. You gotta promise me, you get an urge to booze or use, you call me. I don't care whether it's four in the morning or fucking Christmas Day. You call me, okay?"

Pony nodded. "Okay."

Cam put out his hand again.

Pony shook it, cocked his head and smiled. "Lemme get this straight. You gonna be like... my sponsor?"

"Fuck yeah, man. Why not?" Cam said. "You'll be my first of many."

Chapter 40

C am liked to hang out at the Clairmount library. For one thing, it stocked the *Wall Street Journal,* so he could keep up with all things financial and news in general. For another thing, even though he didn't broadcast it, he liked to read.

He had read the *Journal* and the *New York Times* and had leafed through a few magazines. *Forbes,* of course, but also the *New Yorker* and *Harpers.* Ted had walked up behind him one day when he was reading a short story in the *New Yorker.*

"Pretty high-brow, Cam," Ted said. "You're probably gonna need a dictionary."

"Nah," Cam said, "I'm just looking at the cartoons."

He had gotten the latest Jack Reacher novel by Lee Child and a crime novel by James Lee Burke and was going up to the front desk to check them out.

Avril was there with two books.

He walked up behind her. "Hey, whatcha got there?" he asked, trying to get a look at the books covers.

She smiled. "S'up, Cam." She showed him the books.

Infinite Jest by David Foster Wallace and *The Corrections* by Jonathan Franzen.

"Jesus, Avril, how long do you plan to stay in this place?"

"What do you mean?"

"Well, I mean that's about two thousand pages of reading you got there," Cam pointed out. "Plus, neither one of those five-pounders are what you'd call page-turners."

Avril laughed. "What are yours?" She looked down at his books. He held them so she could see.

"For those of us who are more at home with car chases and loud explosions," Cam said.

The librarian was waiting for them to check out their books.

"Oh, sorry. Here you go. "Avril thumped her books down on the counter.

"I don't know about you," Cam said, pointing at the Wallace book, "but I'm a little distrustful of writers with three names."

Avril turned back to him. "Oh, are you now?"

"Yeah, well, except for maybe William Carlos Williams," he said. "'Cause he *had* to have three."

"Why was that?"

"Well, who's ever gonna go around with the name William Williams?"

"Good point."

The librarian held out her hands. "Can I check those out for you, sir?"

"Sure can." Cam handed her the books, then turned back to Avril. "There's another guy like that."

"Like what?"

"Who had three names and really had to be three names."

"Who?"

"Ford Maddox Ford," Cam said. "Can you imagine....*hi, I'm Ford Ford*. I mean, what the hell were his parents thinking?"

Avril laughed. "You know, for a guy who likes car chases and explosions, you kinda know your stuff."

"Anything you want to know is on the internet," Cam said.

They walked out together.

"Nah, you just don't want people to know," Avril said with a smile.

He held the door for her. "Know what?"

"That you're a closet intellectual."

Cam shook his head and laughed. "Yeah right. I've been called a lot of things, but never that."

Chapter 41

A woman whose voice Rachel didn't recognize knocked on her door and told her she had a call.

"Did he say who?" Rachel asked, opening her door. It was Darlene with the high-pitched voice.

"No," she said, smiling, "but he sounded nice."

Rachel walked down the hallway to the phone. "Hello?"

"Hey, baby," Harlan said.

"I told you not to call ever again."

"But I'm coming there to see you."

She didn't hesitate.

"The fuck you are. How 'bout losing my number, and don't ever call me 'baby.'"

He laughed like he thought she was just messing with him.

"How we gonna get married if I don't see you?"

"We're not. Ain't gonna happen. I don't know where you got that. Where are you anyway? Still out west?"

"Yes, matriculating at USC. I've decided I want to major in microbiology and go out for the football team. I'm thinking linebacker."

"You're not funny," Rachel said. "No college would let you anywhere near them after your little stunts at Harvard."

"What little stunts?"

"Well, your pole dancer friend, for starters."

"How'd you hear about that?"

"What do you mean, how'd I hear about it? You told half the town. Like you were proud of it."

"Well, it's not true. What really happened was my roommate met this exchange student from Bahrain in chem lab. Chained her to his bed, and I got blamed."

Rachel wondered why she'd ever found him amusing. "You need help, Harlan. Where are you really?"

"I told you, on my way to see you...to get married."

"Well, do me a favor. Turn around. Wedding's been called off." Rachel slammed the receiver down and marched to the dispensary to get her nightly meds.

Esther was in line, her back to Rachel.

"Hey, Esther," Rachel said in a monotone.

Esther turned around. "You all right?"

"I'm okay." Rachel nodded.

"You look kind of... I don't know?"

"It's just..." Rachel said and shrugged her shoulders. "Nothing."

Then, she just started trembling.

"What's wrong, hon?" Esther put her hands on Rachel's shoulders.

"Harlan just called."

"Guy with the screws loose?"

"Yeah. Told me he was coming here to marry me." Rachel said. "I just had this dream that he wanted to do something bad to me."

"Jesus, where'd that come from?"

"From this article I read."

"What did it say?"

"About how people get when they can no longer have someone they used to have..."

"Keep going."

"How they want to destroy the other person. Figuring if they can't have them, nobody can. It was about this guy in Florida whose wife left him. So, he rented this condo on the eighteenth floor of this building, then went and kidnapped his wife and two kids. Had a gun and everything. Took them up the service elevator so the doorman wouldn't see them. Then he tied 'em up with duct tape, put it across their mouths so they couldn't scream—"

"—Oh my God, I read about that," Esther said. "Threw 'em off the balcony of the building. One after the other."

Rachel nodded, grim faced. "Then he jumped."

"That was so horrible," Esther said. "Person on the second floor, I remember, described what it sounded like, them hitting the ground. Big thumps, like dropping a sandbag on the floor. Then the last one, the guy I guess, sounded like branches breaking...except it was his bones."

Rachel shivered and held up her hands. "Okay, Esther, I'm really glad I brought it up."

Esther took her hands off Rachel's shoulders, then took a step back.

"You know what my shrink would call your flashback?" Esther asked.

"Paranoia?"

"No, catastrophizing. Imagining the worst possible scenario and thinking that's what's gonna happen. I s'pose you could make a case for paranoia too."

"I don't care what you call it. I didn't tell you half the stuff."

"Like what?"

"Like the first time I told him to stay away for good, after he told me what happened to his dog."

"What happened to his dog?"

"Hung itself, according to Harlan. By accident."

Esther grabbed Rachel's arm. "What are you saying? His dog hung itself?"

"That's what he told me. Said the dog was in his bedroom and he's got these Venetian blinds, and there was like this loop of cord that hung down close to the floor—"

Esther nodded tentatively.

"—and somehow the dog, this gray poodle, got its head caught in the loop and got twisted around—"

Esther shook her head violently. "No way that coulda happened. That's bullshit."

"That's what he told me. He seemed really broken up too. Crying and stuff."

Esther put her hands on Rachel's knee. "This guy's creepin' me out big time. It ever occur to you maybe he hung the dog? I mean, can you honestly see a dog doing that?"

"No, and the fact is he didn't hang the dog, and the dog didn't hang itself."

"What do you mean?"

"'Cause there was no dog."

"What?"

"He'd never even mentioned a dog before, and I just figured that was how Harlan was. Didn't talk about his family, his home life at all. I mean, I hardly ever saw his parents. So why would he ever talk about his dog?" Rachel bit a thumbnail. "So anyway, I ran into his mother at the supermarket, said I was really sorry about their dog. She looks at me funny and goes, 'What dog?'"

Esther's hand shot up to her mouth. "Wow. He is one seriously disturbed individual."

"Yeah," Rachel said, "not exactly marriage material, right?"

Chapter 42

Avril went to her mailbox in the foyer just off the living room. Her box was between Bryn's and Lindsay's. She saw a letter from her sister. Terry was about the only thirty-two-year-old woman she knew who still wrote letters. Alongside the letter lay a brown manila envelope.

She opened the manila envelope flap and pulled out a note and a DVD.

The note was from Dr. Holmgren. Weird, she thought, that he'd send something through the mail.

Then she realized it was probably because they weren't meeting again until the beginning of the following week.

It was addressed to "Avril." She read the note:

> Avril,
>
> I thought this might be beneficial to you vis-à-vis your bipolar disorder. Admittedly, this is a rather odd format for a doctor to dispense information, but I believe you will find it most helpful. It is a movie—made in the seventies, if memory serves—that has a very effective message about dealing with the onslaught of bipolar. (Don't be put off by the poor production quality and also don't let the somewhat random sex and gratuitous violence distract from the film's many cogent points.)

Let's discuss it at our next session.

Dr. Holmgren

A rush of heat filled Avril's chest. She couldn't wait to see it despite his warning that it wasn't exactly PG. She walked to the DVD machine in the living room. Terry's letter could wait. She just hoped no one was using the machine.

She was in luck.

She shoved the DVD into the player and fast-forwarded it.

"Hey, whatcha watching?" asked a voice behind her.

Avril swung around. It was a new girl, Laura. Avril wanted to watch it alone.

"It's... I don't even know the name of it," she said. "You probably won't like it. It's got a bunch of violence."

Laura pulled up a chair. "Not like I got a whole lot else goin' on."

Avril groaned but Laura didn't seem to hear.

Avril sat down and pushed Play.

Poor production quality was an understatement. It was grainy and dated looking. Two twentyish hippie girls were coming onto an older guy in a bar. The bar's patrons looked foreign, and sure enough, there was a sign in Spanish.

"What is this anyway?" Laura asked, trepidation in her tone.

"Just watch," Avril snapped.

The scene changed, and the man and one of the hippie chicks were taking off their clothes. The other hippie chick was in the kitchen getting a meat cleaver out of a drawer. Avril wondered how many twenty-three-year- old girls had meat cleavers lying around the kitchen.

Next scene: the girl who was in the kitchen raised the meat clever over the head of the unsuspecting man. Next scene: graphic blood spilling from the head of the man slashed by the cleaver.

Laura turned away from the TV.

"Jesus, Avril," she said. "What *is* this garbage?"

Avril didn't answer.

It seemed like the meat-cleaver scene was the ending, because the credits started rolling.

The "cogent points" Holmgren had referred to had thus far eluded Avril.

As in a lot movies, there were outtakes. The first one was of the director and a hippie girl. He crept up to her with the meat cleaver behind his back. He pulled it out and raised it high in the air and slashed down on the girl's head.

It ripped into her skull. Blood squirted in all directions.

Laura shrieked and ran out of the room. Avril closed her eyes, her fists tight, nauseated.

What she had just seen, she realized, was *real*. It was not acting. She opened her eyes.

The actress lay on the floor covered in blood.

Twelve words slowly scrolled across the screen:

Snuff, an Edgardo Mestreux film. *Shot in Ecuador, where life is cheap.*

Chapter 43

Dr. Holmgren had his hands together as if in prayer. He always looked empathetic, but now he looked tremendously pained, as if he had just suffered through the whole incident side by side with Avril.

Avril bit a fingernail and nervously twirled a strand of hair.

"Can you understand why I want to get out of here?" she said, shaking. "I mean, that is just about the sickest thing. Who would do something like that?"

Holmgren held up his hands.

"Avril, I totally understand what you're saying. And of course, we're trying to find out who did it. I think, though, that you're making real progress here. If I thought that Clairmount wasn't helping you, trust me, I would suggest that it might be best if you left."

"It's kind of hard *not* to read something into it...some sicko kills an actress in *real life*."

"Are you sure that's really what happened?" Holmgren asked.

Avril tried to swallow, then nodded. "I called a friend who knows movies cold. Told me that's the first snuff film ever made. Do I know it for sure? No. But how do you fake someone smashing a meat cleaver into someone's head?"

Avril covered her eyes, wondering if she would break down again or be sick.

Holmgren put a consoling hand on her shoulder. "I met personally with George Wittman, head of Clairmount, who suggested you have special security—"

"No, no, no," Avril shook her head vehemently. "That's the last thing I want. If I'm going to stay here, I just want to blend in. I don't want some freak in a bad suit tagging along behind me talking into a mike on his collar."

"Okay, I understand, but will you stay? I really do think you're making good progress."

She looked out the window and flashed to what happened after she watched the movie that had been supposedly sent by Holmgren. Cam had heard about it somehow and raced over to Brook House. He just walked into the living room there, asked someone where her room was, and ran up the two flights of stairs, disregarding every rule in the book.

He knocked on her door, and she opened it. She fell into his arms, neither one saying anything for a few moments. Then she thanked him for coming and said he better leave before they both got kicked out. He'd started to leave, then she'd taken a few steps toward him, kissed him on the cheek, and thanked him again.

She looked up at Dr. Holmgren and forced a smile. "Yeah, okay, I'll stay," she said. "Thanks for everything, Doctor. I just hope they catch that bastard."

Chapter 44

C am hadn't left Brook House when he'd come to see how Avril was. He just went downstairs to the living room and opened up the first book he saw. Three hours later, he was still there. He wasn't quite sure what he was doing there. After starting two books he didn't like, he came across a dog-eared *The Catcher in the Rye*.

He figured he had read it at least eight times before. It was pretty easy to relate to Holden, a lovable, disturbed fuck-up who, lo and behold, ended up at a mental institution. He knew whole passages by heart. Particularly the one where Holden said, *I keep picturing all these little kids playing some game in this big field of rye and all...I'm standing on the edge of some crazy cliff... I have to catch everybody if they start to go over the cliff...I'd just be the catcher in the rye and all. I know it's crazy, but that's the only thing I'd really like to be. I know it's crazy.*

Cam remembered a date with Charlotte—when he was drunk, at a place called Doubles. He'd reeled off that quote apropos of absolutely nothing, maybe trying to impress her. Other guys could do that with a classic snatch of dialogue from *Ghostbusters* or *Pulp Fiction* and get a laugh or two, but Charlotte just looked at him like he was speaking Farsi. So, trying to salvage something, he echoed Holden, *I know it's crazy*, and she just looked at him and said, 'No, you are.'

He looked up from the book a little later and saw a woman he had met before coming toward him.

"Oh, hey," she said to Cam.

"Hey," he said. "You know how Avril's doing?"

"She's kinda freaked," the woman said. "Like you'd expect. Think she's gonna stay in her room awhile. You goin' to DBT?"

"Nah, think I'll just stick around here."

Two hours later, Cam was on his second book when Avril came down the stairs. It was the first time he had seen her when her hair didn't look perfect.

She smiled when she saw him.

He stood and walked over to her.

"You okay?"

Her eyes drifted away. "Yeah, I'm fine. Is the word out?" Then she caught herself. "Of course, it is."

He patted her shoulder. She smiled up at him.

"Have you been here all this time?"

He nodded.

She smiled at him. "Thanks. You're a damn good man, Cam."

Chapter 45

Later that day, Rachel went down to Brook House and asked a woman if she would ask Avril to come down from her room. She waited for her in the living room.

"Are you okay?" Rachel asked when Avril came down the steps. "I heard all about it."

"Not really," Avril sighed. "I mean, can you *fuck-ing* imagine?"

"No, it's so fucked," Rachel said. "I'm getting sprung from Acute and coming down here. I'll kill the motherfucker."

Avril smiled and patted her hand. "Thanks. Thanks for coming."

"So, I was thinking, wanna be my roomie?" Rachel asked eagerly.

Avril laughed. "You kidding? The two of us...oil and water?"

"That's mean."

"Besides," Avril said. "I got a 'roomie' I'm very happy with. However, she does discharge day after tomorrow, so maybe... I don't know. Maybe dealing with you and your prepubescent behavior might be easier to put up with than some of the nut jobs here. I'll think about it."

"I can catch you up on the latest OCD John and Manic Hispanic stories."

"Can't wait," Avril said.

"Hey, but first you gotta do something about that pathetic shower of yours, huh?"

Avril groaned. "I just said, I'll think about it," she said, lowering her voice. "You gotta promise me you won't be snorting anytime soon."

"I promise—that drug dealer's history anyway. Probably 'cause Cam kicked his ass," Rachel said.

Avril laughed. "Hey, what about your loony tune boyfriend?"

"That's another story."

"Tell me."

"He keeps calling. Says he's coming to see me."

"For real?"

"Yeah, he's really freakin' me out, man. I dunno...something in his voice."

"What?"

"Like the guy's nuts, crazy, fucked up in the head, dangerous for all I know."

"You have his number?" Avril asked.

"Uh-huh."

"Give it to me."

*****

A few minutes later Rachel returned to Acute Care. Avril went to the phone and dialed the number Rachel had given her. It rang about ten times. Just as she was about to hang up, a man answered.

"H'lo."

"Harlan?"

"That's me, sugar tits. Who's this?"

"My name is Colleen. I'm a friend of Rachel's."

"Well, any friend of Rachel's is a fr—"

"Cut the shit, asshole, and don't even think about hanging up until I tell you to. I have a friend. Lives out west," Avril went on. "Guy's like a bloodhound. Tracks people down. People who pull bad shit. Then when he finds 'em, and he always does, well, you can use your imagination."

Avril paused, deep into the role. "You still there, Harlan?"

"Yeah," Harlan said. "Why you telling me this?"

"Why? Because, Harlan, you're a sick fuck and Rachel told you to stay the fuck away from her."

"But she's my—"

"She's your nothing, asshole," Avril said. "And if you think I'm bullshitting you, I'll give you the number of a guy in the L.A. police force. Ask him to tell you about Raymond Ballenger. Meat Hook is what he goes by."

Long pause. "Harlan?"

"Yeah, I'm here," Harlan said, all the bluster had seeped out of him.

"Good. So, bottom line, you *ever* think about calling Rachel again, you *ever* get within a hundred miles of her again, your nuts'll be hanging from a barbed-wire fence. Okay, asshole, we're done now. You can hang up."

He didn't have to be told twice.

She hung up and beamed. Ol' Av... girl still had the chops!

Chapter 46

Back in ACU, Rachel was still in disbelief about Avril's snuff-film incident. Who could have come up with something as sick as that?

A res knocked on her door and said she had a call. Harlan?

"You know who it is?" Rachel asked, opening the door.

"Sounded like an older man," the res said.

"Okay, thanks."

She walked by the observation deck, gave OCD John—circling as usual—a wave, and picked up the phone.

"Hello?"

"Hi, Rachel," Judd Kornbluth said.

"Hi."

"How you doing?"

She sighed. "Oh, you know, one good day, next one sucks. Have any more conversations with my a-hole stepfather?"

"Everything is all taken care of. Phil's getting a stipend, and hopefully you'll be done with him."

Every time OCD John went around, he'd flash his off-kilter smile. "What's a stipend?"

"Meaning not very much."

"I know what it means. But how much?"

"Thirty thousand dollars. I negotiated him down," Kornbluth said.

"Oh, okay. Well, thanks."

There was an awkward pause.

"All right, well, I should be—"

"So, I was wondering—your bad days there, what are they like?"

"You really don't want to know."

"Yeah, I do. Tell me."

He sounded genuine.

"Why?" A tinge of exasperation in her voice.

"I guess... 'cause I'm a concerned parent maybe."

Rachel laughed. "You mean after being such a concerned parent the last five years?"

"You don't have to be so sarcastic."

"The fuck I don't. It's my armor."

Kornbluth sighed. It had a softening effect on Rachel.

"Fine. Bad days... are when I feel all alone in the world," she said, "and just don't see the point in being alive."

She'd meant to tone down the drama.

"I understand. I've been there." Kornbluth said.

"But why? You had parents, a normal home."

"I had parents who quietly hated each other and drank themselves into a stupor every night. 'Normal?' Trust me—that's the last thing it was."

Ed and Sarah Kornbluth had divorced ten years before. They now lived five blocks apart, passed each other on the street, and never spoke.

"I know one thing: they sucked as grandparents," Rachel said. "How about a call on my birthday... Granny?"

"Sorry. You kinda of struck out in the grandparent's department."

"No shit. At least Mom's parents called me a couple of times," she sighed. "Can we be done with this depressing conversation?"

"Sure. What else?"

"Not much. I been thinking about getting my own apartment when I get out of here."

"The good news is you can afford a really nice one. Would you live in the city?"

She was hoping he'd offer advice instead of asking questions. "Yeah, I guess," she said.

"What about...any thoughts about college?"

"Funny you should ask, I got into Skidmore."

"Hey, congratulations, that's great."

"I just don't know if I can handle college."

"Come on, that's the perfect school for you."

"How the hell would you know? You don't know me."

It came out colder than she meant.

"That's where you're wrong. I know you're creative as hell. Play a mean bass guitar, I heard. Paint incredible landscapes."

"You're a little out of touch. I don't paint anymore."

"Well, you should. You got talent."

"What, at painting sticks with leaves on 'em?"

"You wouldn't get in to Skidmore if you weren't creative."

"That place is a second-rate college."

He paused. "Is this what you do all day long?"

"What?"

"Put yourself down. Beat yourself up."

"Pretty much."

She heard a long sigh from her father. "You've got a lot to live for, Rachel."

She returned his sigh. "Oh, yeah? Like what?"

"Imagine this," Kornbluth said. "You go to college, get a great education, find what you really love to do, meet a guy, graduate— what the hell, magna cum laude—move to a really nice apartment 'cause you definitely can afford it. The guy moves in with you—which I'm not endorsing, by the way—and after a couple of years, he asks you to marry him and you say yes. Three years later you have a son, name him after me, of course, and live happily ever after. You defy your long-standing family tradition of divorces, suicide, drugs, and alcohol."

Rachel remained silent.

"Can you just imagine how good that would make you feel?"

She just thought for a second. "You been rehearsing that?"

"No, but I've been thinking about it a lot. Sounds pretty good, huh?"

"Sounds like Fantasyland."

"See, that's the thing, Rachel." His voice amped up a few decibels. "You're conditioned to think of everything as bad or broken. Like that's the way it should be...the natural order."

"Ah, yeah, thanks to you in part."

"Okay, guilty. I've been a shitty father. But I got news for you—a lot of people turned out just fine with shitty fathers."

"What about with shitty fathers, shitty stepfathers, shitty boyfriends, a not-so-hot mother—"

"Okay, I get it. So, after eighteen years of shittiness your die is cast. Is that it?"

He had a point. "So, you're giving me the 'it's time to turn your life around,' speech?"

Kornbluth laughed, then paused for a second.

"I guess I am. Why not?"

"'Cause it's a bitch when you got no role models," she blurted.

Kornbluth was silent, then finally: "Maybe it's not too late."

"What do you mean?"

"I could try to be one. If you'd just give me the chance."

Chapter 47

Ted felt like he was on the animal side of the bars at a zoo, as the women of Brook House gawked at and ogled him.

"We welcome you, Ted," Tanya said, sitting in the circle of women in the living room. "Our last man departed the house about two weeks ago."

"Not soon enough," Lindsay muttered, knitting something that looked like brown chocolate pudding with twigs in it.

"Lindsay, please," Tanya said.

"Guy was a major freak show," Lindsay said, looking up at Ted.

Ted smiled at Lindsay. "I'll try to just be a *minor* freak show."

Avril laughed. "You seem better," she told Ted.

"Thanks."

"I knew this man back in his zombie phase," Avril said to the group.

Ted smiled. "Like you should talk."

"Okay, Ted, so what we do at this meeting," Tanya said, "is tell the rest of the house what our goal of the day was and whether we achieved it, then what our moment of the day was."

"Okay," Ted said.

"Amy, lead us off," Tanya said.

Amy said her goal of the day was to try not to answer the voices in her head.

Consensus was that was a good idea.

"Bryn, how 'bout you?"

Bryn looked over at Avril, for courage maybe. Making eye contact didn't seem quite so tough for her as before.

"Okay," she said, taking a deep breath. "Well, this is my next-to-last day and my goal is to just be positive, stay in the moment, and have fun with my housemates, who I'm gonna miss like crazy."

"That's good. It is so critical to stay in the moment," Tanya said.

"I know," Bryn said, glancing at Ted, "'cause I find myself thinking a lot about what it's going to be like out there. You know, the real world. It's hard not to project into the future. I get really scared."

Avril, sitting next to Bryn, patted her on the hand, "You'll be fine."

Bryn's eyes darted to Avril's. "You think?"

"I know."

Ted smiled. Place might be okay, he thought.

*****

Ted went up to Avril right after the meeting.

"How are you doing?" he asked. "I heard about that video."

"I'm fine," she said, waving a hand. "Just some sicko's idea of a joke."

Ted nodded.

"So, tell me about you?" Avril said. "I just got bits and pieces. What's your story?"

"Is this what happens when us rookies show up?" Ted asked. "We gotta tell you veterans our whole tortured history?"

Avril smiled. "Of course. How else are we gonna cure you?" she asked. "Seriously, why are you here, Ted?"

Ted scratched the back of his head. "You want the reason or the real reason?"

"Start with just the 'reason.'"

Ted began to say something, but stopped. "Don't take this the wrong way, but are you just bored or curious or what?"

"Partly, yeah, but also it definitely helps to talk about whatever your thing is. Just like with a shrink, except maybe I can relate a little better and won't charge you three hundred bucks an hour."

"But there's more to it, right?"

Avril smiled again. "Yeah, okay, probably a selfish thing: *I* feel good about myself if *I* can help someone feel better. Know what I mean? Emphasis on the *I.*"

Ted smiled and nodded. "Okay, the 'reason' for my depression is I lost everything I had. My company, all our money. Our house is next unless we do something to save it. The worst part of it was we had to move away from the place we loved, where all our friends were, to about the only place I could get a job. Which, by the way, I hated. I was a real estate broker... *was.* Currently unemployed. I used to do something I loved. Building houses. This place where we live now... we can't stand it. No friends, the weather's always eighty-five and sunny, no seasons, no deciduous trees. Sorry for the long, rambling answer."

"Don't be," Avril said, nodding. "Okay, and the *real* reason?"

Ted looked around the room. There was a fireplace with a guitar next to it, which leaned up against the wall. On either side of the fireplace there were built-in bookcases filled with books left there by patients over the years. There was also a piano donated by a famous musician who did a stint there.

"The real reason"—a wave of emotion washed over him—"the real reason is the guilt I have for what I did to my wife. I took away everything she loved, and she never complained. She never blamed me, never accused me, never made me feel bad, hardly even talked about it. Just put her head down, plowed ahead and made the best of it—"

Ted put a hand over his eyes and tried to compose himself. "My daughter, on the other hand, didn't let me off the hook so easily. Who can blame her? She...isn't talking to me these days."

Ted sighed. "Meantime, I felt sorry for myself. I wallowed in self- pity. I couldn't put it behind me and move on...I...I fell apart."

Avril patted him on the shoulder.

"Did you notice the *I?*" he said, trying hard to smile, "Emphasis on the *I.*"

Chapter 48

"Okay," said Joyce the DBT teacher to the twelve people from Brook House gathered in a circle in the small classroom, "try to remember a place where you felt really happy, a safe place, a serene place. Then, just close your eyes and try to picture it for a few minutes."

Joyce always started off the class with some form of meditation.

A few minutes went by.

"Did that work for you?" Joyce asked. "Did you find a place that made you feel safe and comfortable?"

Varying degrees of nods.

"Ted, how about you?"

Ted, sitting next to Avril, smiled.

"Yeah, but I had to hunt around awhile. Nothing came to me right away."

"Mind telling us about it?"

Ted scratched the side of his head.

"No, I don't mind. It was the back porch of my house. This big porch that looked out over the backyard and the pool. Lot of great trees, real quiet. I used to read out there. My dog always used to lie at my feet. I think she liked it almost as much as I did."

"Aw," Bryn said, smiling.

Ted looked over at her and smiled.

"Yeah, so after the dog died—one of the toughest days of my life, by the way—I buried her about five feet away from the porch. So, she could be close to me when I was out there. Had this tombstone, with these little dog paws carved into it. I remember what it said: 'Our beloved Maizie, never far from our hearts.'"

A chorus of "aws."

Ted put up his hands. "Sorry. didn't mean to turn this into a soap opera. It's just—"

"Ted, that was really lovely," Joyce said. "I think if you kept going, we'd all be in tears."

"I love that name...Maizie," Lindsay said.

Next, they did their goals for the day, then their moments of the day, and now were saying their goodbyes to Bryn, Avril's roommate. Bryn was leaving the next day, and the goodbye was a ritual Brook House patients had been doing for years.

Ted sat in the middle of a sofa between Avril and Bryn in the living room at Brook House.

Tanya asked Laura to lead it off.

"So, Bryn," Laura said, fifties, wiry, painfully shy, "here's to you. I just have one thought. There, um, used to be this advertising campaign—I can't remember what it was for—but it had this line, 'You've come a long way, baby.' And you...you really have. So, Bryn, good luck out there. You're gonna do just fine."

"Thanks, Laura. I really appreciate it." Bryn hopped up and hugged her.

Lindsay was next.

"Bryn," she said, twirling a strand of hair, "I think you're amazing. When I think of how you were when you first got here. I mean, let's face it, you were a frickin' disaster—"

Bryn nodded and laughed.

"And now you're so much better. I mean, you used to be scared of your shadow. But I think now you're ready to go out there and deal with your stuff. At least a lot better than before. So, go for it girl. I know you can do it."

Bryn smiled and nodded.

"Thanks. I hope so."

Next came Amy. "I'm going to make this short, Bryn," she said. "At first I thought, 'Wow, never been anyone I had less in common with.' Then we hung out a little, doing that stupid jigsaw puzzle and stuff. I got to know you and...sounds lame, but I consider myself lucky —incredibly lucky—to have spent twenty-three days, I think it is, with you. You da bomb, girl. Good luck to you."

Bryn smiled her splayed, goofy grin. "Thank you...thank you so much."

Tanya smiled. "Meghan, you're next."

Meghan, always dressed in black, had tattoos and attitude and didn't share the love.

"Bryn," she said slowly and deliberately, "gotta hand it to you— you're the all-time master at running the sympathy con. At playing the fragile little bird who everybody has to protect and defend. Well, let me tell you, your whole act really wore me out, and I for one am happy to see you get your sorry ass out of here."

Bryn looked ambushed, like she didn't know whether to flee, cry, or scream.

She just froze.

Ted was about to say something.

Then Avril spoke up, softly at first.

"You feel good about yourself now, Meghan? Got that off that scrawny little chest of yours?"

Meghan's head swung around defiantly at Avril.

Avril kept going. "You feel good about trying to ruin someone's last night here? After all the nice things that were said"—she spoke in a tone Ted had never heard, hypnotic in its unemotional, flat force— "well, here's the thing, Meghan, it's not gonna work. 'Cause Bryn *is* strong. She's *not* a fragile little bird and *can* deal with all the unhappy, cheerless people like you who feel better about yourselves by trying to make others feel shitty."

Avril just kept her eyes riveted on Meghan's. "So, nice try. You gave it your best shot. Might have worked on somebody, just not Bryn."

Ted felt like jumping to his feet and leading a standing O.

Avril looked over at Bryn.

Bryn glanced back at her, blew her a kiss, and shot Meghan a defiant, raised fist.

Chapter 49

Cam walked Avril back to Brook House after lunch. He had just told her that Arthur was his prime suspect in the snuff-flick incident.

"*Really?* You actually think he'd do that?" Avril said. "I think of him as just kind of a sad, lonely little guy who doesn't know how to relate to people."

"Come on, Avril. That's bullshit. Guy's one of those people who hates the world. He told us this story about putting a cherry bomb in a tennis ball, then throwing it for his dog to run after. Blew his dog's head off, he said, like he was proud of it."

Avril's mouth dropped, and she stopped walking.

"You really believe he did that? I've heard some of his stories. They all sound pretty farfetched."

"Yeah, well, someone sent you that thing and I sure as hell don't have anyone even close as another suspect," Cam said. "Do you?"

Avril cocked her head to one side, then glanced off in the distance.

"No, nobody. It's just so totally alien."

"That's our boy, Arthur," Cam said, nodding slowly. "A total alien."

"You sure it's just that you never liked him?"

"I never liked him for a lot of good reasons," Cam said. "Want to hear my laundry list?"

"No," Avril said. "Can we just change the subject?"

"Absolutely," Cam said. "So, I've been wondering about that DBT stuff they teach you. Is it working for you?"

"Yeah, I think it helps. I mean, the concepts all make sense. The big thing is you have to use 'em and practice after you leave here. That's gonna be the tough part. You know, when there aren't any teachers around to drum it into your head."

Cam nodded as they approached the road bisecting the Clairmount campus. Avril turned away from the street. Cam knew it was her automatic instinct, not to be recognized by any passing motorists.

"I see you ditched the beret and shades?"

"Yeah, going rogue these days."

Cam laughed and looked both ways down the road.

"Okay, coast is clear."

She turned, and together they crossed the street.

"I've been dying to ask you a show biz question," Cam said.

"Fire away."

"My teenage heartthrob was Demi Moore," Cam said. "Ever do a movie with her?"

Avril stopped and put her hands on her hips. "Jesus, Cam, how old do you think I am?"

"I don't know, early thirties?"

"No, just barely thirty," Avril said. "Thirty and two months to be exact."

"Okay, okay," Cam said, raising his arms. "I got no problem with older women."

Avril huffed. "How old are you...Junior?"

"Twenty-nine and four months."

"Okay, so I'm ten months older than you," she said.

"Like I said, I got no problem with cougars. But what about Demi?"

Avril smiled. "I've never been in anything with her, but we met once. I liked her. Girl's got her issues though"—Avril caught herself and laughed— "Like I should talk. The poster child for issues."

"Guarantee you," Cam said. "I'd give you a run for your money."

"I doubt it," Avril said. "As far as Demi goes, she's way too old for you, Cam."

"Yeah, well, she seems to go for the young pups, so I always figured I had a chance," he said as they reached the back door of Brook House. "Hey, I'm moving down here later this afternoon."

Avril turned to him with a big smile. "I know. It's going to be you and Ted and all us babes."

"AKA heaven."

"Speaking of babes," Avril said. "One of the old girls was telling me this morning about something called delusional parasitosis. Ever hear of it?"

"No, couldn't even spell it."

"You think you got bugs crawling all over you," Avril said and shuddered.

"That's one I haven't had...*yet* anyway.*"

Avril laughed as they stopped at the back door of Brook House. "You know, you have an incredible laugh," Cam said.

"My sister told me I laugh like a camel."

Cam cocked his head and looked into her eyes. She had so much more sparkle and fire than when he met her that night at AA.

"A camel, huh? When was the last time she heard a camel laugh?"

Avril shrugged.

Cam spotted the res studying them through a window, like she was trying to figure out whether they were breaking any rules.

"We're being officially observed," he said.

Avril looked toward the window and saw the res. "That's Sarah. Watch out. She's a real ball buster," she whispered.

*****

From a window in the library, Arthur had watched Cam and Avril as they strolled down the hill. Arthur saw them walk past the road and disappear out of sight, Cam seemingly doing all the talking. Arthur shook his head in disgust. The guy and his half-assed pretty-boy grin...It made him sick. The fact that Avril was buying it, lapping it up even. Couldn't she see the guy was about as deep as a puddle?

A few minutes later he was out back telling Dr. Crockett all about what he had just seen.

"People at this place disgust me," he said to the doctor. "Like Cam-whatever-the-fuck-his-name-is."

Crockett rolled his eyes. "Come on, Arthur. You know perfectly well what his name is. You've sung his praises before."

"Yeah, well, I was watching the brain-dead schmuck give Avril the full-tilt snow job a little while ago. They were walking down the hill and he was working his bullshit charm, and she was clearly diggin' it."

Crockett was tired. Slept bad the night before. Had a dream he was on the football team at Dartmouth but could run only in slow motion. He decided to just let Arthur go on autopilot for a while.

Arthur slid the Adirondack chair closer to the doctor. It scraped on the flagstone. "I could just picture it," Arthur said. "Him telling her about all the money he makes. He's one of those hedge fund cocksuckers. Telling her about his G-5 jet, how he's gonna fly out to Hollywood, take her out to dinner at Spago or one of those bullshit places. Probably asking her out to his big motherfucker house in the Hamptons—you know, infinity-edge pool, grass tennis court, all that lame shit."

Crockett just let him go on his rant. Patients had to unload, even if it was on a fellow patient.

"Hedge fund cocksuckers," Arthur repeated, spit starting to fly. "Probably got a Ferrari that goes zero to sixty in three-point-eight seconds...Wish the motherfucker would slam into a bridge abutment going a hundred miles an hour."

Chapter 50

Her sister ran up, bear-hugged Avril, and practically lifted her off the ground. Avril was holding open the front door of Brook House.

"I don't care what you feel like—you look hot as hell," Terry said, stepping back and taking in Avril.

"Thanks, you too. Pisses me off how you keep pumping out kids and look so good."

"The G word," Terry said, then whispered, "girdle."

Avril put her arm around her sister's shoulder, and the two headed into the living room of Brook House.

"Come on in to my little slice of heaven," Avril said.

They walked in and saw Lindsay on the black leather couch, knitting.

"Hey Linds, this is my sister, Terry," Avril said, gesturing, "and that's Lindsay."

"Hi," Terry said.

"Hi," Lindsay said, staring. "Are you famous too?"

"Nope, just a plain old housewife."

Lindsay looked down at her knitting. "Well, you look like you could be."

"Thanks," Terry said. "One per family."

"Not the Kardashians," Lindsay said.

"Got a point there," Terry said.

Avril gave her sister a flick of the head and started walking out of the living room.

Terry followed, then turned back to Lindsay. "Well, nice to meet you."

Lindsay gave her a wave. "I just want to be a housewife one day too."

Avril gave her sister a quizzical smile.

"Sweet," Terry whispered as they entered the hallway outside the living room.

"Strange," Avril whispered back.

Terry laughed. "Show me your room."

"Okay," Avril said, and they walked up the two flights.

Avril opened the door and let her sister go in first.

Terry raised her hands. "Hey, beats a lot of dumps I've lived in. Nice bed..."

Terry looked at the other bed, half the size, with a pronounced sag in the middle. "How come—"

"Who said all patients are created equal?" Avril said. "I couldn't possibly sleep in the thing that was here."

Terry laughed. "Room's nice and light anyway."

"Best way to sum it up... it doesn't suck *too* much."

"Exactly."

Terry opened the door to the bathroom. "A little on the small side."

"Ya think? I practically have to go in sideways. Hey, let's go out back. There's a nice porch that looks out over this brook."

They walked downstairs and went out to the porch.

"This *is* beautiful," Terry said, taking in the view, then sitting. "I love big New England trees. And you got your very own babbling brook...*How cool is that.*"

Avril sat down in a green Adirondack chair.

Terry pulled her chair close to her sister and patted her arm. Neither one said anything for a few moments. They looked out over the wide green lawn and the brook beyond. Avril watched a leaf fall into the water and get quickly carried along until it was out of sight.

"So, are you any better since we last talked?" Terry asked.

Avril had decided she was definitely not going to go into the snuff flick. She knew her sister would want her to leave if she heard that.

"Honestly, yeah. I mean, a little," Avril said. "But I gotta tell you, it was the mother of all depressions."

"But you're better than when I first talked to you?"

Avril nodded.

"Like, how?"

Avril thought for a moment. "One thing, I'm forcing myself out of bed in the morning."

"That's a start, right?"

"Yeah, I used to just—I think I told you—just lie around and ruminate."

"That's probably the worst thing you can do, huh?"

"Yup. Got to the point where I was absolutely convinced nobody would ever offer me a part again. And you were gonna get sick of all my whining and cut me off. I was gonna lose all my money, and a few days later I'd be camped out in some discarded refrigerator box."

"Jesus, that's scary."

"I know. My mind can really mess me up when I lie around. So, I gotta get up, which isn't so easy when you think there's nothing worth getting up for. I read this article about Sigmund Freud, how he had this horrible cocaine addiction. Did you know about that?"

"No."

"Well anyway, he decided the only way to beat it was to make sure he had something to do virtually every minute of the day. So, I figured, that's what I have to do. Now I wake up at seven, get in the shower, put on my clothes, go to breakfast, come back here, take a run, read for forty-five minutes, go to knitting class, then the library, check emails, get a new book from the library."

"You're wearing me out."

"Any downtime at all and my imagination just goes crazy. They tell you stuff here like, 'live in the moment,' 'be mindful,' which means don't go back, don't go forward. You dwell on the past or the future and it's all *baaaad* shit."

"Makes sense to me," Terry said. "Was the manic thing worse than the others?"

"Bad, but I've had worse."

Terry smiled at her sister.

"What?"

"Like that time you went and charged up two hundred thousand dollars' worth of stuff on Rodeo Drive, then took everyone you knew for dinner at Towers. And ended up having sex—"

"Please, don't remind me." Avril put up her hands. "You don't get how I have absolutely no control. I, like, go into this new mind and body."

"Oh, trust me," Terry said, leaning forward and patting her sisters arm. "I get it. You don't think I know you? How the real Avril doesn't really like to shop and never has sex until like the twentieth date. Believe me—I know you."

Avril leaned forward and kissed her sister. "I love you."

"I love you too," Terry said, then she snapped her fingers. "Oh God, I didn't tell you...'Member Mandy Galbraith?"

Avril nodded. "Yeah, in your class in high school."

"Well, she called me up, said she was coming out to L.A., and I could tell she was trolling for a bed. So, I figured, what the hell and asked her if she wanted to stay at the house. So, it was her first night there, Tim's gone to bed, and she and I got heavily into the Pinot Grigio. She starts going on about Alan Streeter—"

Avril's shoulders and head jerked back at the mention of the teacher. The man who had scarred her for life. She started to tell Terry she didn't want to hear it, but let her go on.

"Mandy heard he was selling cars for a while—that didn't work out—then he was a waiter somewhere—"

"You're kidding. I can't picture that."

"Yeah, well, neither could the guy who owned the place. So, long story short, he ends up basically homeless, soup kitchen and all, and this guy Frank from my class runs across him and talks to him. Bought him lunch or something, and he starts talking about you."

Avril held up her hands. "Is this going to upset me?"

"I'll stop if you want."

Avril took a deep breath. "No, go on."

"He goes off on this rant about how you're responsible for everything bad that ever happened to him. If it weren't for you, he'd be back teaching school, leading a nice normal life."

Avril's hands shook. Terry reached over and held them in hers.

"Sorry. I shouldn't have brought it up. I just thought maybe it would help to know how fucked up the guy is. You always felt somehow it was partly your fault, which is completely insane."

Avril turned her hand over and squeezed Terry's. "I know. I know, but I don't think that anymore."

"Good. So, let's not talk about it. Hey, look," Terry said, pointing at the family of seven ducks that were marching across the lawn.

"It's the Joneses," Avril said. "A girl here gave them all names. Reggie is the father. Greta, I think, is the mother. She feeds them graham crackers twice a day. She has names for all the babies too. Says she can tell 'em apart."

Terry laughed. "But they're identical. There's no way."

Avril shrugged. "What can I tell you? A firm grasp on reality is not all that common around here."

They heard footsteps behind them. "Hi, Avril," said a voice.

Avril turned.

"Oh, hi, Amy. This is my sister, Terry."

"Hi," Terry said, looking up and shading her eyes.

"Hello," Amy said. "Time to give the Joneses their dinner."

Terry noticed the graham crackers in her hand.

Amy walked down the steps to the lawn. Avril and Terry watched as the ducks waddled over.

"Hi, guys," Amy said. "Here you go. Greta, ladies first." She tossed a corner of a graham cracker to the mother. "And, Betsy, since it's your birthday, you're next."

She flipped a piece of graham cracker at the feet of a duckling. Avril and Terry just looked at each other and smiled. "Sweet," Terry said.

"Strange," Avril said.

Chapter 51

Rachel noticed that Darlene always seemed to be the one to answer the phones at Acute Care. Her working theory was that Darlene knew the calls were never going to be for her but wanted to talk to someone—anyone—and total strangers would do just fine.

"It's your father," Darlene said to Rachel, who was in the living room reading the last chapter of her Tina Fey book.

"Thanks."

"He sounds nice."

Rachel bounced to her feet and walked quickly to the phone. "Hi."

"Don't even think about hanging up on me," Phil Eppersley growled.

"'My father,' right. What do you want, Phil?"

"I want you to talk to Kornbluth and tell him unless I get two hundred fifty grand, I'll sue the estate. And I want you to convince him I deserve every nickel."

"But I thought—"

"I changed my mind. Listen to me. I'll sue the shit out of you, and you'll end up in court. You'll get asked a million questions about your mother. Furst will put you through the ringer, and I can promise you it won't be fun."

Rachel felt an instant migraine coming on. She couldn't stand the idea of her past being dredged up.

"But you and he agreed on everything?"

"I thought it over and changed my mind, so this is plan B," Eppersley said. "Soon as I hang up, I want you to call him."

Rachel wondered if Furst had put him up to this.

"Rachel, did you hear me? You wanna go to court? Want a bunch of painful memories dredged up?"

She couldn't imagine what he was referring to, but took a deep breath and exhaled. "I'll call him."

She hung up, then picked up the phone and dialed her father's cell.

"Hi, Rachel," Judd Kornbluth answered.

She started crying and couldn't get a word out for a few moments. "You... you... you need to give Phil—"

"Calm down, just calm down," Kornbluth said. "It's okay. It's going to be okay."

Rachel glanced over at the far wall so no one could see her crying.

"It's not okay. We need to give him two hundred fifty thousand dollars, or he'll sue me and—"

"Rachel, please honey, I hate to hear you upset like this. Listen to me, okay? Just listen for a sec."

"Okay," she said, wiping the tear-stained phone on her T-shirt.

"You better now?"

Rachel stopped crying. "Yes."

"Good. Phil Eppersley is just a loudmouthed jerk who throws around a lot of hollow threats. There's a reason he's calling you, you know. Figures he can scare you into getting what he wants."

"Yeah, well, it's working."

"Shhh, shhh, just listen. Christ, I'd like to kill that guy."

Rachel gave a weak laugh. "Be my guest."

"Here's what it comes down to—it's all a bluff. Guy's not gonna sue. Last thing he wants is to go to court. You really think a judge is gonna be sympathetic to *him*? Your mother left him out of her will because she couldn't stand him and because he physically abused both of you. That sound like a guy who's going to win over a judge?"

"No." She had a flashback of her father holding her hand and smiling down at her as he walked her to the first day of third grade.

"You gotta trust me on this, Rachel. I'm gonna go see him, not just talk to him on the phone. Guarantee you he'll never call you or try to see you again."

Rachel had another flashback: her father telling her how fantastic she was in a school play where she had messed up one of her two lines of dialogue.

"You gonna beat him up?"

"He's bigger than me, but I fight dirty."

"Like kick him in the nuts?"

"Rachel!"

"Sorry."

"Actually, that's not a bad idea. Hey, I would really like to come see you there, if you'd like me to."

Yes was her emphatic first reaction, but the man had hurt her terribly.

"Yeah, sure, I guess."

"Maybe I could come up this weekend?"

She tamped down her enthusiasm. "Oh, okay."

"So how 'bout, say, three on Saturday?"

"All right," she said evenly, not letting her joy show.

*****

Rachel and Dr. Davidenko were outside sitting in two chairs facing each other.

"I haven't seen you like this before, Rachel. Is it because you're getting out of ACU?"

"Seen me like what?" she asked, wired from the phone call.

"You seem so... up? Happy, even."

"Me? Happy? You got the wrong girl, Doc."

But she was within a stone's throw of it.

"Well, your eyes look—"

"Blue?"

He laughed. "See, even your sense of humor seems, I don't know, more animated."

"Awesome."

He smiled at her expectantly, like he was waiting for her to say how his remarkable care had something to do with the new Rachel.

"It's partly because you're leaving here, right?" Davidenko asked again.

"Partly," Rachel said, crossing her arms.

"And the other part?"

She leaned forward. "Know how I told you when I first got here, I had no relationship with my father?"

He nodded, but she wasn't sure he actually did remember.

"Well, maybe there's the start of something between us."

He gave her a thumbs-up, her least favorite gesture.

"I'm very happy for you. That's terrific."

"Well, it's not terrific yet, but definitely better."

"What exactly happened?" Davidenko asked, looking over at the smokers coming out on smoke break.

"Well, let's just say he stepped up when he had to. Something he never did before."

Davidenko patted her on the knee. "Maybe he's changed?"

"I hope."

Chapter 52

Turned out Cam and Rachel arrived within an hour of each other at Brook House. Cam was alone in the living room. He looked at his watch: five past seven. He was sure the resident had told him there was a nightly meeting at seven. He was looking forward to new faces. Apprehensive too. He had no idea what to expect at the meeting. They rarely had meetings at Main House.

He was sitting on a black couch, hunched forward, when Ted entered the room.

"Hey, Black Cloud, how ya doin', man? Thought this thing started at seven?"

Cam stood up and shook hands with Ted.

"S'posed to," Ted said, "but it's kind of like a cocktail party, always starts fashionably late."

Cam nodded then lowered his voice. "Hey, we gotta figure out a way to get Arthur for that snuff thing."

"You sure it was him?"

"Who else is that sick?"

"Nobody I know," Ted said.

"Yeah, and no tellin' what kinda shit he'll pull next," Cam said. "Hey, how is this place anyway?"

Ted cocked his head.

"It's pretty good," he said. "Lotta wacky broads, what can I tell you."

"I heard that, Ted," Avril said, as she walked into the room with Rachel.

"Who you calling wacky, old-timer?" Rachel said to Ted.

"Hail, hail, the gang's all here," Cam said, then turning to Avril. "How you doin' anyway?"

"Fine," she said.

He gestured for her to sit down next to him. Rachel sat in a club chair across from him.

"I would have figured you for a Schechter guy," Rachel said to Cam.

"Me too. But like I told Avril, I'm very well rounded. I got all kinds of baggage," he said, then gestured to Ted, "plus Black Cloud needed me here to even out the odds."

Avril looked over at Ted. "The old codger's doing a lot better."

Cam nodded. "I can tell."

Other women had been coming in, in ones and twos. Finally, Tanya walked in and sat down at 7:10.

"So," Tanya said, "I'd like to welcome two new people tonight. First of all, Rachel. Welcome, Rachel."

Rachel put up a hand. "Thank you."

"Then Cam," she said. "We welcome you too."

Cam nodded. "Thank you. It's good to be here… I think."

Tanya explained the purpose of the meeting. They went around the circle and Ted said his moment of the day was finding out Cam was coming to Brook House. A little later, Avril told the group hers was seeing Rachel bounce into her room in black spandex pants and an Arcade Fire T-shirt.

"I don't know if you remember," Avril said to the group, "but when I first got here, I said my moment of the day was getting away from all the drama queens at ACU"—several heads nodded— "well, I just want you to know that the queen of queens has arrived."

Rachel hopped to her feet and curtsied. "I'm so flattered," she said. "Thank you."

After the meeting, Rachel asked Ted if he wanted to take a walk and catch up. He said sure, and followed her out the French doors of the Brook House living room.

"You're not the same guy I saw two weeks ago at AA, Ted."

"Thanks."

Rachel stopped, looked at the brook off in the distance, then back to Ted.

"I'm serious. You were like this total zombie, no clue where you were. I should talk, complete pain in the ass I was."

Ted laughed as they walked out to the back lawn.

"I have absolutely no memory of those first few days," Ted said. "Hey, so you're Avril's roommate. That's one to write home about."

Rachel laughed, flicked a strand of hair out of her face. "Yeah, like I have someone to write home *to*. It'll be a trip living with her. Our relationship started out—let's just say—a little rocky, but now it's good. Fought like a bunch of she-cats at ACU."

"She can be tough. Got a great heart though."

"I know," Rachel said, stopping at a lilac bush. "This sucker could use a little water."

Ted pointed. "Watering can's over there. Faucet's on the corner of the house."

Rachel filled up the watering can and watered the lilac bush.

She looked at Ted and smiled. "That oughta keep it going. So, is your wife coming to visit at all?"

"No, we live in California. It's a long haul, and we can't really afford it."

Rachel nodded. "I got my father coming up this weekend."

"Oh, that's nice. He live around here?"

"Yeah, Tarrytown, not too far. First time I've seen him in, like, years."

"Why's that?"

Rachel's eyes narrowed. "When my parents got divorced, he just sorta...disappeared. Had his own problems. Kinda slipped out of my life."

Ted stifled a sigh. Rachel could tell she had triggered something. "What's wrong?"

"Oh nothing, you just kind of hit a nerve."

"Tell me."

Ted blinked a few times. "Me and my daughter, we haven't spoken in a long time."

"Aw, Ted, I am so sorry. Why not?"

Ted looked off in the distance. "For reasons I haven't completely figured out."

She nodded. "You'll work it out, Ted. I'm sure you will."

Ted didn't look sure at all.

Chapter 53

Avril was in the Brook House living room reading *Variety* on her Macbook Air when her agent, Marv Garfield, finally checked back in.

It was early Sunday afternoon when he called, so her first reaction was that because of the unusual hour, he might have some news. Good news would be nice.

"How would you feel about doing Broadway?" Garfield asked her.

His tone implied that she had just gotten Scarlett in *Gone with the Wind*, but her first impression was that it was not good news.

"So, I haven't gotten any scripts," she said. "Is that what you're telling me?"

"Sure you have. Just not the right ones."

"What is it, Marv? Am I radioactive?"

Marv sighed. "You know what I did?" he said. "I Googled bipolar and printed out a bunch of articles. What you just asked me is what they call 'all or nothing' thinking."

"I'm familiar with the concept, Marv, and you might be on to something."

He laughed. "And are you familiar with the concept of going from movies to theater, then coming back to movies? I mean, Meryl and Mirren come to mind."

"All right, all right, the answer is I'd feel pretty good about the theater if it was a good part."

"It is, and here's the kicker: Nick Sebastian is practically begging to get the male lead."

"You're kidding," Avril yelped, mashing the phone up against her ear.

"You believe it?" Marv said. "Three years ago we would have said, 'Are you fucking kidding me?' Nick Sebastian, the kid from the boy band—"

"And *Star Search*," Avril chimed in.

"Guy's come a long way."

"He was amazing in *Beggar's Banquet*, s'posed to be a dream to work with too,"

April was over the moon. "Keep going and don't spare the juicy details."

"Okay, it's called *Visual Effects*, by that limey dude, Connor Shea."

"He's a mick dude, Marv."

"Yeah, well, across the pond somewhere. I'm gonna Fedex it to you."

"I'm so excited I think I might pee my pants."

Marv snorted a laugh.

"That's why they got those plastic sheets you were telling me about."

*****

Cam knocked on Ted's door. "Yanks game in five, Black Cloud."

He was wearing a New York Yankees shirt with number 12 emblazoned on it when Ted opened his door.

"Might have a little problem with the *TV mafia*," Ted said.

"The what?"

"Let's go downstairs. If we're lucky, they won't be there."

Cam gave Ted a fist bump on the shoulder. "Season opener, man. Sabathia's pitching."

"Don't get your hopes up."

"What are you talking about?"

The walked down from the third floor and into the living room.

Six women were playing Monopoly with the TV on behind them. It was a replay of *The Golden Girls*.

Ted turned to Cam and lowered his voice. "That's the TV mafia," he said. "They always watch the shittiest shows on TV."

"Yeah, but they're not even watching it," Cam said

Ted shrugged.

Cam walked in and flashed the biggest smile he could muster.

"You ladies mind if we put on the Yankees game?"

"Damn right we do," said one, looking up from the board. Another one eyed Cam and slowly shook her head. "You think you can just come in here and rule the roost?"

"No, I just—"

"Sorry, we're watching it," said a third, whose back was to the TV.

Cam looked distressed.

Ted lowered his voice. "They outvote us. That's how it works."

"No offense, ladies," Cam said, "but you don't really seem to be watching it."

He had been looking forward to the game all day.

"Okay, then," said one. "We're listening to it. How's that?"

Cam started to say something, but bit his tongue. He turned to Ted and muttered. "This fuckin' sucks, man."

Ted nodded.

"How 'bout if we just watch the first three innings?" Cam asked, thinking if they could just gain a toehold maybe the women would forget about it.

"Now listen, dammit," one said. "You're disturbing our game *and* the show."

"Democracy rules," another one said.

"If you want to watch your baseball game, why don't you go to a bar?" one said. "Oh, but you already tried that, didn't you?"

All six of them caterwauled.

Cam was about to lose it, but bit his tongue again.

He turned back to Ted. "You believe this shit?"—then he had an idea—"Follow me."

Cam, with Ted in his wake, walked up to the second floor and knocked on a door. No one answered. Then he knocked on the door next to it. A woman poked her head out. "Hi," Cam said. "I'll give you twenty-five bucks if..."

Five minutes later Cam was out a hundred and twenty-five bucks but had five new friends. More importantly, a majority. He and Ted watched the Yankees beat the rival Red Sox.

Ted turned to the Monopoly players halfway through the game and said with a wide smile, "I kind of Miss Betty White."

Chapter 54

Rachel was out in front of Brook House at 2:45. Judd Kornbluth was supposed to get there at 3:00.

At 3:15, she started to tremble and an all-too-familiar anxiety enveloped her.

At 3:25, a knife-like migraine had replaced the racing anticipation that she'd felt so intensely a half hour before.

At 3:35, she turned, head down, and walked toward the front door of Brook House. She had her hand on the knob when she heard a car honk behind her. She turned and saw a gray Saab and a man emerge from it. He had less hair than she remembered but a mile-wide grin.

"Hey!" he shouted.

He was stocky with almost no neck, and was wearing khaki pants with a sharp crease and a polo shirt that looked starched.

Rachel could see he had made a real effort to look like a father who was trying to impress and win back a daughter he hadn't seen in years.

He ran up the stairs, took a few steps toward her and threw his arms around her. But Rachel kept her hands to her side.

"Oh my God, I'm taller than you," Rachel said.

Kornbluth smiled. "Got your Mom's genes," he said, pulling back from Rachel, then giving her a kiss on the cheek. "I'm so sorry I'm late. Bad traffic on the Taconic."

"That's okay. I wasn't sure—"

"I was going to come?"

Rachel nodded.

He put his hands on her shoulders. "That father's in the past. The new father just doesn't anticipate traffic so well. Please try to forgive me for all those years. I just had to work out my own stuff before I could be any kind of a father to you."

"You could have been working it out and seeing me at the same time."

"I guess," he said, glancing down, "but there was something really hard about seeing you or even talking to you when I felt so damn... hollow. Like such a failure."

"You think I would have cared?"

"Just chalk it up to insecurity."

"Can we just talk about the weather or something?"

"Yeah, you look unbelievable, by the way. My gawky little thirteen-year-old grown up to be this tall, red-headed beauty."

He gave her a proud smile. "So show me around this place." They walked through the front door of Brook House, and Rachel felt as though a dark, dismal void might finally be filled.

"Okay, well, this is the living room," Rachel said, holding out her hand. "Duh. Where we play games, watch the tube, have meetings. Scene of a lot of drama, they tell me."

"What kind of drama?"

"Well, just imagine sixteen people with every kind of issue, addiction, and affliction known to man. All under the same roof. Bound to be fireworks, wouldn't you say?"

"I hear you," Kornbluth said, putting his arm around her shoulder.

"Come on. Let's go out on the back porch. It's nice out there," Rachel said, feeling secure in the gentle weight of her father's arm.

They strolled through the small dining room. At one end of the large table was a half-finished jigsaw puzzle. One resident had told Rachel it had been started a year and a half ago.

They walked out onto the porch and sat side by side in the two Adirondack chairs.

The brook was running high because it had rained the night before. It rushed faster, louder than usual.

"It's beautiful," Kornbluth said, pointing. "Those trees look like they've been there a million years. You ever see any animals out there?"

"Just this family of ducks. They show up for handouts when they get hungry. Supposedly deer and wild turkey too, but I haven't seen them yet."

Judd turned to Rachel and put his hand on her hand, which rested on the flat surface of the chair.

"So, what can I do?" he asked.

"You've already done a lot, all that stuff with Phil. I really appreciate it. Just make it so I never see him again. Deal?"

"Deal. I went to his house, told him to leave you alone, or I'd take legal actions. He told me to get out of his house, or *he'd* take legal action."

Rachel smiled.

"Wait. You just waltzed right into his house?"

"Yup."

"Right on," Rachel bumped fists with her father.

"Told me if I had anything to discuss, to take it up with Furst. I said there was nothing more to discuss. That he better agree to the thirty thousand, or I was taking it off the table."

"Good job."

"So how we gonna get you better? Give me a little history. I know it's painful."

"No, it's okay," she said, pausing. "You want me to leave you out? Fact that I had this father, then I didn't."

She wasn't going to just give him a pass.

"Fair enough. It's up to me to make up for that." Kornbluth rested his hand back on hers.

"You better. Anyway, after Mom got killed, I hit rock bottom. I mean, first you, then her. I couldn't eat, couldn't sleep. I just drank, did drugs, and cried. All I had left was this loser stepfather I hated. What was I s'posed to do? Get some pathetic job or go to a college I wasn't psyched about? Plus, I had this really bad relationship I just got out of. I mean, my life was a flaming train wreck. So I pretty much just"—she paused, and a few tears rolled down her cheeks— "lost it. Broke down. Hated myself, my life. And that's...when I did it."

Kornbluth glanced down at her wrist and said in a sad, pained tone. "I am so, so sorry, but you're alive. And you're going to get well. I know it."

She leaned toward him to give him a kiss but caught herself. "I can't do it alone. I need all the help I can get," she said. "I mean, what happened to Mom, that's still—"

"I understand. It's got to be incredibly painful. I'll help. I promise I will."

Rachel suddenly looked up and pointed. "Look, the ducks."

Kornbluth looked out over the lawn.

"Wish I grew up in a nice functional family like that," Rachel said, then smiled. "Lots of brothers and sisters, a mother and father. No stress, just eat, swim, and fly. What a perfect life."

"Yeah, and fly down to Florida for the winter."

Rachel stood up. "Let's go feed 'em."

Kornbluth smiled and nodded.

"They like graham crackers," Rachel said, going into the house. "Be right back."

She returned a few moments later, handed her father a cracker, and started down the steps.

"No stress, no addictions, no bipolar, no depression," Rachel said, "and somebody feeds you breakfast, lunch, and dinner. What a life."

They were about ten feet away from the ducks.

"I think that one on the right's the father," Rachel said, pointing. Rachel threw a piece of graham cracker at one of the ducklings' feet. The father saw it and swooped down with his big bill and beat the duckling to it.

Chapter 55

Cam and Ted had had a long talk on the Brook House porch about Avril and the snuff flick. There was no way they could prove anything, but they were convinced Arthur was the only one who could have sent it. Since they couldn't go to the Clairmount authorities and say, 'We don't have proof. We just know it's him,' Cam decided the only thing to do was take the law into his own hands. He told Ted he was going to Arthur's room and see if he could find something incriminating. He had a few ideas. But they'd have to wait until the time was right.

He and Ted were waiting for a scheduled group to begin.

Ted was grousing again about how everything started late at Clairmount. They were all paying good money, so if it was supposed to be a sixty-minute group he wanted it to be *a sixty-minute group*. It never was. He insisted that if you billed yourself as a place with a rigid structure and dead-serious objectives, then you ought to damn well stick to a tight schedule. But Lisa would always drag her ass in ten minutes late to teach Group and do a variation on the same joke about being "time-management challenged." Then she'd look at her planner and say something like, "Ted, I've got a meeting with you tomorrow at three, which we all know really means three-fifteen." Yuk-yuk-yuk.

Lisa was already ten minutes late when Avril walked in.

A minute later, Lisa came in, sat down, and crossed her legs. "Okay, guys, I'd like to introduce you to our newest member." She pointed. "This is Mark. Go around the room and introduce yourselves, please."

Mark was Pony's real name. He and Cam and Ted had already caught up outside in the hallway before the session.

Ted started it out. "Welcome, Pony," he said. "As you know, I'm Ted, the one who *doesn't* cheat at Scrabble." Then to the group: "Pony and I were at Main House together. Never knew his name was Mark."

Then a few others spoke until it was Cam's turn. He looked at Pony and said. "I'm Cam, the guy who gave you your nickname. Also, the guy who always wins at Scrabble. Playing fair and square, of course."

Pony flashed him his *yeah, right* smile. Then the rest of the group introduced themselves.

"Okay, Mark," Lisa said. "Now it's your turn. Tell us a little about yourself."

"I'm Mark, or Pony, as those knuckleheads call me. Anyway, I'm an alcoholic with a side of depression, and, well, I just hope to get better. Oh, and another thing...I thought I was going home 'cause I couldn't afford to pay for the program. Insurance didn't cover it, so out of the blue my doctor told me some anonymous donor had stepped up and paid for it."

He turned to Cam. "You wouldn't know anything about that, would you, Crawford?"

Cam's eyes got wide, and he looked at Pony.

"Me? No, I think that's great, though. You need it, man."

Pony smiled.

Avril glanced up at Cam.

"Okay," Pony said, opening his hand toward Cam. "I'd like to introduce my anonymous donor. A good guy who doesn't want you to think he is."

Cam leaned forward in his chair. "Hey, Pony, glad you think that, but you got the wrong guy. My soon-to-be ex-wife is cleaning me out. I couldn't possibly afford you *and* her."

Pony laughed. "Yeah, yeah, whatever you say."

*****

Cam was working out in the gym after group.

Avril came up to him, wearing black sweat pants and a white hoodie with the hood up over her head.

"So, you back to disguising yourself?" he asked.

She laughed and pulled the hoodie back. Her naturally blond-streaked hair shined like the sun was beaming down on it.

"That was a really nice thing."

"What was?" Cam asked.

"Don't play dumb. Paying for that guy's program."

Cam exhaled loudly. "Hey, it was no big deal. He would have fallen back if I hadn't. Guy needed it bad. I just put myself in his shoes."

Avril smiled. "You don't have to apologize for doing something nice. It's not unmanly, you know."

He laughed. "I know. I know. Just...it was no big deal."

"Okay, 'nough said. So, what do you do in here?"

"You mean besides get beat up by drug dealers?"

"Yeah, exactly."

"Well, I used to kick box. So I take out my aggressions on that bag over there."

Avril looked over at the big leather heavy bag about the size of a cow's torso. It hung by links of chain from an I-beam welded to a steel plate. She had seen some guys with leather gloves go a few rounds with it.

"What about you?" Cam asked. "What do you do?"

"I try to get here every day. You know, the dreaded bathing suit scenes."

222

What had been motivating her most was a movie she'd seen just before checking in to Clairmount, where an actress walked across a room completely naked. Avril knew the actress was at least twelve years older than her but was in way better shape. Avril was particularly concerned about the onset of jiggly-upper-arm syndrome.

"All right then, go for it," Cam said, walking away.

Avril ramped up her work out a notch and sweated more than usual. She watched him do battle with the bag. He wasn't bad. He used his legs much more than his arms, getting off the ground with slash kicks that made a solid thump as he connected with the bag.

She went over to him after she did a set of crunches.

"You're pretty good."

His shorts and shirt were completely drenched in sweat. He was breathing in short bursts. He bent down and put his hands on his knees.

"Thanks. Showin' off a little"—shaking his head—"that was heart attack material."

She laughed. "You some kind of belt?"

"Nah." he said. "If I was, I would have done a little better with that guy Todd."

He was still breathing heavily.

"Still, I wouldn't want to tangle with you in a back alley."

"It's all show."

"You do any not-so-violent sports?" she asked.

"Golf. And a little tennis."

"Any good at tennis?"

"Nah. Lousy forehand, okay backhand, pathetic serve."

"I keep walking by that beautiful old tennis court nobody ever uses," she said. "Want to play one day?"

"You're on."

"I'll kick your ass."

"Well, we'll just have to see about that."

Chapter 56

After the back-to-back rounds of DBT every afternoon came "Group." The purpose of Group was to cement some of the ideas you had just learned in DBT and try to make them part of your daily routine.

Lisa led the group that Ted, Avril, and Cam attended. Rachel took part in another one. Lisa, as far as Avril could recall, had not conducted one group session without talking about her almost groupie-like obsession with Steven Tyler of the band Aerosmith. The second day after Group, Lisa followed Avril into the ladies' room. Avril beelined to the nearest stall. She had just closed the door and locked it when she heard Lisa's voice.

"I hope it's not a weird question," Lisa said into the gray metal door, "but have you ever crossed paths with Steven?"

Avril had always figured a stall was a safe haven.

"Steven Tyler, you mean?"

"Yes. I just thought maybe since you were married to Renny Justice," Lisa said.

"That lasted a nanosecond," Avril said. "Nope, never had the pleasure. S'posed to be a nice guy, I hear."

"Yeah, well, just wondering. Didn't mean to bother you," Lisa said, and she was gone.

Lisa's other obsession, though a distant second to Tyler, was mindfulness. She advocated relentlessly in every Group that living in the present, focusing on that moment, not a second ago or a second from now, was the cure for most anything. Especially depression, bipolar, drugs, and alcohol. She liked to sprinkle her sessions with different games, which she called "mindfulness exercises."

In one, she'd pass out rubbery, elongated toys that looked like squishy jellyfish. Everyone would toss them back and forth in the classroom where they were sitting in a circle. The point was to focus exclusively on what you were doing—at that moment—or else you'd take a rubber jellyfish to the chin.

Another game that didn't seem to have a name had to do with geographic places.

Avril had just started the game. "Winnipeg," she said. The next person had to name a place that started with the last letter of the word before.

"Gettysburg," the next person said.

"Germany," said another.

It was Cam's turn. "Yakituba," he said without hesitation.

"You just made that up." Avril shook her head.

"No, I didn't. Look it up. It's in Japan. Quangtu province."

"Bullshit," Avril said. "You made both those up."

Lisa laughed.

Avril turned to Ted. "I see what you mean about your friend here."

"Told you," Ted said. "Guy's a serial cheater. Can't help himself."

Cam swung around at Ted. "I resent that. You're besmirching my character," he said. "Yemen, then."

"Oh, I get it," Avril said to Ted. "All his chatter is a way for him to buy time to think up a real answer."

Ted nodded. "You catch on quick."

Avril smiled and looked at Cam. "You deserve to be besmirched."

Cam managed to look greatly offended.

They went around the circle until, finally, Ted couldn't come up with the name of a place.

The next part of the mindfulness exercises was something that Avril had nicknamed, "What's Callie's Problem?" a name she kept to herself.

"Does anyone want to share something that's troubling them? Maybe the group can help," Lisa would start out.

She would invariably get as far as "So does anyone want to share?" when Callie would blurt out something that was weighing heavily on her mind.

Today her problem was scary dreams.

"I mean, last night it was this very realistic, bloody plane crash," Callie said. "Night before that, I was in my backyard, and it suddenly turned into this giant sinkhole—"

"—Remeron," Cam said.

"What?" Callie asked.

"Helps you sleep," Cam said. "Also gives you the most incredibly happy dreams. In 3-D and surround sound."

Avril laughed. "Yeah, but you put on weight."

"What's a few pounds to have Technicolor dreams?" Cam said, then added, "Jesus, is there any drug you haven't taken?"

"Done 'em all," Avril said. "A drug store is a gal's best friend."

Lisa smiled and pointed to Ted. "Ted, it looked like you had something to say."

Everyone's eyes swung to Ted. He often volunteered solutions but never before a problem.

He rubbed his hands together uncomfortably.

"My daughter," Ted said, barely above a whisper, "she...she...doesn't talk to me."

"Why?" Lisa asked.

"She said in an email that I didn't 'man up.'"

Cam leaned forward in his chair. "What the hell's that s'posed to mean?"

"That when the shit hit... when I lost everything, I just, you know, wallowed in self-pity. Didn't fight, just kind of gave up. Depression kicked in big time."

"Hey, man, you got slammed by a tsunami real estate market," Cam said.

Ted shrugged. "I know."

"Not too compassionate, that daughter of yours," Cam said. "I mean, depression can be so brutal."

"Maybe she's right," Avril said, and everyone turned to her.

"Go ahead," Lisa said to Avril, her left leg bouncing up and down like a jackhammer.

Avril looked tentative. Like she was wondering how much Ted could take.

Then she turned to him. "I don't know. Maybe it is time you did 'man up.'"

Cam started to say something but Avril held up her hand, riveted on Ted.

"You told me about how your wife gave up her perfect life," Avril said. "Moved away from her friends and the house she loved to come be with you when you took a job three thousand miles away."

Ted nodded uneasily.

"The job that was going to get you back on your feet," Avril said, "The start of your financial comeback. Instead you fell apart, stayed in bed all day, lost the job. Your wife had to get one herself—"

"Avril, the idea here is to help the man," Cam said.

Avril shot a look at Cam. "Will you stop being his apologist."

Cam shrugged. "Will you stop tearing him down."

"Stop," Avril said, putting up her hands. "Ted can take care of himself. And if he can't, he damn well better learn."

"So who are you?" Cam asked. "The queen of tough love?"

"Yeah, maybe so," Avril said. "Something you could probably use since everyone's always telling you what a fucking prince you are."

"Whoa. Where the hell did that come from?" Cam said. "You got a little pent-up anger there."

"Maybe I do," Avril said, her eyes fiery. "Why? You want some more?"

"For Chrissakes—"

"Let her talk, huh Cam," Ted said evenly.

Cam shrugged. "She's doing a pretty good job of that."

Avril sighed and glanced back at Ted. "There's really nothing more to say," she said. "Except you owe your wife, Ted. You owe her *big*."

Ted nodded slowly.

"See, Ted, you spend way too much time feeling sorry for yourself," Avril said. "How 'bout feeling sorry for her. No, better yet, do something to get her out of the mess you put her in."

The room fell dead silent. Slowly, heads began to nod.

Chapter 57

Cam and Ted snuck into Arthur's room that night. They knew he'd be at AA because he liked to badger speakers and give them a hard time.

Cam told Ted to be a lookout in the hallway and make sure no one was coming. Then he slipped into Arthur's room. The room was neat as a pin, which surprised him, because Arthur dressed kind of sloppily and didn't shave every day. Cam didn't really know what he was looking for. He just hoped that he'd find something incriminating.

He opened the top drawer of Arthur's bureau. A neat row of underwear, then balled-up socks to the right. The next drawer held shirts, then the third drawer, long pants and shorts.

He went over to Arthur's desk. A paperback, a *Playboy*, and several pens in a plastic cup. He opened the drawer to the desk and saw a yellow legal pad, a stack of envelopes, a manila envelope, and a roll of stamps in the front left corner.

He glanced back at the manila envelope.

That was a start.

He looked under the pad and behind the envelopes, but didn't find what he was looking for. Something that Arthur had written. A handwriting sample. Then he checked the top of Arthur's desk again but didn't find anything.

He looked back down at the stamps and had an idea. He thrummed his fingers on the desk a few times, looked back down, and had another thought.

He picked up the yellow pad. Then he pulled up his shirt and slid the pad under his shirt. He did the same with the manila envelope, and tucked his shirt back in. He walked toward the door, opened it, and went out into the hallway.

Ted was a few feet away. He didn't look like a lookout. More like a loiterer.

"Any luck?" he asked Cam.

"I think so," Cam said.

"What do you mean, you think so?"

"Depends on how good a bluffer I am," Cam said. "I want to go see that note Avril got."

*****

The two of them came back to Arthur's room two hours later. In the meantime, Cam had gone down to Brook House and asked Avril to show him the note that came with the snuff flick.

Cam knocked loudly on Arthur's door.

"Go the fuck away," was Arthur's response.

Cam pushed it open, and Ted followed him in.

Arthur lay on his bed, reading a paperback, his legs two feet short of reaching the end of the bed.

He looked up and scowled. "Figured it was a tech telling me to take my happy pills," he said. "What the hell do you mooks want?"

"We want to have a man-to-midget talk," Cam said.

"That's not very politically correct, Cameron." Arthur sat up and swung his legs over the side of his bed. "What do you want to talk about?"

"That snuff flick you sent Avril Ensor," Cam said.

"Are you out of your fucking mind?"

"That's about what we'd expect you to say," Cam said. "Thing is, we got three things that'll hang you. This is the first one. Let's call it Exhibit A."

Cam looked over at Ted, who pulled the folded-up manila envelope out of his back pocket. "Just so happens," Ted said, "this is the exact same kind of envelope used to put your little love letter to Avril in."

Arthur shook his head and sneered. "That's bullshit. Those things come in two sizes, and they're all the same. You got nothing, old man. Now why don't you clowns get the hell—"

"Then there's this." Cam took the roll of stamps out of his breast pocket. "Bet you never thought of a stamp as a DNA carrier?"

It seemed to register with Arthur.

"Didn't think of that, did you?" Cam said. "That your dried saliva is all over the stamps sent to Avril."

Arthur shook his head. "Go ahead and test it. It ain't mine."

"That's your story," Cam said. "Then there's Exhibit C, the yellow pad I liberated from your desk. I got it back in my room 'cause I didn't want you trying to destroy any evidence. Same yellow paper used in the note, and what hangs you is how your handwriting is indented on the top page of the pad. *"Avril, I thought this might be beneficial to you vis-à-vis your bipolar disorder.* Well, you know the rest, asshole, since you wrote it."

Ted stepped forward. "Bottom line, Arthur, we're your judge, jury, and executioner, and you just got convicted. We want you out of here in three hours, or we go to the authorities."

"And, hey, here's a fun fact for you," Cam said, "since this involved the US mail, the feds go after you for this."

Arthur gave Cam a nasty look. "You guys are so full of shit."

But clearly some of the bravado had seeped out of him.

Cam figured it was time to leave. "Okay," he said, "then stick around and find out just how full of shit we are."

Ted started to leave, but turned back and tossed the envelope on Arthur's desk. "We're gonna miss you, Artie," he said. "Don't forget to write, you sick sonovabitch."

Chapter 58

Ted was out behind Brook House snipping some lilacs. He had never really been much of a gardener before, but was beginning to get into it.

He didn't hear Cam come up behind him.

"Whatcha doin' there?" Cam asked.

"What's it look like?" Ted said. "Making a bouquet for you."

"I'm touched," Cam sniffed the lilac bush. "Seriously, what's with you and horticulture all of a sudden?"

"So I like flowers," Ted said. "What can I tell you?"

Ted, flower clipper in one hand, lilacs in the other, bent down and arranged the lilacs in a clear vase on the ground that was half-filled with water. He signaled to Cam to follow him as he strode toward a bush that had white and purple flowers.

Ted snipped a clump of purple flowers and a white bunch and added them to the vase.

"Pretty nice," Cam said. "Any idea what they are?"

"No clue," Ted said, sniffing them. "Smell good, though."

They walked along the brook a little farther.

"I know what those are," Ted said, pointing.

"Well, no shit, even I do." Cam reached for one of the red roses.

Ted snipped two red ones and two pink ones and added them to the vase, then picked up the glass container and looked at Cam.

"I hear our little friend checked out," Ted said.

"Yeah," Cam said, "good fucking riddance."

Ted nodded and smiled.

The two walked back up to Brook House. Ted went up the two flights to the third floor, set the bouquet outside the top-floor room of Rachel and Avril, and slipped a piece of paper in between two of the roses. On it he had written:

> *Dear Rachel,*
> *Missed you and your irascible personality at the meeting this morning. Avril said you had a bad migraine. Hope you feel better soon.*
> *Ted*

*****

"Irascible," Rachel said to Ted, "I like that...course, I had to look it up."

They were sitting off in one corner of the Brook House living room. A noisy group of other patients were watching *Jeopardy* on the other side. It was shortly after the Brook House night meeting.

"Yeah, sure you did. You got a bigger vocabulary than me." Rachel still had a migraine but told him it was better.

She looked up at Ted. "Thank you so much. That was really, really sweet. And those flowers are sick."

Ted laughed. "My daughter used to say that word. I kept thinking something was wrong."

Rachel laughed, stretched her long legs out and swung them up onto a coffee table. "I know where you got the lilacs, but what about the roses?" she asked.

"Down by the brook. I saw them on my nature walk."

They talked about how Rachel had to see her doctor about getting new medication for the migraines, about how they just came out of the blue sometimes with no apparent cause. Ted caught her up on what they had gone over in DBT that day.

Rachel stared into Ted's eyes. "And how are you doing?"

Ted was more comfortable talking about her. He picked up an empty CD case on the table next to him and fidgeted with it.

"Okay...better, I think,"

"But one part of you," she said, trying to see the name on the CD, "one part of you is *not* okay."

Ted nodded.

"Your daughter, right?"

Ted put the CD down. "How do you know that?" he said, then nodded. "Oh, of course, Avril."

"Sorry. Girls talk."

Ted smiled. "I know my daughter's mad at me," he said, picking up the CD again, "but can't she at least talk to me? Hell, I'd even settle for a little yelling and screaming."

"You think talking to her...might make it worse?"

"No."

"Why?"

"Believe it or not, because of DBT."

"How?"

"See, the pattern is my daughter and I start going at it from the git-go. First, she says something that sets me off, then I lose it—you know, say something stupid, without thinking. No governor. So, she lashes back, and all of a sudden we're off to the races, going for the jugular. And neither one of us gives an inch. So I figure if I change my style and say something like, 'You know, Christie, you are *absolutely* right' a few dozen times—even if I don't actually mean it—we might get somewhere."

"That makes sense," Rachel said. "I gotta remember that."

"I mean, I know I could have a good conversation with her. Mend some fences."

Rachel turned her head and looked up at Ted with a lopsided grin. "Know what it sounds like to me?"

"What?"

"Sounds like your daughter's got a fair amount of *irascible* in her too."

Chapter 59

Cam was trying to eavesdrop on the dinner conversation at Main between a woman and the New York congressmen who had just been admitted to Clairmount. The congressman had just gotten caught with his pants down. Literally. He was an insatiable sex glutton who had xeroxed his penis and sent copies of it to girls all across America.

Johnson-gate, they called it.

The two sat one table away from Cam and Ted at dinner. Guests and family members could join patients for dinner on Wednesdays and Fridays. It was Friday.

"All I can tell is she's his lawyer," Cam whispered to Ted, across from him.

"My favorite rodent," Ted said.

"Hi, boys," said a voice behind Cam. "Mind if I join you?"

Cam smiled up at Avril. He stood and pulled out the chair next to him.

She put her tray down, and Cam looked at her plate. Nothing but salad.

"Bathing suit scenes?"

She smiled at him. "No, I'm in training."

"For a part?"

"No, for a tennis match." She picked up a fork. "Rachel and I are challenging you boys to a Battle of the Sexes."

Ted gave Cam a thumbs-up.

Cam turned to Avril. "You're on… I cheat, you know."

"Oh, do I ever," Avril said, looking around. "Hey, I haven't seen Arthur lately. You guys seen him?"

Cam shook his head. "Now that you mention it, no."

"Yeah, where is that little rascal?" Ted asked innocently.

"Hi, sweetie," said the voice behind Cam.

Cam swung around in disbelief.

Charlotte Crawford was falling out of a low-cut sleeveless top and short skirt.

Cam stood up and grazed her with a kiss on the cheek. "What are you doing here?"

He hadn't spoken to her since their division-of-assets conversation the week before.

"Just thought I'd surprise you," Charlotte said. Then she spotted Avril, who had just popped a forkful of lettuce into her mouth. "Oh...my...God."

Charlotte put her hand over her mouth and froze.

Cam looked at Avril.

"Oh," he said. "This is Avril, but I guess you figured that out. Avril, this is my wife Charlotte. And that's Ted."

Charlotte didn't even look at Ted but reached over and pumped Avril's hand. "Nice to meet you," Charlotte said, "I don't mean to act like some starstruck fan...just...Cam never told me."

"Well, thank you for that, Cam. Nice to meet you too," Avril said coolly.

"Char, you never saw her, okay?" Cam said, figuring she'd be on the phone with her girlfriends before she drove out of the parking lot.

"Oh, of course," Charlotte said.

"Thank you," Avril said, then muttered, "World's worst-kept secret."

Charlotte finally looked across at Ted.

"And I'm Ted," he said again.

"Hi," Charlotte said and, still in disbelief, glanced back at Avril.

"How 'bout some dinner?" Cam asked her.

"Why don't I just sit with you?" Then, looking down at Avril's salad. "Or maybe I'll have a salad. Got romaine, I see."

Cam motioned to her. "Come on. Follow me."

"Be right back," Charlotte said to Avril.

Avril nodded without enthusiasm.

As soon as they were out of earshot, Avril leaned across to Ted. "Aren't they supposed to be getting a divorce?" she said, her eyes squinty.

"That's what Cam told me."

Avril raised both hands and gave Ted an *I don't get it* shrug.

"Just what I pictured she'd look like," Avril said. "A Dallas Cowboy cheerleader."

Ted laughed. "Now, now. Remember your DBT."

"Fuck that shit."

"And you were making *such* good progress."

Avril eyed Charlotte as she and Cam came back to the table.

"So... how was your drive up?" Ted asked.

"Easy breezy," Charlotte said. "GPS is right up there with the lightbulb. I used to get lost going to the post office."

Ted laughed politely.

"So, Char, Ted and I were just challenged to a tennis match," Cam said.

"By a bunch of *girls*," Ted added.

Avril shot him a nasty look. "Okay, old man, we're taking no prisoners now."

"Wait. You're playing them?" Charlotte asked Avril.

"No, we're kicking their asses," Avril said. "I got a ringer for a partner."

"Rachel's good?" Ted asked.

"Full-boat tennis scholarship at Skidmore," Avril said.

"Yeah, right, like they even have sports at Skidmore," Cam said.

Charlotte smiled. "This place seems like fun," she said, taking a bite of her salad.

Avril laughed. "Oh, yeah, barrel of monkeys."

*****

Charlotte and Cam were walking down the hill toward her car.

"She likes you, you know," Charlotte said. "A girl can tell."

Cam didn't want to go there.

"What did you really come up here for, Char?"

"You're always so suspicious."

"Seriously, why?"

She reached out and took his hand.

He hoped Avril wasn't looking.

"I brought the papers with me."

"Divorce papers?"

"Yes, but I was thinking on the way up—"

"You could have Fedexed them."

"You didn't want to see me?"

"It's not that. It's just... over."

The words sounded like Cam had declared war. Not the way he meant it to come out.

"Yeah, but like I was saying, I started thinking maybe we should give it another try, you know, a... rapprochement?"

"A rapprochement, huh? Did you get that word from your artiste friend Antoine?"

"Stop. What do you think of the idea?"

Cam thought for a second.

"Here's what I think, Char," he took a deep breath, "I think we live in two separate universes. You're an amazing woman and I was damn lucky to have been married to you, but I *know* you can do a whole lot better."

Chapter 60

"Ted, you got a call," Amy said. "Your wife, I think."

Ted and Cam were playing Scrabble at the table near the piano. Ted stood up and pointed at Cam. "Now don't go changing any letters or anything. I'm onto your tricks."

Cam feigned shock. "Ted, would I do something like that?"

"In a heartbeat."

Ted walked through the kitchen and picked up the phone that was sitting on the stool. "Hi, honey."

There was a pause.

"Daddy, it's me," Christie Purvis said, her tone businesslike.

"Oh, hi, Chris," Ted said uneasily.

"I got a call from someone there, said she was a friend of yours."

"You did? Who?"

"Her name was Rachel," Christie said. "We talked awhile, and I decided to call."

"I'm glad you did." Ted's heart beat faster. "Wonder how she got your number?"

"No clue," Christie's tone warmed slightly. "She's very convincing. Told me about her relationship with her father—or lack thereof— how they finally patched things up, how much better it is now."

"That was all it took?"

"Well, truth is, I almost called a dozen times, just to see how you were, but I'm still so damned pissed."

"About what?"

"You know."

He had a pretty good idea.

"About Mom, about what she's been through. No, I'll be more blunt—about what you *put* her through."

Ted exhaled deeply and remembered what he had said to Rachel. Bite your tongue. Don't lose it. Emotional Regulation.

"I mean, what did you want me to do, Dad?" Christie said. "Call you up and ask how the food is?"

Her tone had sharp elbows.

This was where he usually lost it.

"You there?" Christie asked.

"I'm here."

"You taught me not to mince words. You created this monster."

Ted laughed. "Okay, sweetie, go ahead and give it to me with both barrels."

"It's not that I want to kick you when you're down," she said. "I know you're going through a terrible depression, have been for a long time, but don't you think Mom has too?"

He had never thought of that. Maybe because she never complained. But how could she not be depressed?

"I mean, correct me if I'm wrong, but you lost your business, we had to sell the house in Maine, then you moved to California to get that job. Mom went out to be with you 'cause that's what a good wife does. Right now she's fighting to hang on to the New York house"— she paused and sighed—"Christ, why am I telling you this? You know it all."

"Yeah, and it's not as if I don't have enough guilt."

"See, Dad, that's the point. Guilt can be a great motivator. But what happened to you—and this may hurt but I'm gonna say it anyway—you let the depression beat you. Stayed in bed all day, three psychiatric hospitals, lost your job. So Mom went out and got one while you slept all day and felt sorry for yourself."

Ted's first reaction was to lash back. But he held his tongue.

"Point in me saying all this is Mom needs you and I need you too. I know you think you're too old, can't cut it anymore, lost your confidence, whatever, but you can do it. You have to. For Mom, for me. I don't mean material stuff. We just need the guy back who went out there every day, got scuffed up a little, but did the best job he could. "

Ted just waited.

"I know this kind of sounds like a pep rally," Christie said, "but am I getting through at all?"

Ted nodded even though she couldn't see him. "Yes, honey, loud and clear."

"Well, good," Christie said. "So, the last thing I'm going to say is, Mom can adjust to a new life. I mean, what choice does she have? But she needs to do it alongside a man she can count on, like she used to be able to"—she took a long breath— "and as for the depression, well, excuse my language, but *fuck* the depression."

Ted suppressed a laugh. "Wow," he said, watching a res walk past. "I really *did* create a monster."

Chapter 61

Word had gotten around. It was the Super Bowl of Clairmount. Avril and Rachel versus Cam and Ted. The perimeter of the tennis court was lined with spectators in beach chairs, metal folding chairs, even a hunter-green sofa dragged out of the living room of Schechter. There were cheesy hand-lettered banners backing both teams—one read, *Go ball busters! Av & Rach!* Another one said, *Serve it up, bushwhackers.* Four shirtless men stood side by side next to the tennis court, each with a word crudely magic-markered on their chests: *Go Ted And Cam.*

Pony was the *And.*

Even OCD John had gotten into the act. He endlessly circled the perimeter of the tennis court but seemed to have absolutely no interest in watching the play.

There were two linesmen, a man in cutoffs and a woman in Gucci pumps, whose job it was to call balls in or out. At mid court was a jury-rigged scorer's chair—a barstool requisitioned from God knows where. In it sat Esther, Rachel's old friend from Acute Care, who had once identified herself on the phone as the "fat girl with a self-deprecating sense of humor." Esther had stenciled black referee stripes onto a white T-shirt and in her right hand she held a cheap plastic wireless microphone.

She had welcomed the fans, complimented the Tommy Bahama- clad kazoo player from Barrow House for his outstanding interpretation of the pre-match "Star Spangled Banner," and was now refereeing the tightly contested match.

The score was six-all in the first and only set. Avril and Rachel, dressed in matching red gym shorts, tight fitting tops, and red baseball caps turned around backward, looked over at the referee, Esther, for instructions.

"Ladies, we're going to let you make the call to see who serves first in the tiebreaker," Esther said, and flipped a quarter in the air. "Call it."

"Heads," Avril said.

"Tails," Rachel said.

Esther knelt down to see.

"Tails it is. Ladies win."

"Hey, wait a min—" Cam started to contest it but knew he didn't stand a chance.

The girls won the first point when Ted whacked a ball into the net.

The winner of the match would be the first to get seven points and had to win by two.

It was Ted's serve. He threw the ball up and struck it on the side of his racket. It glanced off Cam's head, knocking his hat off.

The crowd loved it and gave Ted a standing O.

Ted tossed up the second ball and hit it, and it went over the net. Rachel stepped into the ball and returned a looping forehand with topspin. Ted let it go thinking it would go out. It hit three inches inside the back line.

"Out," said Ted.

"Way out," Cam said.

"Bullshit," Rachel said.

Cam raised his racket in protest and pointed at Rachel. "Penalty point. Inappropriate language."

"Ball was in," Esther said, checking the linesman's call. "I didn't hear any inappropriate language."

"She said, 'bullshit.'" Cam said, grinning at Rachel.

"Sorry, Cam, you just cursed. Penalty point," Esther said. "It is now two to zero, Pussycats."

Ted groaned, served again, and lumbered toward the net.

Avril lobbed the serve return. Ted reached up for it, flailed, but missed it and the ball sailed over him.

Cam frowned back at his partner.

"What the hell was that?"

"My overhead smash," Ted said.

Cam laughed. "It needs work."

Miraculously, the men—dubbed Men in Black, for their black sweatpants and black strappy T-shirts—won the next four points.

As Cam walked to his spot to receive serve, he noticed a guy in blue shorts stand up, then sit down, after which the person next to him stood up and sat down, followed by the next, and the next.

The stand-up/sit-down routine circled around one side of the court.

"Is that what I think it is?" Cam watched people go up and down.

"Yup, the Clairmount wave," Ted said.

"It needs work," Cam said.

Rachel served a hard one to Cam. He blocked it back with his backhand. Avril took two steps back, reached up high and hit it over-head. It caught the top of her racket and just barely made it over the net on Ted's side, where it spun backward and died.

Avril stuck her tongue out at Cam. "That's what you get for try-ing to lob me."

Cam laughed. "Lob you? I was just trying to get it back."

"Lucky thing you did," Rachel said with a snicker. "Sucker was going about a hundred miles an hour."

Ted won the next two points on his serve when Rachel hit one into the net and Avril's backhand return went wide.

On the next point, Rachel lobbed a ball up over Ted, who swung and only got a piece of it. The ball careened into the fence.

"In golf that's called a shank," Cam said, shaking his head.

"Ladies and gentleman," Esther said, "it is now six to five, Pussycats. If they win the next point, they win the first annual Swingers with Issues Classic."

Avril served. Ted returned it to her. Avril ran toward it, swung, and hit her other elbow with her follow through.

"Shit!" she said.

Cam came up to the net. "You okay?"

"Yeah, just hit my funny bone."

Esther stood up. "Injury time out."

She looked over at Dr. Holmgren, who had joined the match late. "Doc, care to examine the patient?"

Holmgren nodded, opened the gate on the far side, and went over to Avril.

She looked up and smiled. "I'm fine."

"I know you are," Holmgren said, then whispered, "just a little medical advice—keep lobbing Ted."

Avril nodded as she noticed some commotion behind her.

"Ladies and gentleman, as the doctor attends his patient, won't you please welcome our cheerleaders, performing live and in person, the electrifying Tess and the D'Urbervilles."

Tess was extremely large breasted and wore a USC Trojans T-shirt. The three cheerleaders took their positions on the back line and sprang into action.

"Rah, rah, rah, shish boom bash, Pussycats, Pussycats, kick some ash."

"Poetry in motion," Avril said to Holmgren as Rachel, beside her, laughed.

Tess and the D'Urbervilles did a spirited out-of-step kick, shook their pom-poms, and ran off the court to rousing applause.

To counter Tess and the girls, the four men who had *Go Ted And Cam* magic-markered on their bare chests came out and did some bizarre tribal dance. The only problem was they were lined up wrong, so their message now read *And Ted Cam Go*.

Avril thanked Holmgren, and she and Rachel took their positions, ready to receive.

"It is now six to six," Esther announced. "First to get two points in a row is our winner."

Ted served to Avril, who whistled a hard forehand at his backhand. Ted fanned on it and looked at his racket like it had a hole in it.

He shook his head, then stepped up to the line and served to Rachel.

Rachel hit a high lob. Cam backed up and Ted ran to his right. It looked like it would sail over Cam's head, but he jumped up for it as Ted went after it at full speed. The crowd saw it coming and gasped as Ted plowed into the airborne Cam. They landed in a heap, and the ball, untouched by either one of them, fell in for a winner.

Avril and Rachel ran around the net to check on their vanquished opponents.

Cam looked over at Ted. "Talk about train wrecks."

They got to their feet and dusted themselves off. "Congratulations," Cam said, kissing Avril's cheek. "You guys are too damn good."

"Game, set, and match," Esther said. "Ladies and gentlemen, you have just witnessed undoubtedly the greatest sporting event in Clairmount history."

"And I'm guessing," Cam whispered to Avril, "the only one."

Chapter 62

Rachel held the phone between her shoulder and neck and gestured with both hands.

"So, I nailed this forehand right down his alley, the guy had no chance," Rachel told her father. "Then we finished 'em off on the next point. I hit this lob, and they both crashed into each other tryin' to get it. It was classic."

"I still can't believe she's there," Judd Kornbluth said.

"Yeah, my roomie," Rachel said. "Couldn't stand her at first. Same way she felt, I'm sure. But now, we're like...buds."

"That's great, honey. You have to introduce me. Hey, on another subject...I don't want to bring you down," Kornbluth said, "but we may have a little glitch with Phil."

"Oh God, what?"

"Maybe nothing," Kornbluth said, "but he claims to have a letter from your mother saying he's entitled to half her estate should she predecease him."

It hit Rachel like a Louisville Slugger to the gut.

"Why would Mom do that? No way she'd ever give him half. She was trying to figure out a way to dump him but was too scared what he'd do."

Kornbluth didn't answer right away.

"She never said anything about this?" Kornbluth asked. "You think maybe Phil forced her to sign something?"

"Maybe. I don't know."

"His lawyer told me this letter exists. But I haven't seen it yet."

"Think it's possible he just... made it up?"

"I don't know Phil like you do. Is it?"

"Oh yeah, anything's possible with that effing creep."

"But eventually he's got to produce the document, and if he does, I'll determine whether it's legit or not. Let's not worry about it now."

"You'll let me know?"

"Uh-huh," Kornbluth said. "Hey, I was wondering, you got any plans this Saturday?"

The tension over Phil's letter started to fade. "I s'pose I could squeeze you in," she said.

*****

Kornbluth called back two hours later.

"Rach, I just got a fax of that letter from Phil's attorney. There's no mistaking your mother's signature."

"Damn. So, what do we do?"

"I want to talk it over with a few other attorneys here. Then I'll let you know where we stand. Worst case: How would you feel if you ended up with nine million dollars?"

"You think I really care? I can make nine bucks go a long way."

Kornbluth laughed.

"It just gets me crazy, though," Rachel said. "I mean, no way that jerk deserves a penny."

"I'll talk to you about it when I get there. Can't wait to see you."

"Same here."

She wanted to jump up in the air and click her heels together. Even though she might have just become $9 million poorer.

Chapter 63

Ted and Rachel were sitting across from each other, having dinner at Main.

"What do you know about the law, Ted?"

Ted worked a mouthful of ribs. He held up his hand and finished chewing.

"One should always obey them," he said finally.

Rachel laughed. "Good one."

Ted shrugged his shoulders. "What's the question?"

"My stepfather has a letter from my mother that says if she dies before him, he gets half her money."

Ted perked up. "What's the will say? You know?"

He grabbed another rib.

"That I get all of it. That's what she told me anyway. She was thinking of divorcing him but was scared what the guy might do."

Ted finished chewing.

"I'd say the will prevails. You get the dough. But I'm no lawyer," he said, "nor do I play one on TV."

She rolled her eyes. "You're on a roll."

Ted banged on Cam's door forty-five minutes later. "You in there?"

Cam opened the door, a towel around his waist.

"Gotta run something by you," Ted said as he pushed his way into the room.

"Can't it wait till I get dressed?"

"No."

"Okay, then what is it?"

"Rachel ever talk to you about her father or stepfather?"

"No."

"Well, her father took off when she was like twelve. No contact at all since. Never called, never saw her, nothing. So, fast-forward, her mother dies leaving an eighteen-million-dollar estate."

"You're shitting me," Cam said.

"She won the lottery, if you can believe it."

"Hey, beats workin'."

"So Rachel calls the father 'cause she needs a lawyer to settle her mother's estate, and he's a lawyer. And lo and behold, after never calling her in years, the guy gets back to her. Says sure, he'll help. Then he tells her that her stepfather, who sounds like a total Neanderthal, has a letter saying if her mother dies before him, he gets half."

Cam scratched his head. "What's the will say?"

"Exactly. So Rachel says her mother told her she was going to leave her everything. Apparently, her mother was all set to divorce the stepfather."

Cam cocked his head. "Can I ask you a question?"

"Sure."

"Why the hell are you getting involved in this? I mean, shit, man, take care of your own shit."

Ted thought for a second. "You might be right, but the thing's got a real bad whiff to it."

"So what, it's not your—"

"I know, but I'm making it mine."

Cam held up his hands. "All right, all right, so cut to the chase. What do you think's going on?"

"I don't know. I just have this gut feel—"

"And in your official capacity as protector of the innocent, you want to make sure nobody's putting one over on your little friend."

"Well, yeah, something like that."

Cam put a hand on his chin. "Just so happens, I got the perfect guy to dig around and get the skinny."

"You do?"

Cam nodded. "Guy used to be my brother Charlie's partner in New York."

"Charlie...the homicide cop?"

"Yup, now his old partner's a PI. On my other brother's payroll."

"You mean, Evan...the dick."

Cam smiled and nodded. "He looks into our competition, finds out where the bodies are buried."

Ted eyes widened. "Think he can get on it pretty quick?"

"I'll call Evan right away. Uh, okay, if I get dressed first?"

"No," Ted said, handing Cam a cell phone.

Cam chuckled. "Hey, you're not s'posed to have that here," he said. "Shame on you, Ted."

Ted smiled. "It's just for emergencies."

Chapter 64

"You believe I never saw a shrink before I came to this place?" Cam said.

Dr. Holmgren eyed him like he wasn't all that surprised. They were sitting in his office.

"Not like I couldn't have used one of you guys to help me get my shit together," Cam said, "Just that my old man—not the world's most enlightened guy—drummed it into my head that only pussies go to shrinks."

Holmgren smiled. "Yeah, well, he's not the first guy to think that."

Cam nodded and leaned back in his chair in Holmgren's bare-boned office. Not a lot of diplomas or pictures of the wife and kids. He liked that.

"So I think it may be workin'. The DBT, meditating, and all the other shit. It's pretty good stuff."

Holmgren put his hands together and did his little nod. His head barely moved. "So. I'm curious—what is the single most important thing you've learned here, Cam?"

For a moment Cam's eyes searched the ceiling.

"Single most important...That's tough." Then Cam locked onto Holmgren's eyes. "But maybe that it's okay to talk about stuff that I normally would *never* talk about."

Holmgren nodded.

"You mean, the stuff your dad would think only pussies talk about?"

Cam laughed. "Yeah, exactly. *Feelings* weren't exactly dinner conversation in the Crawford household. Your *problems*, or whatever bothered you, were just things you had to figure out on your own. Like if I said, 'Hey, Dad, I'm depressed,' he probably would have said, 'Well, hell, go take an aspirin.'"

Holmgren suppressed a laugh.

"Fact of the matter is, I'm actually not the fuck-up my father and oldest brother made me out to be. See, between the two of them, they did a hell of a number on me. I mean, the classic one-two. My brother'd say, 'What's the problem, Cam? All C's. You're an embarrassment to the family.' So I'd study my ass off and still get C's. Was I stupid? I thought so, and my old man wasn't about to tell me otherwise. He was a tough old military bastard."

"So, what effect did that have on you?"

"You know, self-esteem shit. Didn't think I had what it took. High school, college, life... I mean, the reality is I'm as good at what I do as my brother, Einstein, is at what he does. But he always made it seem he got me into the company as a charity case, 'cause nobody else wanted me."

"What about your other brother, Charlie?"

Cam smiled. "Charlie was always in my corner," he said. "But he was away a lot. Lacrosse camp. Football. You name it."

Cam's eyes scanned the ceiling again. "It's amazing how smart people can get things totally fucked up."

Both Cam and Holmgren nodded.

"The power I gave my family," Cam said. "I mean, Jesus."

Holmgren nodded again. Cam looked at him and laughed.

"Look at us, nodding like a couple of bobblehead dolls."

Holmgren smiled, stood up, and thrust out his hand. "I'm glad we had this talk, Cam. Fact is, you're making very solid progress, so keep up the good work," he said as they shook. "Now, if we could just do something about that tennis game of yours."

Chapter 65

Ted heard footsteps in the Brook House living room. He looked up from his book and couldn't believe it: It had been more than a year since he had seen his daughter.

He stood up, and they hugged. Like they were going to squeeze the air out of each other. Neither one of them said anything for a few moments. Ted had to fight off tears. That was one of his new resolutions, the new Ted... knock off the tears, for God's sake.

"Oh, honey, I don't know what to say. It's so good to see you," Ted stroked her cheek. "You look great."

"Thanks, Daddy. I've missed you. You look pretty good yourself. Lost some weight?"

"Maybe a little. Going to the gym here. Even played tennis the other day."

"But you're a golfer."

"Yeah, well, I didn't say it was pretty."

Christie laughed.

"Wanna go for a walk or something? It's kind of nice around here."

"Yeah, sure. You have a decent room?"

"Room's fine. The trick is not to spend too much time in it."

They walked toward the back door of the living room. Ted held open the French door for his daughter.

"How's that going anyway?"

"Staying in bed, you mean?"

She nodded as they walked down the path, the brook on their right.

"I just force myself to get up when the alarm clock goes off. Sometimes it's pretty hard."

"How come?"

"'Cause I don't know...it's easier just to lie there than get up. But the good news is, some of the stuff they teach here is starting to kick in."

"Like what?"

"Well, just ways to look at things, deal with 'em better. Plus, I meditate, do some deep breathing. But tell me about you—how's biz? And your love life?"

Christie laughed.

"Oh yeah, like I'm gonna tell you about my love life. Business is okay. You know, people aren't buying as many books. But I got a couple of new authors I'm pretty excited about."

"That's fantastic," Ted said, looking up and seeing Rachel coming toward them on the path.

"Hey, there she is. The one who made this little reunion possible."

Rachel stopped and smiled.

"Christie, this is Rachel," Ted said.

"Oh, hi," Christie said. "God, I had no idea you were so young."

"Wise beyond my years." Rachel laughed. "It's so nice to meet you."

Christie pushed a strand of hair behind her glasses. "I'm really glad I talked to you."

Rachel slapped Ted on the shoulder. "Anything for my old buddy here. Dude's the best."

Christie smiled.

"He tell you about the old-fashioned ass whooping we gave him on the tennis court?" Rachel asked.

"He mentioned playing," Christie said.

"But not losing to a couple chicks, right?"

"Are you kidding? He could never live with himself."

Rachel chuckled. "Well, I gotta go water my lilacs, give 'em a blast of Miracle-Gro," Rachel said. "It was really nice meeting you. See you up at dinner?"

"Yeah, we'll be there," Ted said.

"Okay, see you in a few." Rachel walked away.

Ted checked his watch. "It's five. You hungry at all?"

Christie nodded. "It's a little early, but I could eat."

"Get to meet some of the crew."

"I'd like that."

Ted put his arm around her shoulder as they walked up the hill to Main House.

"I just want you to know when I get out of here I'm going to do whatever it takes. Work eighty hours a week. Whatever I have to do to take the pressure off your mother. Give her hope we'll get back home again."

Christie turned to her father and kissed him. "I know you will, Daddy. I know."

*****

"Your friend Cam is a real babe," Christie said.

Ted and Christie were sitting out on the back porch of Brook House in the two Adirondack chairs, after dinner.

"The movie star thinks so too," Ted said, patting his daughter on the knee.

"Really, they're an item?"

"Well, let's just say a quiet item."

"I was disappointed, not seeing her."

"Yeah, I don't know why she wasn't there," he said.

She put her hand in his, looked up, and saw a woman walk across the lawn below them. She was wearing sweatpants and gesturing wildly with her hands, her mouth opening and closing.

Christie looked up at her father.

"She's talking to herself," Ted said.

"So I noticed," Christie said.

"Doesn't even seem so strange to me anymore."

Christie laughed, then pointed. "Oh, look at those ducks. How cute are they?"

The ducks had just come out of the water and were shaking themselves off.

"Can we go see them?" she asked.

"Sure, let's go," Ted said, getting up. "I'm going to get some graham crackers in the kitchen."

Ted got the crackers and then walked down the steps to the lawn.

"They get a little nasty if you get too close," Ted said.

"I know. Start hissing and get all aggressive."

Ted nodded and handed Christie a cracker.

They broke off pieces and threw them to the ducks. One of Ted's pieces landed on one of the baby's back. The mother's beak came down and picked it off.

"What do they eat besides graham crackers?" Christie asked.

"You got me. Worms, maybe?"

Christie shrugged.

Ted flicked the last few pieces of his cracker and looked at all six ducks.

"One big, happy family," Christie said.

"Yeah," Ted said, walking away from her.

"Where you going?"

"A secret mission."

He walked over to the rose bush and inspected all the roses, then looked back over his shoulder. Christie was busy feeding the ducks. He picked a rose, turned and walked back with it behind his back.

Christie looked up as she finished tossing the last of her crackers.

"Whatcha got there, Pops?"

He smiled, brought the rose out, and handed it to Christie.

She took it.

"Aww, Daddy, thanks."

"I'm glad you came," he said, hugging her again.

"Me too."

Chapter 66

Christie had left an hour ago.

Pony had come over and rousted Cam and Ted out of their rooms. A fierce Scrabble game was in full swing. They were at a table in the dining room.

"Got weak genes, huh, Black Cloud?" Cam said, looking up from his Scrabble letters.

"What are you talking about?" Ted asked.

"Your daughter looks nothing like you," Cam said, remembering when he saw Ted's wife, Katie, his first day at Clairmount. "Thank God she got your wife's looks."

Ted smiled.

"How 'bout fixing me up on a double date when we get out of here?" Cam said. "You and Katie, me and Christie."

"What? Hit the local drive-in or something?"

Cam cocked his head. "I'm serious," he said. "Never seen a woman look so hot in glasses before."

"Hey," Ted said, cuffing Cam on the shoulder, "you're talking about my daughter. A father doesn't want to hear how hot his daughter is."

Cam laughed. "Sorry, just tellin' it like it is. You okay with me looking her up in the city when I get out of here?"

Ted frowned. "Do me a favor, make sure you're divorced first."

"Almost a done deal."

Pony looked over at Cam. "So, Cam, I gotta hit you up for a twenty."

"What for?"

"To make good on the tennis bet I made on you and Black Cloud."

Ted laughed. "Why would you ever bet on us?" he said. "They were a couple of hustlers."

"Call me crazy," Pony said, looking at Cam, "but I figured you'd at least be able to cheat better than them."

Cam looked over at Ted and shook his head.

"God knows we tried," Cam said, then caught Ted's eye and lowered his voice. "Which reminds me. That little covert operation of ours? I got my brother's guy on the case."

Ted nodded. "Good, keep me posted."

"I will."

"What are you talking about?" Pony asked. "What covert operation?"

"Something you don't need to know about, Pony. You got loose lips," Cam said.

"Come on, man," Pony said.

"Nope. Hey, it's your turn," Cam said.

"Help!" boomed the unmistakable voice from out in the hallway. It was Avril.

She came around the corner into the living room, a look of panic on her face. Right behind her was a cop in uniform. Cam bolted out of his chair, Ted right behind him. "These are my friends," Avril said to the cop.

"What...what happened, officer?" Cam asked.

The cop looked around the room. "This lady was caught shoplifting in White Plains," he said.

Avril arms started flailing wildly. "See, I went to get some presents for me and the girls," she said. "And for you guys too. But once I got them, I realized I didn't have my purse or any credit cards—"

"'Cause they take them at Admissions," Cam said.

"I caught her in the parking lot with a thousand dollars' worth of stolen goods," the cop said.

Cam walked up to the cop. "I'm sure we can get this straightened out, officer"—then under his breath—"you know who she is, right?"

"Of course I do," the cop said. "Doesn't matter who she is. You can't walk out of a store with a thousand dollars' worth of stuff you haven't paid for."

Cam put a hand up. "Just one second, officer."

He turned to Ted and said under his breath, "You gotta go distract the res. She walks in here, and Avril's history."

Ted nodded and headed to the stairway, which went to the office on the second floor.

Cam turned back to the cop. "How much did all the stuff cost?"

The cop reached into his pocket and pulled out a piece of paper. "Okay, she had this receipt. Nine hundred thirty-seven dollars and forty-three cents."

Avril started waving her arms. "I went up to the cashier," she said, "planning to pay. But then I remembered I didn't have...I was going to send a check to the address on the receipt."

"So you just walked out with everything?" Cam asked.

Avril nodded sheepishly.

"Sorry about this, officer, but I'll take care of it," Cam said. "Can you give me a minute?"

"What are you going to do?" the cop asked.

"Go get the money," Cam said.

The cop didn't react as Cam walked toward the stairway.

Cam always kept a lot of cash on him. Just before checking in to Clairmount, he'd gone to his bank and stocked up on hundreds and fifties. He didn't want there to be a credit card receipt for his brother to see if he ever sneaked off to a liquor store. When he first arrived at

Admissions, just before Ted took a nosedive onto the Berber carpet, Cam had snuck sixteen hundred dollar bills and eight fifties into his shoes. Just in case. After all, Johnny Walker Blue wasn't cheap.

He walked past the office of the res. Ted was chatting her up.

Cam went into his room and peeled back a corner of the carpet. He took the bills that were there and counted them. There were only sixteen hundred dollar bills. Then he remembered: *oh yeah, the bar in the city and Hank the driver.*

He ran back downstairs.

He walked up to Avril and the cop.

"Can you make change for a hundred?" he asked, the wad of hundreds in his hand. "I'll give you ten hundred-dollar bills."

The cop pulled out his wallet. "I've got three twenties."

"Perfect," Cam said handing him the ten hundred dollar bills. "I'll let you slide on the three bucks."

Avril grabbed Cam's arm. "Thank you so much, Cam," she said. "I'll pay you back."

Cam smiled. "I know you're good for it."

The cop handed Cam three twenties.

"There was also a cabbie who drove her up there," he said. "He was waiting around to take her back here. He showed me his meter. It was two hundred forty dollars."

Cam turned to Avril. "Jesus, girl, you're gonna wipe me out."

Avril bowed her head. "I'm so sorry, I—"

"It's cool," he said, peeling off three hundred-dollar bills. "In for a penny, in for a pound."

He handed the bills to the cop. "The rest is tip."

The cop motioned with his head. "I need to talk to you. In private."

The cop and Cam walked away from Avril to a far corner of the room.

Then the cop turned to Cam. "I really don't want to arrest the lady, but fact is, she committed a crime. I can't just pretend it never happened."

Cam scratched the back of his head. "What's your name, officer?"

"Cato. Wayland Cato."

"Officer Cato," Cam said, "I'm just asking you for a little compassion. The woman's clearly not a criminal. You heard her. She was going to send them the money. You know she meant it too. She's just, well, she's here for a reason. She's got some issues but she's getting them attended to. I'm just asking you to let her... let her continue to get the help she needs."

Cato sighed and looked up at the ceiling.

"Please?" Cam pressed. "I mean, what is to be gained by arresting her? That would be a huge set-back for her. Please, just—"

"Okay." Cato's eyes came back to Cam's. "But you gotta keep an eye on her, right? Make sure nothing like this happens again."

"You have my word," Cam said. "Thank you so much."

Cato nodded and he and Cam walked back to Avril.

"Ms. Ensor," Cato said, "we're going to forget this ever happened, but if it ever happens again—"

"Oh, don't worry, sir, It won't," Avril said. "I promise you that."

"Okay, well, I'm going to get going then," Cato said, then to Cam:

"Maybe you guys can get the bags out of my car?"

Cam nodded.

He took a few steps, then turned back to Avril. "My wife is a big fan of yours, Ms. Ensor. I don't suppose I could get an autograph?"

*****

"Jesus, Avril, what were you thinking?" Cam asked, after they went and got the bags and Cato left.

She was sitting at the Scrabble table with Cam and Pony.

"I don't know," she said. "I just got it into my head to go buy a bunch of things. So, I went to a few places in New Canaan, then to Greenwich, but they didn't have what I was looking for, so then I went to this mall in White Plains."

"Whoa, whoa," Cam said. "But what possessed you to call a cab and go on that jag in the first place?"

"I just had this urge. I got this idea in my head that I wanted to get the girls and me these bags that I saw in this catalog. I wanted to get you guys something too, and—"

"Avril, Avril." Cam put a finger up to his mouth to shush her. "Quiet, the res'll hear you."

Avril nodded.

Cam shook his head and put his hands on her shoulders. "You can't just call a cab and go to a bunch of stores."

"Too late," she said with a shrug.

Cam looked at Pony and shook his head.

Avril leaned forward and kissed Cam.

"That was a serious violation," Cam said, rattled. "What made you think that was a good idea?'

"Kissing you?"

"No, no, taking off in a cab," Cam said.

"I don't know. It was stupid—I admit it. I just couldn't help it. I had an urge to get those bags and also get you guys—"

"Avril," Cam said and shook her gently.

"What? What's wrong?"

"Are you in a manic state?"

She looked at Cam, then Pony, then back at Cam. "I guess...I guess maybe I am."

Cam leaned closer to her.

"I know it was a while ago," he said, "but did that movie have something to do with this?"

She blinked several times, opened her mouth but nothing came out.

"I tried to forget about that," she said finally, her voice low.

Cam's face moved close to hers. "Are you all right, Avril?"

She nodded, but her eyes didn't look so sure.

"I think you should go up to your room," Cam said, "take a nap maybe."

Avril nodded.

*****

Cam went to the office of the res next.

Tanya looked up at him with a big smile as he walked in.

"Oh, hi, Cam," she said. "I've just been having the most wonderful conversation with your friend, Ted."

"Sorry to have to drag him away," Cam said. "But his services are required at the Scrabble board."

Ted shot up out of his chair. "Well, Tanya, it was nice chatting with you," he said, following Cam out of her office.

Cam turned to him when they were out in the hallway. "How'd it go with Tanya?"

"Man, I really took one for the team there," Ted said, shaking his head.

"What do you mean?"

"A ten-minute monologue about her great-aunt Trudy's funeral."

Cam laughed.

"Well, at least it didn't cost you thirteen hundred bucks."

Chapter 67

The girls at Brook House loved their bags. Of course. What was not to love? They cost over $150 apiece. Avril had also bought Cam a pair of size ten-and-a-half size shoes that looked expensive, and Ted a lizard belt. Cam had no idea how she knew his size.

Avril had talked to her doctor, who had upped her dose of Abilify and put her on Divalproex, which she had used in the past for manic bursts of bipolar. Still wired and hyperactive, Avril asked Rachel if she wanted to go for a run, then hit the gym afterward. Rachel said sure, but her father was coming at four. Then she listened to Avril pinball from subject to subject for twenty minutes without giving Rachel a chance to wedge a toe into her nonstop monologue.

They were running a loop around the outer perimeter of the Clairmount grounds, and Rachel was struggling to keep up.

"So this is what bipolar is all about," Rachel said, breathing heavily. "You turn into Wonder Woman."

"Yeah, it's not all bad. I have more energy that I know what to do with. I'm smarter than that guy in the wheelchair—"

"What guy in the wheelchair?" Rachel asked.

"You know, what's his name? Steven Hawkins."

Rachel didn't bother correcting her.

"Also, I'm the sexiest woman on the planet, and I don't even notice my crow's feet and wrinkles. And we know all about my tennis game. Poor Serena Williams. I'd take her love and love."

"Jesus, girl, take a breath."

*****

Judd Kornbluth handed his daughter the baby-blue Tiffany & Co. box in the living room of Brook House.

"Oh, wow," Rachel said.

"You don't even know what it is yet."

"Yeah, but I know it's from Tiffany's."

"Unless it's from JC Penney in a Tiffany box."

She laughed and opened the box lid. Inside was a pair of diamond-studded earrings.

"Oh God, I love them," she said, her eyes blazing. "'Understated elegance' as my oh-so-sophisticated roommate would say."

"Five years worth of missed birthdays," Kornbluth said. "Put 'em on."

She did.

"Red hair and diamonds, a hell of a combination." He clapped his hands together.

Rachel kissed him. "Thank you so much."

He smiled and nodded.

"Something else I want to talk to you about," he said.

Rachel felt the cold shudder of fear she always got when something came up blind. "Bad?" She winced.

"Good."

She exhaled. "Oh, thank God. What?"

"What would you think about coming to live with me?"

It had flashed through her mind once, but now she was caught totally by surprise.

"Oh my God."

"Is that a yes?"

She nodded and smiled. "Yes, yes, and yes."

Chapter 68

Ted and Cam were coming from the library. Cam had just spent an hour on the internet. He wanted to see what was going on in the outside world, particularly on Wall Street. It was a day of free fall for the market. Ted had gotten a new book. Reading had become easier, and his concentration had improved considerably.

"So, my brother's mole got inside Rachel's father's office," Cam said.

"How'd he do that?"

"Just called up, said he had to see a lawyer right away. Made up some bullshit story, then slipped a bug under the guy's desk. Piece of cake, he said."

"You're kidding."

"He's trying to get a bug in the stepfather's house too," Cam said. "Maybe he won't need one."

"Hey, thank your brother for me."

"I will," Cam said, pointing to the tennis court as they walked by it. "The scene of our epic humiliation."

But Ted was too preoccupied to hear. "So he'll let you know when he has something?"

"Absolutely."

"I just hope for Rachel's sake, the guy's okay," Ted said.

*****

Avril was in the living room at Brook House when Ted and Cam walked in.

"Hey, listen," she said, her hands whirling excitedly. "I just wanted to thank you both and let you know that I promise not to get all crazy or go on any more expeditions. And also tell you the doctor thinks he's got things under control, and if I'm lucky, this thing will be short-lived."

Cam looked at Ted, then back to Avril. "I remember when you were a woman of few words."

She laughed. "Yeah, well, not when I'm manic."

Ted patted Avril on the shoulder as he walked past her. "You're gonna be fine. I've got to call my wife."

"See you later, Ted."

"So, you feel better?" Cam asked, running his hand through his hair.

"I think so. Hey, listen, when I was AWOL yesterday, I also went to this little market and got two steaks, some portobello mushrooms, and a couple of artichokes."

"Wait. How'd you pay for that?"

"I had like fifty bucks I didn't give those Nazis at Admissions," Avril said. "I don't know about you, but I'm kind of sick of the mess hall, how 'bout I cook you dinner here?"

"Um, tough decision," Cam said, putting his hand on his chin. "It's meat loaf and cabbage night, you know."

Avril laughed. "I'll take that as a yes," she said. "Dinner's served promptly at seven-thirty. I'm going to grill the steaks out on the back porch."

"Why don't I do that?"

"You're on."

"Medium rare good?"

"Perfect." She smiled at him. "Think *Char* would mind?"

Cam thought for a second.

"*Char* has a new man in her life. A guy who doesn't drink, do drugs, or have a closetful of issues."

Avril gave him her crinkly little frown. "Sounds like a real bore to me."

*****

Cam and Avril were finishing up dinner outside on the porch. It was almost completely dark.

"I want you to know I'm trying really hard to not yap your ear off with a bunch of manic nonsense and I really love my flowers and the fact that you dressed up for dinner."

"That's a run-on sentence, you know," Cam said.

"Yeah, well, it's a short one for a manic."

Cam had followed Ted's lead and picked a bouquet of flowers, leaving only three roses left on the rosebush. He had dressed in the blue blazer and khakis he'd worn the day he was admitted, and a white linen shirt.

"Ordinarily I would have brought a couple of bottles of red wine, but since I don't do that anymore, red roses will have to do," he said.

Avril leaned across the picnic table and put her hand on Cam's. "How do you think it's going to be, not drinking?"

Cam raised his arms. "Right now I have absolutely no desire. Don't miss it at all. I'm not saying it's going to be easy, but it brings out this guy I don't want to be anymore."

"The guy crawling on the floor of Main House, you mean?"

Cam shook his head. "You're worse than my brother," he said. "Yeah, *the crawler*. But I'm telling you—I am *so* done with it. Besides, I can't be drinking if I'm gonna be Pony's sponsor."

Avril raised a glass of Pellegrino. "So here's to you and sobriety."

Cam raised his glass and saw Tanya inside looking out at them.

"And to you," Cam said, "lower highs and higher lows."

She smiled, and they clinked glasses.

"Amen," she said. "Hey, how about a little after-dinner walk."

"Sure," Cam said, then leaned toward her. "Did you see Tanya?"

"Yeah, she keeps peeking out at us. Last time I checked, there was nothing in the Clairmount handbook that says two patients can't have dinner together."

Cam stood up. "Or take a walk. Come on, let's go."

They walked down the steps to the big lawn separating the house and the brook.

"How long do these manic things last?" Cam said, reaching down and putting his hand in hers.

She gave his hand a squeeze. "Oh God, sometimes only a few days, sometimes seems like forever."

She stopped and turned to him.

He put his right hand around her shoulder and leaned forward and kissed her. She responded as if it was something she'd long been waiting for.

Then she pulled back.

"I think we might be violating a rule in the Clairmount hand-book now," he said. "Something about 'patients must refrain from shows of affection.'"

"Yeah, but let's take our chances. Live a little dangerously," she said.

He put his other arm around her, held her tightly, and kissed her. A few moments later she pulled her head back and looked him in the eyes.

"You know, when you get manic, you get horny," she said.

"I promise I won't take advantage of that knowledge."

"Aw, shucks."

She pulled him to her and they kissed again. A sharp crack sounded on the other side of the brook.

Cam thought he saw the figure of a man running.

"Jesus," Avril said, turning toward it, "what was that?"

"A grizzly bear?" Cam said, downplaying it.

Avril laughed. "Seriously?"

"'We're in the middle of suburbia. Probably a deer or something."

"So call me chicken, but mind if we go back?" Avril said.

"Damn, just when it was getting good."

"If you're very lucky, you might get another chance."

Chapter 69

"Cam...Cam."

Cam was dreaming of the place in New Hampshire where he went to camp when he was twelve. The bizarre thing was Ted and Avril were there too, swimming in the lake with him and the other ten-year-old campers. He felt a warm body in bed next to him.

"Jesus Christ." He bolted up.

"It's just me," Avril whispered.

"What the hell? You can't—"

He felt her hand softly touch the side of his face. "Remember what I said about living a little dangerously?"

"Yeah, but—"

"Shh, shh, shh, nobody's gonna be the wiser," she said.

It was the most seductive voice he had ever heard.

Her lips were on his.

Cam put his arms around her and rolled her slowly on top of him. He felt the curves of her body and the soft sweetness of her kiss. Her breasts pressed into his chest. Cam reached around and felt where her bra fastened. Then he pulled away from her.

"We can't do this."

"What do you mean?"

"We get caught, we're out of here. Besides—"

She put her finger on his lips.

"Relax. I propped your chair up against the doorknob. A tank couldn't get through."

"You told me earlier how you get when you're manic."

"Yeah?" she said with a little laugh. "You have a problem with that?"

"Yes," Cam said. "I mean, no. Christ, this is so unlike me."

Avril rolled off him and laughed.

"This is truly a first," she said, shaking her head playfully.

"For me too. I just don't want you to regret—"

He stroked the back of her neck.

"What if we just...kiss a lot?" he asked.

He could see her incredulous smile.

"You sure are one strange bird, Cam."

They kissed. Again. And again.

Cam woke up later to Avril snoring lightly.

He couldn't move because she had both arms wrapped around him, her head on his shoulder. He had his arms wrapped around her too. It was not a comfortable sleeping position by any stretch, but it made him feel good. They were a man and a woman who had found each other at a very tough time in their lives. Maybe it was something that could last.

Maybe they could even help each other get better. Maybe love each other too. And if not conquer their respective diseases and addictions, then at least make the suffering less painful, their struggle less solitary.

Cam fell asleep with her in his arms.

Two hours later he awoke again. They were as tightly clenched as before.

"Avril, psst, hey," Cam whispered.

One of her eyes opened.

"Hi," she said and smiled.

"Much as I hate to, I gotta kick you out."

"Why?"

"Because, for one thing, I don't think it would be good for Rachel to wake up and see you *not* in your room—she might think you went midnight shopping. And for another, I don't know if I'm going to be able to exercise my remarkable self-control much longer."

She ran her forefinger along his cheek. "Okay, but you had your chance."

"I know."

"May never get another one."

He put his hand on the back of her neck and stroked it lightly.

"Come on—no rain check?"

"We'll see," she said, flicking her long eyelashes.

"Did anybody ever tell you, you have the most amazing eyelashes?"

"You mean, besides George Clooney?"

"Really?"

She laughed. "Never met the man. Got you jealous though?"

"Nah, guy's way too old for you," Cam said, kissing her on the lips, then sliding around to the edge of the bed. "All right now, you really gotta go. Shoo, shoo, shoo."

Chapter 70

That morning Cam took a call from Don Fleming, his brother's private investigator. Fleming said he hadn't been able to get a bug into Phil Eppersley's house, but didn't need to.

"Rather than sum up what I got," Fleming said, "I'm just gonna let you hear it from the horse's ass."

"Is it bad?"

"Depends how you look at it," Fleming said. "I think it's good. Proves Kornbluth's a complete scumbag."

Cam sighed, knowing this would shatter Rachel. "Tell me," he said grimly.

"Hang on. I'm gonna play it."

A few moments later, Cam heard a click.

"This is him talking," Fleming said.

"I'm going to get Rachel to sign the papers later today."

There was silence.

"I can't hear anything," Cam said.

"Keep listening," Fleming said. "Bug only picks up what Kornbluth says."

"She doesn't care as much about the eighteen mil as getting you the hell out of her life."

There was a pause.

"No, Phil. Fifty-fifty. Not a fucking dime less. I'm the one getting the deal done. I'm the one who got her to trust me."

A long pause.

"You really think that bullshit forgery of Evelyn's signature is gonna go anywhere? You're deluding yourself. Listen. I could make a case I should get the lion's share. You bring very little to the table. Bottom line is, it's all about my daughter trusting me."

Another pause.

"Don't fuckin' lecture me about fatherhood. You didn't do such a bang-up job."

A short pause, then Kornbluth's voice again.

"Yeah, then you can go out and buy all the fucking motorcycles you want."

Cam heard a click.

"That's basically it," Fleming said.

"What a complete shithead," Cam mumbled, his mind leaping ahead.

"I told you," Fleming said. "Sounds like money first, daughter second."

"No, daughter *last*. And this is a kid with serious issues," Cam said.

"Hey, I appreciate it, Don. Send me the bill, okay?"

"Not Evan?"

"No, this has nothing to do with him."

*****

Cam told Ted about the recording as they walked up the hill on their way to lunch. Ted took it really hard. His face went white. He had gotten so close to Rachel in such a short period of time. He knew how devastated she would be.

"I gotta tell her," Ted said.

Cam nodded.

"Christ," Ted said, "eighteen years old and every man in her life's either been a deadbeat loser or out to exploit her."

Cam leaned forward. "I think you gotta be there when the guy shows up. Confront the slimeball."

"Yeah, I know," Ted said, scratching the back of his head.

"You want backup?"

Ted shook his head.

"She's gonna really need you, man," Cam said. "The alternative is you just sum up the conversation between Kornbluth and her stepfather—"

"Nah, I gotta confront him," Ted said solemnly.

*****

Ted was headed back from lunch alone when he heard someone walking behind him on the path.

"Yo, wait up."

It was Rachel.

"Hey," Ted said.

"You okay?" She searched his eyes. "Sounded like the old depressed Ted for a second."

"You got that in a 'hey'?"

"One word is enough for my keen antennae."

"Well, just for the record, I'm fine," he lied.

"So let me tell you the latest," she said in a gleeful tone, "my father asked me if I wanted to come live with him."

"I thought you were going to college."

"Yeah, maybe, but even if I do, sooner or later you go home. Hello, Ted...remember Christmas break?"

"It's been a few years."

Rachel laughed. "Pretty cool though, huh?"

Ted had to fake it. "Sure is."

"He's coming again tomorrow night. I'd love to introduce you two."

"Wasn't he just here?"

"Yeah, but tomorrow night he's coming because I need to sign something. And, of course, 'cause he can't get enough of me."

"Of course," Ted said.

"What time?"

"Six."

"I'll be there."

Chapter 71

Ted's stomach felt as though it had bats crashing into its walls. He wasn't looking forward to meeting Rachel's father. Unmasking Kornbluth was going to be a raw, brutal blow to Rachel. He had enlisted Avril to console Rachel in the aftermath of his confrontation with her father.

First, he'd asked Avril how her mania was doing, and she'd told him that she had woken up and felt like she was no longer going ninety miles an hour. Just a tad over the speed limit, she'd said. Then he told her the whole Judd Kornbluth story. She was heartbroken for Rachel. Said she'd do everything she could, but knew Rachel was going to be devastated, a basket case. They'd have their hands full taking care of her. They decided Avril would wait upstairs in her room and Ted would get her when he needed her.

At six o'clock, Ted walked into the living room. Rachel was there, dressed up, made up, and amped up.

"Wow, you look fantastic."

He was sad she'd gone to so much trouble for a bum.

"Thanks. I'm going out front to wait for him," she said, twitchy with excitement. "Can't wait to introduce my two favorite men."

She clapped her hands together and walked out.

Ted wanted to be a million miles away.

He sat down and thought about Christie. How he would never let her down again. How somehow he would solve the money problems. How he would be there for Katie, reassemble all his shattered parts, put himself back together, respect himself again. He mentally prepared himself for a new job he might not like. It was time to put into action the adage one of the shrinks had flogged him with: 'fake it till you make it.' It was time to step up, man up, do whatever it took.

Ted looked at his watch. It was 6:20. He went over in his mind what he was going to say to Kornbluth. But he couldn't really script it. He'd have to play it by ear.

Rachel came into the living room at 6:30. "I'm sorry, Ted. What can I say? Man's just habitually late."

She raised her hands over her shoulders.

"Don't worry about it. I'm not going anywhere."

Rachel turned, and Ted heard her open and shut the front door. Ted thought about New York and how he had to get Katie back there. To all her friends who loved her. To the boards and committees and clubs she contributed so much to and took such pride in giving all of her extraordinary talents to. And most importantly, so she could be near Christie again.

At 6:50, Rachel came back into the living room. Ted saw a smudge in her mascara.

"Ted, I'm *really* sorry," she said. "I don't know what to say. The phone didn't ring, did it?"

Ted shook his head.

She threw her hands up in the air, took a few quick steps forward and stopped. "Goddamnit, this is really annoying. Just a little bit longer, 'kay?"

"Sure."

Rachel spun around. Ted heard the front door slam. He went upstairs and knocked on Avril's door. "Ted?"

"Yes, it's me."

Avril came to the door. "What's up?"

"Jerk hasn't showed up yet."

"I've got AA at seven," Avril said, "which I could always miss."

"If he's not here in ten minutes, you might as well go."

"It's no problem. I can skip it."

"He's probably not coming. I mean, he's already almost an hour late."

"Your call," Avril said.

"Just ten more minutes."

Avril nodded.

Ted went back down the stairs.

He returned to the living room and sat down.

At seven, he went out to where Rachel was waiting.

She looked over at him, her eyes downcast.

He just shrugged.

Rachel's mascara was a little more smudged and he could see the pain in her sad, blue eyes.

"That's all right, I'll stick around," he said, trying hard to sound up, "not like I got a lot of pressing engagements."

She nodded her thanks.

He went back inside and up the stairs to Avril's room.

He knocked again.

She opened the door.

"Go to the meeting," Ted said.

"You sure?" she asked.

He nodded. "Yeah, go. You're late. He's not coming."

Avril walked past him and ran down the steps, then turned back.

"How 'bout you?"

"Nah, I'm gonna stay here," Ted said. "They won't miss me."

Ted went back to the living room and perused the bookshelves.

He pulled out a yellow paperback, opened the cover, saw some blurbs, then sat down and started to read it.

Then suddenly he heard Rachel's voice.

"Hey, Ted, Ted." Rachel careened into the living room, holding the hand of a squatty, balding man. "Can you believe it? He had a flat on the Merritt?"

The man thrust out his hand. His handshake was clammy and limp.

"Hi, Ted, Judd Kornbluth. My apologies."

Rachel beamed. "This old codger's my new best friend," she said, clapping Ted on the arm.

That made it even worse.

"Rachel, I hate to tell you this," Ted said, making tight fists, "but I wouldn't believe a word your father says."

Rachel looked like she had just taken a violent jolt of electricity. "What do you mean?"

"Who is this guy?" Kornbluth demanded.

Ted took a step closer to him.

"You and Rachel's stepfather are in collusion to steal half of Rachel's inheritance," he said, steel-eyed.

Rachel's lips were quivering, her hands shaking. "No, Ted. No, you're wrong."

"That's the most absurd thing I ever heard," Kornbluth said.

Ted reached into his breast pocket and pulled out a folded-up piece of paper and stared straight into Kornbluth's eyes. "This is you on the phone yesterday with her stepfather, '*She doesn't much care about the eighteen mil, she just wants to see the last of you.*' He says something, and you say, '*Fifty-fifty, Phil, not one dime less. I'm the one getting this deal done. I'm the one who got her to trust me.*' Want me to go on?"

Kornbluth reached out and put his hand on his daughter's shoulder. "Don't listen to this guy's BS, honey—"

Tear were streaming down Rachel's cheeks. "I can't believe it... not again."

She yanked away violently and Kornbluth's hands slid off her.

"How could you? How could—" she shrieked, then bolted across the room.

She grabbed a golf club next to two umbrellas in a stand near the back door.

Ted ran after her as she raced outside and started slashing wildly at the two lilac bushes. Ted just watched the purple and blue petals slowly cascade to the ground around her.

Then she tossed the golf club to the ground and took off running. There was no way Ted could keep up with her.

Chapter 72

C am sat on one side of Avril at the AA meeting. On his other side was Amy from Brook House. OCD John had come up to Avril and shyly asked her if he could sit next to her. She patted the chair and John eagerly sat down in it.

Jack, the speaker, had been pretty good. Not long-winded and preachy like some. He was in his late thirties and had four years of being clean and sober. He still felt the urge to drink, he said, but had no trace of any holier-than-thou attitude. He told them about falling off the wagon three times—the most spectacular one was at a Phish concert. He explained Phish wasn't exactly a band you got all tanked up for, pot being more their audience's drug of choice, but nevertheless he had put away half a bottle of tequila on the drive to see them. Cam could relate, though he wasn't much into Phish. And tequila even less. The speaker's drive home from the concert was challenging, he related, but fortunately not tragic. He passed out behind the wheel of his car while waiting for a long train at a railroad crossing. After that—as he phrased it—he *put the cork in it* for good. Went to a hundred sixty-one meetings in a hundred sixty-one days. He wrapped it up by saying that since he was a little soft on willpower, he counted on a rock-solid support group, which he had.

The leader thanked Jack and pointed to a raised hand.

"Hi, Anne, alcoholic," a woman said.

A chorus of, "Hi, Anne."

"Great story, Jack, very inspirational," Anne said. "Whenever I get the urge, I do at least two meetings a day, and not just call my sponsor but make sure I go see her. She doesn't let me out of her sight till the craving is gone."

"Thank you, Anne," the leader said. "Whatever it takes, huh?"

Anne nodded.

"I saw another hand," the leader said. "Over there."

"Hi, Jared, addict and alcoholic."

"Hi, Jared," the group said.

"So," Jared said, "I did battle with tequila too. Stuff makes you do weird shit. Like the time I ate the damn worm. Wife got so pissed at me, all I remember was her hitting me over the head with a frozen steak. Anyway, I enjoyed your story, Jack. Guess a meeting a day keeps the tequila away, huh?"

Jack smiled and nodded.

"Thank you, Jared," the leader said, looking around. "Okay, so if that's it, I think we're done—"

Avril heard the distinctive foot shuffling. Then she looked up and saw...Arthur Petit. He was wearing purple corduroy pants and a white button-down shirt. His stubby hands cradled an automatic pistol, as if it was a baby.

"Hi, I'm Arthur," he shouted, brandishing the gun for everyone to see, "with my plus-one here."

Avril's eyes popped and she grabbed Cam's arm.

Several women gasped, another made a whimpering sound, and someone shouted, "No." Everyone else sat dead silent, frozen, watching Arthur take short steps toward Avril thirty feet away. He had the pistol trained on her.

"Probably thought you'd seen the last of me?" he said. "No such luck. I'm back like a bad dream."

Then Arthur glanced at Cam and aimed the pistol at him.

"You don't look so cocky anymore, Crawford. Lemme hear you beg for your life."

Cam just stared back at him.

Arthur took another step forward. "Come on, motherfucker. Beg!"

Cam's lips were pressed tight.

"Your face isn't gonna be so pretty with a couple of slugs in it," Arthur said

He trained the pistol back on Avril.

"The late great Charlie Manson did that actress, Sharon-what's-her-name. Now I'm gonna do you. You're way bigger than her any day of the week."

"And you're a vile little monster," Avril hissed under her breath.

Arthur shook his head and smiled.

"She speaks. Gotta hand it to you, you're pretty ballsy," he said, the muscles knotting up in his face. "Unlike your wimpy boyfriend"— he pointed the gun at Cam— "just sitting there about to piss his pants."

He was fifteen feet away from Avril now, his eyes drilling into hers.

OCD John put his arms around Avril protectively.

"Get your hands off her," Arthur yelled, "you fuckin' mutt."

OCD John did as he was told.

Avril blinked several times but kept staring him down.

Then Cam spoke. "Look, man, just walk away. Nobody's gonna get in your way."

Arthur aimed the gun at him. "Shut the fuck up."

He pivoted the gun back to Avril and took two more short steps.

"This is your last movie, Avril. Got any final words?"

She just glared at him. "There are no words for a sick bastard like you."

Arthur raised the pistol.

He never saw it coming.

Cam slashed at the pistol with his right foot just as Arthur squeezed the trigger. A bullet shattered the window above Avril. Cam dived at Arthur, smashing him in the stomach with his head. Arthur fell backward, his head hitting first. Cam jumped on top of him and looked down at Arthur's grimacing face.

Cam got up into a crouch and rolled Arthur over onto his stomach. As he did, a man came up from one side, pinned his arms back, and handcuffed him.

Cam looked at the man. "You a cop?"

"Yeah," the man said.

"Well, what took you so long?"

"I don't bring my piece to AA," he said. "Always figured it was a pretty safe place."

Then the man pulled out his cell phone and dialed.

Cam turned to Avril. She was still in the same position, like she was in shock.

"You, okay?" he asked, as Amy put her arm around Avril.

"Yes," she whispered. "Thank you."

"You're never gonna have to worry about that sick psycho again," Cam said.

He took Avril's face in his hands and gave her a soft kiss.

Avril looked over at Arthur and just shook her head.

People started filing out of the room, talking quietly or staring blankly ahead. The cop made more calls.

"Let's go back to the house." Cam put his arm around Avril's shoulder.

She nodded, looking suddenly exhausted.

The cop snapped his cell phone shut.

"Thanks for what you did," he said to Cam as Cam walked past him.

Cam nodded. "I know you're gonna want to talk to us. Do we have to do it now? She's pretty upset."

The cop looked at Avril. "That's okay. Just tell me where you'll be."

"Brook House, over near—"

"I know where it is," the cop said.

Cam, Avril and Amy walked out of the auditorium slowly and down the path to Brook House, nobody talking, sirens blaring in the distance.

Suddenly Cam saw Ted up ahead. He had a lost look on his face, like his first day at Admissions.

Ted ran toward them. "You seen Rachel?" he shouted.

Avril's eyes grew wide. "Did her father show up?"

Ted nodded, mouth tight, eyes darting.

"How bad was it?" Cam asked.

"Really bad," Ted said. "She was devastated. Ran off right after I confronted her father."

"Where'd she go?" Cam asked.

"Around back of the house, then I don't know," Ted said.

"Oh my God," Avril said, hand on her forehead.

"How long ago was this?" Cam asked.

"'Bout fifteen minutes ago."

Avril walked fast down the path to Brook House. "We gotta find her."

Amy looked up at Ted, her lower lip trembling. "What a horrible night."

Ted looked at Cam. "Something happen at the meeting?"

"That fucking psycho Arthur showed up with a gun," Cam said.

"Jesus, are you kidding?"

Came shook his head. "Lucky nothing happened. Cops got him now."

"Thank God," Ted said. "Hey, we really gotta find Rachel. She was a total wreck."

Cam and Ted started to run with Avril ahead and Amy behind. They rounded the corner and saw the butchered lilac bushes, purple and blue pieces scattered on the ground like confetti. "Jesus, what happened?" Avril said.

"She just went crazy. With this golf club," Ted said.

"But she loved those lilacs," Avril said.

Ted shrugged. "I know."

"Okay, let's split up," Cam said. "Amy, go look out back. Ted, you go towards Main. Avril, she's got friends over at Barrow House—"

Avril stepped forward, looking sheepish. "Okay, I just need to go to my room first."

Cam looked at her.

She whispered, "I peed in my pants."

Cam smiled and patted her on the shoulder. "I'll go back towards the classrooms," he said. "One of us'll find her."

Avril ran up the steps to her room, taking them two at a time. In front of her bedroom door, she saw one purple lilac petal.

"Rachel!" she said as she burst through the front door.

She saw Rachel hanging from the bathroom door, something thin and black wound around her neck. Her eyes were open, and the tip of her tongue hung loosely.

"Help!" Avril screamed as loud as she could. "Help! Help! Help!"

She ran around the door and saw Rachel's black spandex pants stretched tight over the top of the door, tied to the knob. She fumbled with the tight knot on the doorknob until she was able to loosen, then untie it. Then she heard Rachel's body thump to the carpet on the other side. She stepped around the door, fell to her knees, and untied the other end of the black spandex pants from around Rachel's neck.

She heard someone open the door as she bent over to do mouth to mouth. Rachel's lips were cold. Avril breathed into her mouth, then exhaled, then blew as hard as she could. She saw Tanya out of the corner of her eye, feeling for a pulse. Avril kept exhaling and inhaling. She saw Tanya's grave look as she gently lowered Rachel's arm to the carpet. Avril kept breathing into Rachel's mouth, faster, more determined.

She saw Cam walk in. She heard Tanya whisper to him. Cam put his hand on Avril's shoulder. She looked up and he shook his head. She turned, put her mouth back on Rachel's, and breathed out, frantic now.

"It's too late," Cam whispered.

"No," she said.

She heard the sound of footsteps and hushed voices.

She blew into Rachel's mouth even harder.

Two hands were on her shoulders. Cam knelt beside her. "There's nothing more you can do."

But she couldn't give up.

"Come on," Cam said. "A doctor's here."

Avril pulled back a few inches, breathing heavily, and looked down at Rachel's lifeless face. She picked a deep-blue lilac petal out of Rachel's hair and patted her shoulder. Then she put her arms around her, rested her head on Rachel's chest, and started sobbing.

A few moments later she held her arms up to Cam, who helped her up and took her in his arms. They hugged each other for a long time.

Footsteps pounded up the stairs. "What happened?"

It was Ted.

He saw Rachel's body.

"Oh my God," he said, then looked into Avril's eyes.

He walked across the room, went to the window, and looked out. His shoulders shook as he wept for the girl he had become so close to. Then he turned around, walked over to Rachel, knelt down, and kissed her cheek.

"I am sorry. I am so, so sorry, Rachel."

Chapter 73

Ted's wife, Katie, was on her third cup of coffee. Cam was sipping a glass of orange juice. He hadn't had coffee since leaving Clairmount six months before. Coffee retained a booze connection in his mind, since he used to lace his morning Starbucks with Johnny Walker. He winced, thinking about that. How could that ever have been a good combination?

They were gathered in the small dining room of Katie and Ted's apartment in Tiburon, California. Cam had arrived the night before and had slept in one of their guest bedrooms.

The sun flooded through the window, and Cam shaded his eyes with one hand while he finished off an English muffin with the other. Ted had gone to work fifteen minutes before.

He and Cam had spent the previous night talking and reminiscing about Rachel, their first time since her tragic death.

Cam sighed and said to Katie, "Poor guy was just born with the guilt gene."

"Well, you can understand why he'd feel that way," Katie said, taking a sip from her mug.

"Course I can," Cam said, placing his hand on Katie's. "But you know what? The sad reality is she would have found out she had a worthless bastard for a father sooner or later. It would have put her over the edge whenever it happened."

Katie nodded, clearly sad that she had never met the girl who had meant so much to her husband.

"I promise you," Cam said, "Ted did everything he possibly could. He was there to catch her fall. Plus, he had Avril ready to help, you know, pick up the pieces. It just—"

"I know." Katie patted Cam on the shoulder,

They had all replayed it so many times, always with a different ending.

Ted had had dreams about Rachel every night for five straight months. Now, a month later, he still woke up in the morning, and the first thing he thought of was her. But somehow his memory of her and her brief, haunted life made him stronger. Like he was going to damn well succeed for both of them. He pictured her every time the black cloud passed over him. The luminous smile set off by the tangled swirl of shiny red hair—his vibrantly intense vision of her—had slowly begun to fortify him.

"I'm sorry about the New York house," Cam said.

Katie nodded. "Ted told you?"

"Yes."

Katie smiled. "I lost a house but gained a garden."

"What do you mean?"

"Come out back and see." She waved her hand.

They walked out the French doors to the backyard.

It was a small yard, but there was a neat, green lawn in the middle surrounded by a breathtaking profusion of flowers on three sides. Cam only knew the names of a few of them but was struck at how many different kinds of flowers were blooming. And in every color imaginable.

"It's beautiful," he said.

"Thanks. About two weeks after Ted got back from Clairmount, I saw this U-Haul truck pull up, and Ted gets out. He had gone to a garden center and practically bought the place out."

"Get out of here. Ted got all these?"

"Yep, two trips. Helped me plant 'em too."

Cam just shook his head in wonder as they walked around the garden.

"You know, he was showing signs of being a closet gardener at Clairmount," Cam said, smelling a flower he thought was jasmine.

"He told me that," Katie said.

Cam saw the lilac bush.

"I know what that one is," Cam said, pointing.

"Ted's favorite."

He just nodded.

"So, everything's good with Avril?" Katie asked.

"Oh yeah, amazing," Cam said. "She's loving the *the-a-tah,* guarantee you she gets a Tony nomination."

"Her reviews were incredible," Katie said.

"I know." Cam looked at his watch. It was ten.

They heard the refrigerator door slam.

"Who does Sleeping Beauty get the sleep-in gene from?" Cam asked. "You or Ted?"

Katie laughed. "This is nothing. Back in college she'd come home and sleep till two in the afternoon."

Christie Purvis walked out, rubbing her eyes and yawning.

"Speak of the devil," Katie said.

Christie kissed her mother, then Cam.

"Look at you," Cam said. "Even with messed-up hair and no makeup, you look like a million bucks."

Christie laughed. "What time is it, anyway?"

"A little past ten," Cam said.

"Still early," she said.

"So do we have any plans for today?" Cam asked her.

Christie looked at Cam. "Not really. What were you saying about Alcatraz last night?"

"I'd kinda like to go see it," Cam said. "See the Birdman's cell and stuff."

Christie laughed. "Seems kind of random," she said. "Make you a deal. I'll go there with you, then we check out Haight-Ashbury."

Cam smiled and nodded. "Yeah, sure, why not?" he said. "An old prison, then a bunch of old hippies."

Chapter 74

Six months later, Avril, Ted, Katie, and Christie were seated at a table in a private back room of a restaurant in New York. Avril had arranged it. The dinner featured lobsters, artichokes, and arugula salad. In consideration of some of its guests' personal histories, bottles of Pellegrino and Perrier replaced wine and champagne.

Avril was the first to stand and raise a glass.

"First, I'd like to propose a toast to our dear friend Rachel on the first anniversary of one of the saddest days of my life," Avril said, looking upward. "The day we lost you. We miss you, babe, we all miss you so, so much. A day doesn't go by when I don't think about you and remember your funny, wise-ass, fantastic personality. You had the fastest mouth and biggest heart at Clairmount. I hope you're in a better place now. I'm never, ever going to forget you, girl."

"Hear, hear," Ted said, clinking his glass.

Avril turned to Ted. "And to you, old man," she said, "three hundred ninety-five days clean and sober, right?"

"Yup," Ted said, with a smile. "Gotta tell you, it ain't easy."

"But you're doing it."

He nodded, then stood. "All right, my turn."

"The floor's all yours," Avril said.

Ted slowly got to his feet.

"Okay, I want to propose not one but *five* toasts, so bear with me, because I may—no, I definitely will—get long winded. The first one is to David Pentima—"

"Yes," Avril said, raising a fist.

"Who's that?" Christie asked.

"Fairfield County prosecutor," Ted said. "For his sterling job going after Rachel's bum of a father, Judd Kornbluth. The man worked tirelessly, and even though Kornbluth didn't end up in the slammer, at least he can't practice in the state of New York."

Avril clapped, and the other two women raised their glasses.

"Second toast," Ted said, "is to my friend—" he looked down, paused, and composed himself— "to my dear friend Rachel, who I never got to spend enough time with. But the short, happy time we had together was so incredibly precious to me. We had a special relationship, which I'll never forget. I never really got a chance to thank her for the part she played in one of the most important events in my life—" he smiled at Christie—"bringing us back together."

He bent down and kissed his daughter's head.

"So, to Rachel, I miss everything you were," Ted said, "and, you should know, the world is a far lesser place without you."

"Yes, thank you, Rachel, thank you very much," Christie said, dabbing her eyes with a handkerchief.

Ted patted her on the arm.

"Toast number three," Ted said, walking over to Avril and putting his arms on her shoulders, "is to the belle of Broadway, the toast of the theater world, and—you heard it here first—a Tony in May, an Oscar in the near future— " he raised his glass—"to my dear friend Avril."

She clinked Ted's glass.

"Thank you, Ted. From your lips to God's ears."

Ted patted her on the shoulders.

"And my fourth toast is a two-fer... first," he turned to Katie, "to the woman who stood by me—God knows why—when I was at rock bottom. Who never complained, never got down on me, who always was there, solid as a rock. The woman who helped me dig out of the deep hole I was in." Ted bent down and kissed his wife on the cheek. "Here's to you, honey."

Avril and Christie raised their glasses.

"Bravo," Avril said.

"Thank you," Katie said.

"And next… to Christie. Who did everything to come to our rescue when things went south. Who came to see me at Clairmount and gave me a huge lift, as together we patched things up. So, here's to you, honey, you're the best."

"She sure is," said Katie, and Avril patted Christie's shoulder.

"And lastly," then he paused and began to choke up, his face suddenly wan, "to the man who was always there for everyone at Clairmount—me, Rachel, Pony—"

"Me, definitely, so many times," Avril said.

"The list goes on," Ted said, dropping his head and wiping a tear from his eye. "I can't tell you, Cam, how much we miss having you here tonight…"

Avril dabbed her eyes with her napkin as she slowly shook her head. "It's not the same without you."

Tears came to Christie's eyes, too. "Miss you, Cam…" she said quietly under her breath.

"I called him today," Ted said, "and he said he was sorry he couldn't join us tonight, something about a *prior commitment*—" the three others laughed— "He asked me to give you all his love… hell, even included me…" Ted rubbed his eyes, struggling to hold it together. "Anyway, here's to our much-loved friend Cam, a man with a heart of gold, who had a little stumble—well, let's not kid ourselves—a big stumble, but is back in a safe place. Let's pray it goes well for him. I told him I'd come up and see him over the weekend. Even force myself to eat that awful Clairmount food. So, here's to Cam, one day he'll join us… clean and sober having slayed his demons… but sadly, not tonight."

THE END

Read the first 4 chapters of
Killers on the Doorstep on the following page.

KILLERS ON THE DOORSTEP

Exclusive sample.

ONE

"So, what's up?" Sam Dubin asked as he sat in an Eames chair that commanded a breathtaking view of the Intracoastal twenty-five stories below.

"That's what I love about you, Sam, how chill you are for a shrink," Max said.

"I don't think they say that anymore."

"What?"

"Chill. Pretty sure it's dope now," Dubin said. "But what was your point?"

"I just wonder how many shrinks kick off a session with, 'So whassup'?"

"I didn't say 'whassup,' I said 'what's up?'"

Max zeroed in on Dubin's pants, "Or wear yellow pants?"

"They're cream-colored, wiseass."

"Or calls their clients, 'wiseass'."

Dubin held up his hands. "Okay, okay, Max, let's start over: *has anything been troubling you lately?*"

"Fuck, yeah, everything. Thanks for asking."

Dubin laughed. "Okay, can we get on with it now?"

Max tapped his desk nervously. "Well, I gotta admit, I *was* stalling a little."

"Why?"

"'Cause I'm kinda embarrassed about something that happened the other day. Well, night, actually."

Dubin raised his hands. "Go on, tell me."

Max groaned. "Okay, here goes…you remember my friend, Pamela?"

"You mean, your sex toy, Pamela?"

Max gave a pained laugh. "Yeah, her. Okay…. this may sound like one of those *only-in-Palm-Beach* stories… So anyway, I'm at the Poinciana Club, playing golf with her… now, fair warning, if I haven't made it clear already, Pamela is one of the most unrepressed women I know."

"Unrepressed in what way?"

"The usual way. Sexually."

"Got it."

"Okay, you might blush a little now—"

"You're stalling again."

"I know, I know. So, it's almost dark and we're finishing up. It's the last hole and I can barely see my ball ten yards ahead of me. I walk up to it, pull out my gap wedge, take a practice swing, and, just as I'm about to hit it—" Max shook his head—"I see, out of the corner of my eye, Pamela with her skirt down around her ankles. She's peeling off these black lace panties and a second later she's completely naked. Well, except for this sports bra, I guess it was, which she yanks off in one quick tug."

"This really happened?"

Max nodded sheepishly. "So, I say, 'What the hell are you doing? You want us to get kicked out of here?' And she just gives me this innocent look and kind of…caresses those incredible breasts of hers. Meanwhile, my mind's jumping all over the place, like how I'm on the board at the Poinciana and now I'm gonna get my ass tossed out for lewd behavior or some shit."

"So what did you do?"

"Went over to her, scooped up her skirt, said, 'For God's sake, put it back on.' Instead, she curls her finger and whispers, 'Come on, Max, it's dark, nobody can see.' She presses up against me and I'm feeling the heat and I, I… start to lose it. Sensible, sober, board member Max Barton—" he snapped his fingers—"goes right out the window and my randy alter-ego comes charging in."

Max wiped a bead of sweat from his brow and looked over at Dubin, who was tapping furiously on his iPad.

"'Come on,' she says, and she grabbed my hand and we started running for the green."

Max squeezed a quick sip out of his water bottle while Dubin looked up at him, blinking rapidly under raised eyebrows.

"And?"

"When we got there, it was really dark. So, she just pulled me down on the grass and we proceeded to—"

"No," Rubin said, shaking his head. "Then what?"

"Well, a few minutes later I rolled off her, out of breath, and she whispered, 'Thank you for indulging my fantasy,' and I said something lame like, 'I'm always available to indulge fantasies like those.' And she ran her fingers across my chest and said, 'I always wondered what it would feel like, doing it on a soft, undulating green.'"

Dubin shook his head. "What did you say to that?"

"Nothing, 'cause that's when I heard this noise, a car door slamming, and the sensible, practical Max kicked back in, and I ran back and started grabbing our clothes."

Dubin sighed and typed a few more words into his tablet. "Then what?"

"She came up to me just as cool as can be and put her finger up to my lips and goes, "Want to do it again?"

Dubin shook his head yet again.

"Um, just for the record, Sam, I declined," Max said. "So we got dressed and got the hell out of there."

Dubin put aside his iPad. "That's really crazy, you know, Max."

"You don't hear me defending it," he said. "So, what's your conclusion? Bottom-line it for me. I mean, besides the obvious, that I'm an undisciplined, shallow, reckless man."

"Well… that whole incident is really more about Pamela than it is about you."

Max nodded. "Yeah, I know, but she's not your client…though you might wish she was."

Dubin slowly shook his head. "Okay, I'm just gonna go ahead and state the obvious here: that whole incident wasn't just crazy, but stupid too. I mean, really stupid. How would you ever have lived that down if you had gotten caught? I'm sure your investors would have been thrilled to hear about it." The head shaking ratcheted up a notch. "I mean, Jesus Max, that was something a horny sixteen-year-old with nothing to lose would pull."

Max put up his hands. "Okay, okay, I'm suitably ashamed of myself."

Dubin's eyes scanned Max's office. "You make light of it, but my read is, it isn't so much about risk-taking or thrill-seeking, like that heli-skiing and sky-diving you did a while back, or even that little… splendor in the grass moment itself, but that you're desperate to fill a void in your life."

"I don't really get how you come up with that," Max said, glancing at his watch. "Hey, we got time for another quickie?"

Dubin laughed. "I'm not Pamela, you know," he said. "Fine, but you gotta get it done in… seven and a half minutes."

"No prob," Max said. "So, have I told you about my brief fling with polo?"

Dubin nodded. "Just that you had a friend who played and you were thinking of trying it."

"Let's just call him an acquaintance. Guy who made it big on Seventh Avenue. Sold his business to—I forget which—Kate Spade or Tory Burch's company, one of 'em. Had a lot of money and didn't know what to do with himself. So, he took up polo."

"Sport of kings, huh?"

"Exactly. That's what he kept calling it. Anyway, he talked me into going out to Wellington, where he says they got more polo fields than swimming pools. I immediately regretted it."

"Why?"

"Well, 'cause on the way out the guy's droning on and on about all these old-money, blue blood, WASPy types who used to play out on Long Island in days of old, and it's obvious to me that my buddy— Aaron's his name—wants to reinvent himself as the modern-day equivalent of one of those guys."

"Palm Beach is famous for its reinventers."

Max nodded. "No shit, you can say that again. So, we get out there and this instructor gives me kind of a half-assed lesson on how to hit the ball with a mallet while I'm sitting on this dopey wooden horse."

Dubin chuckled. "Really?"

"Yeah, then when it's over, I watched the second half of the match Aaron was playing in. Talk about watching paint dry."

"Oh, really, it was boring?"

"Christ, was it ever. Then, after the match, there're like these picnics in the back of everyone's hundred-thousand-dollar Range Rover and they break out the bubbly and all this prissy food. I got stuck listening to this guy boast about playing with Prince Harry—or 'H' as he called him—then he reeled off a list of Viscounts, Barons, Earls, and other British aristos he'd whacked the little white ball around with. Meanwhile, everybody's guzzling flutes of champagne and pretending to enjoy these dainty little cucumber sandwiches. I mean, Christ!"

Dubin straightened out the crease in his cream-colored pants. "I'm not seeing how any of this is up your alley *at all*."

"Up my alley? The whole thing's just a convention of fuckin' wannabes," Max shook his head. "Then I started thinking about the poor polo ponies."

Rubin cocked his head. "What about 'em?"

"Well, I gotta think they hate every second of their sorry existences. I mean, what creature wants to get hit in the legs with rock-hard balls, whacked by mallets, and be forced to stop, slow down, then speed up every five seconds?"

"I never thought of that."

"Why would you?"

Dubin leaned forward. "I think it's kind of touching, though, you thinking about those poor ponies."

"Gee, thanks, Sam. Glad you're touched. So bottom-line it for me again: I mean, besides the fact that I'm undisciplined, shallow, reckless *and*...cynical *and* bored. What do you make of this quest of mine for...whatever the hell it is?"

"Fulfillment? Contentment, maybe?"

"Those are such bullshit shrink words."

"Okay, then, like I said before, you're in search of something to fill a void?"

"Back to that, huh?" Max said with a shrug.

Dubin sighed once more. "Look, Max, everything I tell you, you already know. You're a tremendously successful man who's made a ton of money with Barton Resources and can buy or have whatever the hell you want. I'm convinced, though—and I'll say it again—there's a king-sized void in your life that you're desperate to fill."

Max sat back and tapped his desk for a few moments. Then, "Okay, so the obvious question, what is this king-sized void?"

Dubin didn't hesitate. "People."

"People?"

"Yes, meaningful people."

"Sam, I got a company full of people and a ton of friends."

"But in the time you've been seeing me you haven't had a meaningful relationship with a woman, and sorry, the *unrepressed sex toy* Pamela doesn't count."

Max sighed. "She'd be hurt to hear that."

"And what about family? Last time I checked, you got a mother up in Boston you only see on Thanksgiving and Christmas. Not to throw guilt at ya, but you *do* have a private jet."

"All right, all right, I'll try to be more attentive to dear old mom."

Dubin got to his feet. "But that's it, right? That's all the family you got? I mean, not even any distant cousins?"

"Yup," Max said with a nod. "Last time I checked anyway. So what?"

TWO

Barton Resources had the entire penthouse of the east tower of the Philips Point Building at 777 South Flagler Drive in West Palm Beach. But like a lot of companies, in the middle of Covid, they didn't need all the space they had. Many employees worked remotely, from home, or their boat, or, hell, even the beach. Max Barton was considering going to the building's management company and renegotiating his lease to shed some of his unneeded office space. He anticipated some pushback, but he had all the cards. Not to mention the fact that his company's latest earnings had come out the previous month and had been splashed all over the *Wall Street Journal*, CNBC and Bloomberg Business week. They were in the stratosphere, not just up, but up, up and away. Their best quarter ever.

In Max's office now were two of Barton Resources' managing partners, Landon Blau and Jennifer Simmons.

"I want to try something out on you guys," Max said, like it was a casual thought, no big deal. "I'm thinking about taking a year off. Maybe longer. Call it a sabbatical."

Blau's frown was instant. "What are you talking about? You're not serious, are you?"

Simmons didn't react, likely because the news was good for her. More power, more money, big house in the estate section of Palm Beach.

"I'm totally serious," Max said. "I don't remember when my last vacation was. For the last sixteen years, all I've done is work. Hey,

I'm not trying to sound like a martyr, I just want to take it easy for a while."

He glanced around his office at all the tinted glass, expensive-looking wood, and wide-open spaces. He knew that to some employees the office felt like a giant fishbowl with nowhere to hide or nod off for half an hour if, say, you'd had a few drinks at lunch or a late one the night before. He liked it, though; for some reason it felt casual and somehow even cozy to him.

"'Take it easy,' huh?" Simmons responded at last. "What exactly does that mean? What are you gonna do?"

"I don't know yet. I'll figure something out."

"So, who's gonna run the show?" Simmons asked, no doubt figuring there could only be one serious candidate.

"Hey, not so fast, it's not like I'm retiring," Max said. "I'll still be checking in. Keeping track of everything."

Simmons nodded, trying hard to hide her enthusiasm for what she was hearing.

"This is a *very* big deal, Max," Blau said. "What do you think the investors are gonna say?"

"Christ, Bernie Madoff could be running the place as long as they're getting their returns. I didn't hear a lot of bitching about the latest batch of numbers."

"I just don't think it's that simple," Blau said.

"Look, as much as I like to think this place is all about me and my brilliant investment strategies and formidable leadership skills, we all know we're on autopilot. We've got a good, solid system in place and it would take a lot of fuckups to...fuck it up."

"Eloquent, Max," Simmons said with a laugh. "Well, far be it from me to be thinking about money, but since you're going to be on sidelines maybe we split a piece of what you'd ordinarily be making?"

"Fair question, and again, I don't know yet, but suffice it to say, it's in my best interests to keep you guys happy."

Blau laughed. "Yeah, a happy guy is a productive guy."

"Or gal," added Jennifer.

Maximilian Barton was worth a billion dollars, give or take a million or two. (Of course, it didn't take long for a *Wall Street Journal* reporter to drape the form-fitting moniker, *Max-a-billion* on Barton's broad shoulders.) But Barton had absolutely no ambition to claw his way up into the rarified air of Jeff Bezos or Elon Musk. In fact, one of the things he intended to do in his year off was explore ways to give his money away efficiently, so that his funding supported the actual cause itself, as opposed to a large percentage going to nebulous administrators. He had actually hired someone to oversee that process and told her he wanted to give away ten per cent of his net worth a year. He had done the math and was confident he'd never run out of money. But, first things first, he planned to be selfish, think about himself and just have fun for once, instead of being a complete workaholic and obsessing about his damned company all the time.

Leaving his office, Max flashed back to his abortive test run with polo. What a ridiculous bust that whole thing was! He now felt an urge to give a look at something that had long appealed to him. Ever since he was a passenger on a friend's father's beat-up Donzi speedboat as a kid, going like a bat out of hell on a muddy lake in Massachusetts, racing on the water had intrigued him. The fact was, Max had been, for all his life, an adrenaline junkie. Taking major positions in companies and making risky plays on Wall Street had long sated that need, but now that he'd be taking a hiatus from it all, at least temporarily, he needed to replace it with something.

What had sparked his interest was watching jet skis tear around the Intracoastal behind his Palm Beach house. He guessed they were getting up to 50 or 60 miles an hour. It looked like a hell of a rush. So, on a whim, he'd bought a Yamaha GP jet ski and moored it at his private dock, which he had never used before.

What he loved about the jet ski was jumping over waves, getting airborne, the pure thrill of boundless speed. His game plan was to get comfortable on the Yamaha at top speeds, then maybe trade up to one that was even faster. And it didn't take long before he was piloting the Yamaha as fast as it would go…except on those days when the Intracoastal was too choppy.

Then he read an article about a man on a 1200 horsepower jet ski setting the world speed record at just north of 135 miles per hour. He imagined the thrill he'd get from watching the landscape and houses fly by, just a blur on the shore.

Hmm, thought his adventurous side, sounds like a hell of a challenge…. *are you fucking crazy?* his sane side practically bellowed.

THREE

It was only a fifty-minute drive from Providence to Newport. But the Smith Hill section of Providence was a million miles away from the thirty-four-room "cottage" on Bellevue Avenue where the wedding reception of Isabelle "Izzy" Codman and Will Baxter was about to take place. It had been hurriedly moved inside Izzy's parents' house because heavy rains and winds were expected, and even though tents had been erected at Bailey's Beach Club, 50-mile-per-hour winds were in the forecast, and no one wanted the tents to blow down and injure guests or members of the wedding party.

The job was right out of Ronan "the Gent" Quinn's playbook. In fact, he had done one similar to it on nearby Ocean Drive three years before. That one had netted him and his sons a little over a hundred thousand in cash and another $220K in jewelry, which they fenced in Boston so there wouldn't be a trail back to Providence.

The downstairs of the three-story Bellevue Avenue cottage consisted of a massive ballroom, which was separated by eight brawny Ionic columns from a dining room that could accommodate two hundred people, plus an industrial-sized kitchen and an oversized den that had a hand-constructed mahogany bar built back in the 1920s by a renowned local craftsman. The three ground floor spaces would accommodate the three-hundred-person wedding crowd with room to spare.

The new location worked particularly well for Ronan's gang because he and his nine men could easily observe and command the large open spaces and make sure none of the guests had the bright idea of being a hero and calling the cops on their cell phone. The biggest stroke of luck for Ronan had been Covid 19, because of the fact that everyone—members of the wedding party, guests, and staff alike—were required to wear masks, except, of course, when eating or drinking. The second biggest stroke of luck had come when the chefs, waiters, and bartenders were informed at Baileys Beach Club that, for safety reasons, the wedding reception would be moving to the cottage on Bellevue Avenue. Ronan's inside man—the head valet, who had been generously bought off—had gotten wind of this change of venue and texted Ronan, who quickly lined up two white vans. The wait staff climbed into the vans being driven by Ronan's men to make the short drive to Bellevue Avenue but were instead taken to an abandoned warehouse in Middletown, where they were tied up with zip ties. Ronan's remaining seven men took their places as chefs, waiters, and bartenders until the wedding party and guests arrived, at which time, sixty-year-old Ronan, stocky, white-haired, ice-blue eyes, and dressed like one of the guests, tapped his champagne glass with a silver spoon.

"Ladies and gentlemen," he said through his mask in an accent that was anything but blue-blood Newport, "my men and I will now be relieving you of your wallets and your jewelry. So kindly deposit same in one of these canvas bags—" which his seven men quickly produced, along with their Glock and Sig Sauer automatics. "The quicker you do it, the quicker we'll be on our way so you can enjoy the wedding of Will and his lovely bride, Izzy."

There was a collective reaction of inaction. "You heard the man," Ronan's son, Everett yelled. "Hurry the hell up! Now!"

Men's hands quickly dug wallets out of pockets, while women started removing rings, necklaces, and bracelets and dropped them into the nearest bags.

Just to show they meant business, Chuckie Byrne, Ronan's hulking enforcer, slammed his left fist into one of the ushers' rosy-cheeked face. "Don't just stand there, fuckhead! Wallet! Watch! Ring! Come on, man, give it up!"

The usher, wobbly and starting to gush blood from his nose, reached into his pocket.

Byrne's action had the intended effect of accelerating the process, as men flipped their expensive crocodile wallets stuffed with cash and women tossed their jewelry into the dark green bags.

Dontrell Quinn, Ronan's other son, holding a bag in one hand and his CZ 75 nine-millimeter pistol in the other, smiled at one of the pretty bridesmaids. "You get bored here, meet me over at Ronnie's Bar in Gansett." He said it partly because he was a natural-born flirt and liked her looks and partly because he knew she'd repeat what he said to the police, which might lead them on a wild goose chase looking for the non-existent bar. Though, Dontrell knew, they'd have to be pretty stupid to fall for that.

The bridesmaid put an expensive-looking ring and a necklace in the bag Dontrell was holding. Dontrell smiled and thanked her.

In five minutes, it was done.

"Well, thank you, ladies and gentlemen, for your cooperation. Now, let the dancing begin," Ronan said, as he walked up to the bride. "Shall we?"

Izzy Codman looked somewhere between dumbfounded and horrified.

He put his arm around her waist and his hand on hers and led her in a perfect waltz with no musical accompaniment for a full thirty seconds.

Then he bowed and he and his men departed along with three canvas bags full of cash and a collection of Tiffany's finest baubles and beads.

FOUR

Four months later…

Ronan Quinn's latest venture had gone bad. Really bad. He and his gang had gotten into a fierce turf war with an Italian gang, their biggest rivals. The gang was run by a grandson of Raymond Patriarca, the long-time New England crime boss known as Il Patrone. Ronan called the grandson, "the Mutt", but he was really a double-mutt since he was the illegitimate son of Patriarca's illegitimate son. But Ronan couldn't talk, since he had married only one of the three mothers of his three sons. In any case, there had been a bloody street battle the night before that claimed two of Ronan's men and three of the rival gang's. But Ronan had been hit three times, and it seemed clear he was not going to make it.

He was in the Roger Williams Medical Center, which was not the preferred hospital for men with gunshot wounds. You usually went to the Rhode Island Hospital on Eddy Street if you had a bullet in you—or, in Ronan's case, three: one in the shoulder, one in the stomach, and one in the chest. Last rites had been ministered by Ronan's priest, Father Dunster, and now only his three boys remained in his room. They were trying their best to keep it light.

"Get you anything, Pop?" Everett asked. "There's a liquor store a block away."

Ronan tried to laugh, but it came out a gurgle. "Cut the shit," he tried to say, but his voice was barely audible.

"You feeling all right?" Dontrell asked, putting a hand on his father's good shoulder.

"'Cause ya look like shit," Everett said with a forced laugh.

Everett Quinn was twenty-four years old. He was six-one, had prominent cheekbones, and had inherited his father's brilliant blue eyes. Ronan had always berated Everett for spending too much time with the ladies, but they seemed to seek him out, so who was he to say no?

Ronan smiled but it disappeared quickly. "I'm dying, boys," he managed to rasp. "Guinea bastards finally got me."

"We'll get 'em back, Pops, and then some. Don't you worry," said Everett.

"If it's the last thing we do," Dontrell added, nodding.

Ronan only had enough strength for a nod. Then he turned to his third son. "How long's it been?"

The third son shrugged.

"Gotta be twenty years," Ronan said, struggling to get the words out, "right after you went off to that fancy college."

"That was nineteen years ago."

Ronan nodded. "When Everett was six and Dontrell four," Ronan glanced at Everett and Dontrell. "So what do you boys make of your big brother?"

Dontrell glanced over at his older brother, whom he had never laid eyes on before, and shrugged. "Dude's got nice clothes."

"Nice of him to finally make an appearance," Everett said to his father, then turned to Max Barton. "You think you're too good for us or something?"

Max's eyes drilled into his brother's. "No, we just took… different paths."

Ronan smiled. Clearly a painful act. Then he started coughing. Finally, he said: "You can fuckin' say that again."

Everett looked at Max and chuckled. "You probably never heard that naughty word before, huh slick?"

Max rolled his eyes. "I'm familiar with it."

"*I'm familiar with it*," Everett said, in a mocking tone. "What's the different path you took? I never heard or... gave a shit."

"For starters, your brother went to Gorton School, one of the most exclusive prep schools in the country," Ronan said.

"Groton, actually."

"Whatever. Then he, ah, what's the word... *matriculated* at Harvard University in Cambridge, Mass where he was on the crew team—you know, those skinny boats and the long oars—and also played on the squash team."

"Whatever the hell that is," Everett scoffed.

Ronan kept his eyes on Max.

"I actually went and saw you play once. Made sure you didn't see me, not that you would have known who the hell I was. Gotta admit, you were pretty fucking good."

"Gee, thanks... Pop," said Max. "But why the hell are we talking about sports I played a million years ago?"

Everett's eyes got slitty. "You can't call him that...Pops. Not if you were in and out of his life for five minutes."

"That was 'cause of his mother," Ronan said weakly.

"How come you got that fancy-ass name?" Everett asked. "Maximilian Barton. Sounds like you came over on the *Mayflower*."

Max laughed. Surprised his brother had even heard of the *Mayflower*. "My mother gave it to me—" he flicked his head at Ronan—"they never got married."

"How come I got your last name, Pop?" Dontrell asked. "You never married *my* mother."

Everett laughed and glanced at this father. "You kiddin'? Think that old bigot would marry a black woman?"

Ronan held up his hand. "She was the best of the lot."

"Thank you, Pop, that's nice of you to say," Dontrell said.

Dontrell, at age twenty-two, was an inch shorter than his brother, Everett. Dontrell was a light-skinned black man with corn row braids, emerald-green eyes, and a deep scar above his left eye, the result of being slashed by a man wielding a box cutter. Dontrell told people, with a straight face, that he'd cut himself shaving.

"So, you live down in Miami?" Everett asked Max.

"North of there. Palm Beach."

"Heard you're a real baller," Dontrell said.

"What?" Max had no clue what that meant.

Everett laughed. "Means you're rich, dumbass."

"He's a fuckin' billionaire," Ronan said.

And those… were the last words out of Ronan "the Gent's" mouth.

TO KEEP READING VISIT:
https://amzn.to/45T6shh

Audio Books

Many of Tom's books are also available in Audio…

Listen to masterful narrator Phil Thron and feel like you're right there in Palm Beach with Charlie, Mort and Dominica!

Audio books available include:
Palm Beach Nasty
Palm Beach Poison
Palm Beach Deadly
Palm Beach Bones
Palm Beach Pretenders
Palm Beach Predator
Charlie Crawford Box Set (Books 1-3)
Killing Time in Charleston
Charleston Buzz Kill
Charleston Noir
The Savannah Madam
Savannah Road Kill

About the Author

A native New Englander, Tom Turner dropped out of college and ran a Vermont bar. Limping back a few years later to get his sheepskin, he went on to become an advertising copywriter, first in Boston, then New York. After 10 years of post-Mad Men life, he made both a career and geography change and ended up in Palm Beach, renovating houses and collecting raw materials for his novels. After stints in Charleston, then Skidaway Island, outside of Savannah, Tom recently moved to Delray Beach, where he's busy writing about passion and murder among his neighbors. To date Tom has written eighteen crime thrillers and mysteries and is probably best known for his Charlie Crawford series set in Palm Beach.

Learn more about Tom's books at:
www.tomturnerbooks.com

Made in United States
North Haven, CT
24 March 2024

50383842R00200